THE DEVIL'S CHAPLAIN

"Brilliant... It is one of the finest depictions of evil I have ever read... It is also a highly entertaining mystery with a heroine as compelling as she is gutsy."

— Ken Bruen

"Readers of legal thrillers who want cases that are not cut-and-dried but filled with satisfying twists and much food for thought will find *The Devil's Chaplain* a powerfully-wrought inspection of not just legal processes, but social issues revolving around murder, redemption, punishment, and resolve. It's a thoroughly engrossing inspection that's hard to put down: **a riveting story that hinges on clues so elusive that the tension is exquisitely drawn.**"

— Diane Donovan, *Midwest Book Review*

THE DEVIL'S CHAPLAIN

a novel

by

Bruce Hartman

"Without Contraries is no progression."
— William Blake, *The Marriage of Heaven and Hell*

Swallow Tail Press

ISBN-13: 978-0-9997564-0-9

Also available in a library edition and ebook format.

Part I: Actual Innocence

"Humankind's rich repertoire of thoughts, feelings, aspirations, and hopes seems to arise from electrochemical brain processes, not from an immaterial soul that operates in ways no instrument can discover."

Excerpt from "Declaration in Defense of Cloning and the Integrity of Scientific Research," *Free Inquiry*, Volume 17, No. 3 (1997)

Union Correctional Institution,
Raiford, Florida.
Tuesday, May 8, 2012, 1:00 p.m.

The crowds begin to gather in a special section of the parking lot reserved for protesters. They form two groups, separated by a wooden barricade, both motivated by the same concern for the sanctity of human life. SAVE CHRIS RITTER shout the placards of one group, SEND A MURDERER TO HELL demand the others. When the media are absent, the two groups get along well enough, even enjoy a certain camaraderie. But when the TV news vans pull in, the battle lines are drawn: ritual marching, chanting, shaking of placards, shaking of fists.

On this rainy Tuesday there's special cause for excitement: the arrival of the condemned man's new attorney, a tall, striking African-American woman named Charlotte Ambler. They all know who she is: they've seen her on TV. She climbs out of her rented Honda Accord, ignoring both groups, and walks solemnly to the guard station, where she surrenders her briefcase and undergoes a security search. In spite of the wet weather, the protesters climb out of their Volvos and Subarus, their pickups and four-by-fours, to watch Charlotte Ambler as she is escorted into the prison. A middle-aged white woman with puffy blond hair and a sad, defiant expression stands beside her pickup truck with a homemade sign:

PRO-LIFE
PRO-GUN
PRO-DEATH PENALTY

Beside her a man with a beer belly down to his knees stands with his fists clenched, as if to protect her from Charlotte. She glowers at the lawyer and snaps a picture of her with her cell phone. A black woman with her head shaved and wearing a T-shirt that says "Take Back the Night" shouts obscenities in a high-pitched voice.

A hard rain falls and the crowd takes refuge under their umbrellas, with one solitary exception: a balding Asian man wearing a clerical collar who stands apart from both groups of protestors in a lonely vigil. He faces the building where the execution will be carried out clasping his hands in what appears to be silent prayer. The rain splashes against his bald head and drips over his blotchy face. His black eyes are unblinking, even in the rain. Both groups dislike him for refusing to take their side and for having certain privileges they don't have. Sometimes, instead of standing in the parking lot, he presents himself at the guard station and is admitted inside to visit death row. He's the only religious figure the condemned man will talk to. Even the other inmates on death row hate him.

They call him the Devil's chaplain.

Chris Ritter

If the State of Florida has its way, I will soon be deprived of the illusion that I exist.

Eighteen days from today, at exactly 6:00 p.m., I'll be strapped on a gurney and wheeled into a windowless room where a cocktail of toxic chemicals will be pumped into my veins. Only a miracle can save me.

Not that I believe in miracles. I taught my students that the universe is matter and energy acting in accordance with physical laws and constants that never vary. I still believe that. Nature is what exists, and it's all that exists. But as my life went on I became acquainted with something I wouldn't have recognized when I was a student. I became acquainted — on intimate terms — with evil. Not as a supernatural force, but as part of the world, and as part of myself.

Like most academics, I started out naive and idealistic, hardly aware that there might be flaws in human nature or my own. My innocence wouldn't last long. Until the day of my arrest I led an outwardly productive, exemplary life; I was even famous in my own small way. People with my credentials and accomplishments don't end up on death row, do they? Yet here I am, the exception that proves the rule. Beneath the surface I had much to be ashamed of, but I didn't commit the crime they're going to execute me for. I didn't kill Helene Varga.

As my last day approaches, I feel my sense of self disintegrating and spinning off in a thousand different directions. I'll try to hold it together long enough to meet the new lawyer they sent down for the final appeal. Charlotte Ambler. Not that there's any hope of survival in a system where innocence isn't a defense. I spend day and night rethinking the story of my life and how it might have turned out differently. It's a harrowing tale, with enough might-have-beens to stock a parallel universe.

And the crowning irony is that it all began with a stupid prank.

2.

Charlotte Ambler threaded her way past rows of razor-wire fence and electric gates into the prison. The entrance lobby looked like a typical government building with beige walls, bright fluorescent lights and posters warning visitors of the hazards of not washing their hands. But there was the sign — UNION CORRECTIONAL INSTITUTION, in raised black letters on the wall behind the guard station — that said she'd come to the right place, the place where Christopher Ritter was scheduled to die in a little over two weeks.

Two guards waited to escort her farther inside, both of them white, about forty years old, dripping sweat in their short-sleeve blue shirts. One of them greeted her with a wry, patronizing smile, as if to say: Well, what have we here? The other never uttered a word or looked her in the eye. They marched her down a green tiled corridor that smelled like a public toilet, their belts jingling with keys, tasers and other tools of the trade, unlocking and relocking metal doors and sliding gates that blocked their way every twenty paces or so. Not a soul was in sight, and no daylight, just flickering bulbs enclosed in cages on the ceiling. Were they walking underground? Charlotte felt nervous, claustrophobic, a little scared. It was her first time inside a prison. She knew she'd be safe here. But still she asked herself, the girl who wanted to be a concert pianist, who didn't like conflict or confrontation: How had she let herself be talked into this?

The guards took her to a visitors room designed specially for inmates on death row. It was a soundproof cube about ten feet square with windows for the guards to watch through. In the middle stood a wide steel table, with built-in wrist cuffs on the prisoner's side. Chris Ritter had arrived early; he sat shackled at the wrists and ankles. Charlotte was a little unnerved by his appearance. He'd been a prominent biologist at a famous university whose picture was once on the cover of *Time* magazine. From that picture and from news photos taken at the time of his trial, she'd envisioned a handsome, sandy-haired man with a serious, confident expression. But after ten years on death row he looked exactly like what he was: an old con — shorn, unshaven and shifty-eyed. When she sat down across from him he nodded but didn't smile.

"I'm Charlotte Ambler," she said in a friendly but serious tone. "I'm an attorney from the Titus Foundation."

"Nice to meet you." He ventured an unenthusiastic smile. "I'm sorry I can't shake your hand."

Charlotte smiled back. "Nice to meet you too. I hope I can help you."

He rolled his eyes. "I doubt it very much."

"Let me tell you a little about myself. I've been out of law school for six years, working at a big corporate firm in Philadelphia. Before that I clerked for a Federal judge. Right now I'm taking some time off to devote myself exclusively to pro bono work."

"Good for you. I hope you enjoy it."

Charlotte tried not to show her annoyance. "I take this very seriously."

"I'm sure you do." He flashed what she supposed was meant to be a winning smile, as if trying to recapture the charm he'd used on women in his younger days — including, she couldn't help thinking, the woman he'd been convicted of murdering. She felt herself recoiling from his attempt at friendliness.

"Nothing personal," he said, sensing her reaction. "I've had my fill of lawyers, that's all."

"I'm sorry you feel that way." She set her laptop on the steel table. "I assume you know this," she said, "but I have to tell you anyway. The Titus Foundation has a limited mission. They're not an anti-capital punishment group per se. They represent people who've been wrongly convicted; in other words, people who didn't actually do what they were accused of. If someone's on death row because of a procedural flaw, that isn't within the scope of the Foundation's mission. They will only represent you if you are innocent."

Ritter shrugged. "Understood."

"So I have to ask you a question you don't have to answer. Whatever you say is covered by the attorney-client privilege and will never be disclosed under any circumstances."

"Got it."

"Did you kill Helene Varga?"

He challenged her with his eyes. "No, I did not."

"You're innocent?"

"Absolutely."

"OK. That's what I expected you to say." Charlotte watched him carefully. "But you should understand that I'm not obliged to accept your statements. Before I can represent you I have to make my own judgment of whether you're guilty or innocent."

"Just what I need. Another judge and jury."

"It's just a preliminary step. I'm going to talk to Mr. Levy this afternoon."

Sol Levy was an old-school Florida lawyer who'd represented Ritter at his trial — folksy, shrewd, wise in the ways of Southern juries — and naturally he wasn't popular on death row. Ritter's face darkened when Charlotte mentioned the man's name. "I can save you the trouble," he said. "Mr. Levy will tell you I'm guilty beyond a reasonable doubt."

Charlotte tried not to show her surprise. "I'm not obliged to accept his statements either."

"Let me tell you something," Ritter leaned forward, straining against his shackles. "The only reason I'm here is that the great Sol Levy wouldn't let me testify in my own defense."

"Mr. Levy couldn't stop you from testifying."

"No, but he told me that if I insisted on it I'd have to find another lawyer, and I couldn't do that. My wife — my ex-wife now — had all my assets locked up and I was at the mercy of my so-called best friend, who paid Sol to lose the case so he and my wife would never see me again. It worked. They're married now."

"Who's married now?"

"My ex-wife Kathryn and my ex-best friend. It turned out they'd been sleeping together for years. They even had a child I thought was mine."

Charlotte typed some notes into the laptop as she tried to gather her thoughts. Accusations by a prisoner against the lawyer who lost his case are routine and often welcome as suggesting grounds for appeal. But Ritter's complaints seemed so bizarre that Charlotte's first instinct was to dismiss them. She kept her voice steady. "You think Mr. Levy tried to lose the case?"

"Let's just say he didn't try very hard to win."

One of the guards — it was the friendlier one — rapped on the window and cracked the door open. Charlotte explained that this was her initial interview with the client; she needed more time.

"Take as much time as you need, ma'am," the guard smirked. "Mr. Ritter don't have a lot on his agenda. Except, you know…" His smirk widened to a grin.

"No, I don't know." She stared him out the door. "Now leave us alone."

The door clicked shut and she turned back around to face Ritter, who seemed impressed with the way she'd handled the guard. "You were saying?"

"If I'd insisted on testifying," he said, "I would've been stuck with some court-appointed attorney who was probably used to fixing traffic tickets. The guy Sol brought in as the so-called mitigation specialist was bad enough."

"OK." She typed a few words into the laptop and leaned toward him. "You may have an ineffective assistance of counsel defense. Was that the basis of your appeal?"

"Not my first appeal. That was based on technicalities — rulings on evidence, jury instructions and the like. Sol handled that one himself, and he lost, of course. After that appeal was denied, the state assigned a new lawyer named Julie Halkins."

"Julie is still assigned to your case," Charlotte said. She had already spoken with Julie Halkins. "If I come on board, I'll be working under her as co-counsel."

Ritter smiled. "She filed a couple of appeals based on ineffective assistance of counsel. Sol had screwed her in some other case and she really wanted to make him look bad. And she did ; I read the briefs. Sol came across as the laziest, sleaziest, most incompetent lawyer who ever set foot in a courtroom."

"But you lost those appeals."

"Sol is pretty well connected in this state. And the problem is — as I'm sure you know — that advising a defendant not to testify is such standard procedure that no lawyer can be criticized for doing it."

Charlotte had to agree. "If you let your client testify, you're putting everything he ever did under a microscope. You're putting his whole life on trial."

"I was willing to take that risk," Ritter declared with a sudden intensity in his eyes. And as if driven by a compulsion to confess, he started telling Charlotte his life story, beginning with his childhood and continuing into his college years. She listened with growing discomfort, typing notes on her laptop to avoid being caught in his gaze. Working for the Titus Foundation called for emotional contortions that were unusual in criminal work. You really did have to be judge and jury and reach your own verdict at the outset. And you knew that if he was really the psychopath they said he was, he'd be able to wrap you around his little finger and shake you like a puppet before you had a clue.

"Wait a minute," she said, stopping him. "Why are you telling me all this?"

"Because I want you to understand," he said. "I lived a life of lying and cheating and betrayal, which I'm completely ashamed of. But I didn't kill Helene Varga."

Charlotte shook her head. "It's a good thing you didn't testify."

"I want you to hear the whole story."

"The jury wouldn't have accepted that." She wasn't sure she could accept it either. "Don't you see? They wouldn't have believed that this murder was the one exception of innocence in an otherwise shameful life."

Ritter leaned forward as far as his manacles would allow. "I didn't do it. Do you believe me?"

"I don't know if I believe you or not."

He stared back at her as if she were something small and far away. "I know who killed Helene," he said. "There was a man named Craft, an evil man, who got control of my life and stalked and tormented me for years. He's still out there, I'm sure of it."

Charlotte felt a little chill: it wasn't real, of course; the temperature in the room was probably ninety degrees; just a reflection of Ritter's sudden change in tone. "Who is this man? Is there any evidence that he killed her?"

"Does this sound crazy? Is that what you're thinking? That's what Sol Levy thought, he thought I was crazy. He thought I should plead insanity, which I absolutely refused to do. He also thought I was guilty, and that's where he went wrong. Your own lawyer is supposed to believe in you, isn't he? Or she?"

Charlotte hesitated. "I don't have to believe everything you say. I just have to believe in you enough to try and get your execution postponed."

"I'm not interested in a postponement."

"There are cases going up to the U.S. Supreme Court this term that could put an end to capital punishment once and for all. They could be decided within the next year."

"No more delaying tactics. Ten years is enough."

"You could have the distinction of being the last man executed in America. Is that what you want?"

"If it's not me, it'll be somebody else. It'll be the guy in the next cell, the Jamaican drug dealer. He's scheduled to die a week after me — and believe me, he deserves it."

"How can you say that?"

"Listen to me!" Ritter tried to raise his hands but to Charlotte's relief they were stopped by the manacles. "If I let you represent me, don't even think about arguing against capital punishment. Don't even think about arguing that it's cruel and unusual punishment, or the injection's going to be too painful or I'm too crazy to execute or anything like that. Don't even think about it."

Charlotte felt claustrophobic, as if she were the one chained to the table. The guard — not the friendly one — gawked at her through the window. "What do you want me to say, then?"

"The only argument I'm willing to make is that I didn't do it."

Her voice felt weak. "Actual innocence."

"You've got it."

"That's what the law calls it," she said. "Actual innocence. It's the argument that 'Yes, I'm not insane, I was represented by competent counsel, I've appealed on all the technicalities and lost; in other words, I got a fair trial and you'd have the legal right to execute me if I were guilty. But you have to let me go because I'm actually innocent.'"

"That's right. I'm actually innocent."

Charlotte glanced up at the guard. She wanted to stand up and run out of the room. "Believe it or not, that's not a basis of appeal."

"Isn't it the only basis of appeal?"

She took a deep breath. "The courts say the state has an interest in finality that can trump your ability to assert your innocence after a certain point in the process."

"Finality?"

"They say that what the state owes you is a fair process, not a perfect result. So even if all the witnesses recant, even if someone else confesses to the crime, that doesn't necessarily mean you'll be set free. Not if you've been duly tried and convicted, and all your appeals have been denied."

"But would they execute me?"

She snapped the lid down on her laptop and looked away. "You can't get much more final than that, can you?"

3.

Chris Ritter

Life on death row has its consolations. We can have three pictures (most opt for Jesus and two naked women), a 13-inch TV, and two packs of smokeless tobacco products per week. Each six-by-nine-foot cell has a cot built into the wall, with a steel toilet right beside it. The room comes with three greasy meals a day, provided by a pair of surly guards named Filly Bob and Bubba. That's what I call them, anyway. There are actually dozens of them, white, black and Hispanic, with various names, but they all look and sound alike: pudgy, squint-eyed and stupid. If they were laboratory rats, which is what they most resemble, they would probably be in the control group that couldn't find its way out of the maze.

As I sit on my cot, my new neighbor Teague stares at me with the pitiless gaze of a panther eyeing its prey. He's a former drug dealer from Jamaica who murdered his wife and step-daughters when he suspected them of betraying him to the police and later killed a prison guard who wished him a happy birthday. An enormous, powerful man, six and a half feet tall, though all I see of him in the shadows of his cell are his skeleton's teeth and the luminescent whites of his eyes. After fifteen years on death row, he's scheduled to die a week after me, and when he does (I wouldn't have said this twenty years ago), the world will be a better place. He's been in the cell across from mine for two weeks and I have yet to hear his voice. He just stares at me. He stares at me with the whites of his eyes, as if he were peering up from an abyss. He looks like he wants to kill me.

The guards hate Teague and are scared to death of him. Sometimes they refer to him as an animal. "You're just another hunk of meat waiting your turn in the slaughterhouse," I heard Billy Bob telling him one day. "What you've done shows you aren't really human."

"You don't have a soul," added Bubba. "Any more than a chicken."

"So it don't matter if we kill you."

Other times they call him a devil and torment the other prisoners with that belief. "You see that devil over there?" Billy Bob asked me one night as he squinted into my cell with Bubba. "Better take a good look at him. Where you're going, you're gonna be seeing a lot more like him."

Teague stood in his usual place, glaring back at us with a hatred as unfathomable as the deepest reaches of space.

Bubba smirked his pink, puckered smile. "Some night we'll let him into your cage so he can give you a sneak preview of Hell."

How did I get here? I wouldn't tell the whole story to Charlotte Ambler even if she were willing to listen. Lawyers flatter themselves if they think their clients are telling them the truth. On death row you lie about everything, even to yourself. Not because you expect to survive, but the opposite: it's the only way to die with dignity. There are things in every man's life that are best taken to the grave.

I was a happy kid growing up, though I had little reason to be. My father was an alcoholic insurance salesman from a once-proud Virginia family, my mother a savage Cajun beauty he'd found in the bayous while stationed at Fort Polk in the sixties. He believed in doing the right thing, because to do otherwise wouldn't reflect well on your family, and so when she got pregnant he married her. That's what a man did in those days. To my mother, morality was a heavily seasoned gumbo of guilt, compassion and asking what Jesus would do. She was a voodoo Catholic who dabbled in witchcraft, he a Presbyterian who had stopped believing in his own religion but remained confident of its superiority to all the others.

I wanted to be a good person, but neither of them showed me how. By the time I reached adolescence, I spent most of my time in the woods, where no one could see into my heart. I would lie down between the trees and close my eyes and listen to the clamoring crickets and cicadas and blue jays. I felt closer to them than I felt to any person.

Then one day my mother died of a stroke. I was fourteen.

For the next few days I found myself in the midst of a gothic struggle for her soul. The Catholic priest from Roanoke, my father's Presbyterian pastor, and a brooding visitation of my mother's kin from Louisiana who seemed to have crawled out of the earth, all contended over the empty husk she'd left behind. I felt so sad I didn't want to talk to anyone. I stayed hidden behind a mask of shock and grief. When no one was looking I fled into the woods. I listened to my heart and didn't hear anything. I felt isolated inside my soul.

At the graveside service I stood detached, immobile, disconnected. A breeze touched my face. A pair of blue jays quarreled in a nearby tree. I didn't cry. My father's brother, my Uncle Ed, noticed that and remembered it thirty years later at my trial. My mother was dead and I didn't cry at her funeral.

Tuesday, May 8, 2012, 4:00 p.m. 18 days to execution.

The rain had stopped, unveiling a stifling humid afternoon. Charlotte left the prison the same way she came, though less certain that she was doing the right thing. Even if her client was innocent, she felt a little less so, a little soiled by her encounter with him.. She sensed that one of her bouts of depression might follow her from the prison and overtake her in the soupy Florida heat. In the parking lot the sea of protesters parted as she passed, waving their placards, mouthing ugly faces for the media. The SAVE CHRIS RITTER placards seemed more poignant now that she'd met the man, but also a little less convincing. Did these people have any idea who Ritter really was? Did they even care? A burly white man — almost everybody on both sides was white — jiggled his SEND A MURDERER TO HELL sign in her face with a foolish grin, as if he were clowning at a children's birthday party. The woman with the puffy blond hair aimed a defiant expression at Charlotte but stepped aside as she approached. Others waved or smiled or snapped pictures on their phones. To them she was a celebrity, likely to be seen on TV: they were there as fans, not as protesters, execution groupies who followed a prisoner through the system like a rock star. There were some shouts, some gibes, but nothing personal. No one expected her to stop and speak to them. She was a player in the spectacle they'd come to witness and she was expected to stay in character. A TV news reporter blocked her way and asked her to comment on the case, which she declined. Her non-comment would be on the news that night.

Cars and trucks cruised in and out of the parking lot under a state trooper's direction as if it were a theme park or a county fair. The trooper waved to Charlotte as she drove past him in her rented Honda. A red pickup trailed behind her, dropping back and following at a distance as she turned onto the two-lane highway to St. Augustine, where she'd arranged to meet Sol Levy at his office the next morning.

Wednesday, May 9, 9:00 a.m. 17 days to execution.

Sol Levy's office was a white-stucco storefront on a side street near the center of St. Augustine. The old lawyer greeted Charlotte wrapped in a swath of blue seersucker, faded to gray, that looked more like a tent than a suit. His jowls and ears sagged as if cut by the same tailor who'd made his suit. Bushy white eyebrows curled over a pair of uncompromising blue eyes. "Good afternoon, ma'am!" he intoned in a deep Southern drawl. "How can I help you?"

"Mr. Levy?" she stammered, extending her hand. "I'm Charlotte Ambler from the Titus Foundation."

"Delighted to meet you, Charlotte!" He gave her his flabby hand and bowed slightly. "I'm so glad you're here. The Titus Foundation does wonderful work on these death penalty cases. I wish I could help out on more of them."

They stood in a cramped reception area presided over by a well-dressed woman of about sixty. "Charlotte," Sol said, "I'd like you to meet Millie Kirbo, *secretaire extraordinaire*. Millie's the brains of the outfit."

Charlotte and Millie exchanged greetings and observations about the weather, the parking situation and Millie's grandchildren, whose pictures covered her desk. "We're here to help you any way we can," Sol said, leading the way into a cluttered, windowless conference room. "We've got this set up as your temporary office. You can plug your laptop in over there, use the phone, the copier, whatever you need. There's a coffee pot over there that's always full. You just let us know if there's anything else we can get you."

She set her briefcase down on a chair and poured herself a cup of coffee. "I'd like to start by reading the trial transcript. I assume you have it? And the briefs filed in the previous appeals?"

"Sure, I have them," Sol said. "And you're welcome to read them if you want to find out what an incompetent shyster I am." He forced a smile as if to remind her that Southern hospitality has its limits. "That was the basis of the last couple of motions, you know. Ineffective assistance of counsel."

"They've almost got to argue that, don't they?"

His smile tightened. "Once you get settled in here, why don't you step into my office?"

Sol's office was dark and cool, like a cave or a hollowed-out tree, the walls lined with bookshelves that continued into the adjoining conference room. An enormous desk littered with files and loose papers stood in the middle of the room. Behind it loomed a heavy-framed portrait of a middle-aged woman with dark, serious eyes, and below that was a row of smaller pictures, photographs of a smiling boy at various stages of growth. Everything in the office looked as if it had been waiting a long time to be hauled out to the curb.

"You can see I keep pretty busy for a young fella," Sol said as he cleared off a chair so Charlotte could sit down. "Gearing up for a big jury trial in Jacksonville in a couple of weeks."

"I was out at Raiford yesterday," Charlotte said. "I talked to Chris Ritter."

Sol nodded as if Charlotte had reminded him of someone he'd rather forget. "Is he going to let you represent him?"

"I think so. He's a little hard to read."

"Don't waste your time trying to crack the code," Sol smiled. "You're never going to understand it."

"What do you mean?"

He motioned for Charlotte to close the door behind her. "I can say this to you," he said in a low voice, "because you're his attorney, at least provisionally. I can't say it to anyone else, not even to Millie."

"Go ahead."

"The first thing you need to understand about Chris Ritter — maybe the only thing — is that he's a psychopath. I beg your pardon: a sociopath. That's what they call them now."

"That's pretty harsh. I'm not sure how you—"

"And every word he tells you is a lie."

Charlotte's breath faltered as she struggled with the instinct to defend her client, even though Sol must have known more about Ritter than she did.

"He tortured that woman and beat her to death and threw her body in the swamp hoping she'd be eaten by the alligators," Sol went on. "Then he flew back to New York like nothing had happened. That's what I call harsh."

"You sound more like the prosecutor than the defense attorney."

"We're talking about the truth here, Charlotte. Not some lawyer's arguments."

"He says he wasn't even on the mainland when Helene Varga was killed. He'd taken a boat out to an island to do some research—"

"I've heard all that," Sol interrupted. "Charlotte, he wasn't on any island or in any boat. He got that idea from a story he read in the newspaper about a boatload of Haitians who drowned out in the ocean that day. I guarantee that everything he told you about being on that island came right out of that newspaper article."

"I talked to him for a couple of hours. It didn't sound like he was just making it up."

"Like most psychopaths, Chris Ritter is a masterful liar and manipulator. He can be extremely charming and persuasive when he wants to be." Sol smiled with exaggerated warmth, as if to illustrate his point with a caricature of patronizing Southern charm. "Obviously he succeeded with you."

Charlotte bristled at the implication that she'd been taken in by a psychopath. She stood up and edged toward the conference room. "In that case—"

"As he did with me at first," Sol quickly added. "And don't get me wrong: I did my damnedest to save him. I was lead counsel — I handled the guilt phase of the trial — and a very fine attorney named Charlton Morlot, who has since passed away, handled the penalty phase. I wanted to save him, and I still do. He's guilty as hell, but I don't want to see him die."

The old lawyer fished through a stack of documents and pulled out a pair of bulky binders. "You'll see what I mean when you read the trial transcript," he said. "And if you're still not convinced, try dipping into this." He held out a sheaf of photocopied pages clamped together with a metal clip. "It's a copy of Ritter's diary. I was able to keep it out of evidence in the guilt phase by not letting him take the stand. For which his swamp rat of an attorney Julie Halkins, who was assigned after I'd done all I could for him, expressed her appreciation by filing briefs characterizing me as an incompetent hack who shouldn't be allowed near a courtroom."

"She was wrong to do that," Charlotte said.

"I couldn't agree more. But frankly that was the only argument she could come up with. You'll be working with Julie — if she'll give you the time of day — so you can decide for yourself what kind of an attorney she is."

He carried the transcript binders into the conference room and set them on the table.

"Here, Charlotte. You read these and judge for yourself. The jury deliberated just two hours before bringing in a verdict of guilty on all counts."

Charlotte sat down in front of the binders, wishing Sol would go back to his office and leave her alone. She was annoyed by his condescension, his phony courtliness, his air of authority and most of all by the satisfaction he seemed to take in his own client's conviction.

"How much of his story has he told you?" the old lawyer asked. "Has he told you the part about Craft? The demonic figure who led him down the road to perdition?"

"He started telling me about something like that. Is that what he says happened?"

"That's the story."

"You were right, then, not to let him testify. Nobody would have believed that story. It would have completely destroyed his credibility."

"No, you don't understand," Sol chuckled in his condescending way. "In New York it would have destroyed his credibility. Down here the jury would have swallowed it, hook, line and sinker."

"Then why not—"

"They would have viewed him as an agent of the devil and sent him straight to death row."

4.

Chris Ritter

Six months after my mother died, my father took a shotgun and blew his brains out on the front porch. I fell into the clutches of my Uncle Ed, a bigoted religious fanatic with a cold heart and a fiery temper who'd bought a prosperous farm and run it into the ground. Four years later, I won a full scholarship to a famous university in New York. I never went home again.

At the university I worked hard and had plenty of time left over to make friends, chase girls and get drunk on weekends. I took an assortment of courses — literature, history, philosophy, even theology — but soon found myself gravitating toward science, eventually majoring in biology. Nature, I concluded, is everything that exists, and the material world is the only world we have. The only thing I cared about — or so I told myself — was the truth.

My best friends were Doug Leipzig and Tim Salis, and the three of us made a perfect match because we were all so different. Doug was a business major from Boston with a knack for making money and having fun. Tim Salis was the artistic, creative type, a theater major from New Orleans who spent his days reading plays and his nights rehearsing them with one of the campus theater groups. The three of us shared a fourth-floor walk-up on the far West Side. On a typical day I ate breakfast at a steamy hole in the wall on Tenth Avenue called the De Luxe Luncheonette, which was owned by a cheerful Dominican named Oscar Lopez. One morning as I sipped my coffee in a booth near the back, I sensed the waitress standing in front of me. I'd noticed this girl before.

She was about my age, quite pretty in spite of her freckles, with reddish hair and a milky complexion, and to be honest she was one of the main attractions of the De Luxe Luncheonette.

"You're different," she said.

I glanced up and caught her wry smile. "Different from what?"

"From everybody else."

"Highly unlikely. Almost impossible, in fact."

"The way you look at people. It's as if you're studying them."

"I am studying them. I'm a biology major."

She laughed, and that was how it all began. Her name was Kathryn O'Donnell and she was from Racine, Wisconsin. She was a Social Work major, which is probably why she found me interesting. She was slow to laugh but for some reason she thought I was funny.

Not that anything much happened between us. At first — and for a long time afterwards — we were just friends. But we knew our relationship was special and might lead to something. I was one of the few men, she told me, who had ever succeeded in making her laugh. It was like a hidden power I hadn't been aware of. Of course Doug and Tim fell in love with her too, but she never laughed at them. I knew all along that if she ever went to bed with one of us, it would be me.

Wednesday, May 9, 2012, 6.00 p.m.   17 days to execution.

Even before Charlotte had finished reading through the transcripts and briefs, she had all but made up her mind to withdraw from the case and fly back to Philadelphia. Didn't Sol know he was putting her in an impossible situation? Didn't he realize that the Titus Foundation only defended the innocent? If it was so obvious that

Ritter was guilty, she would have to go home. Why had she put herself in this position?

A capital murder trial proceeds in two phases: a guilt phase, in which the jury must either find the defendant guilty or acquit him, and, for those found guilty, a penalty phase in which the jury must weigh both aggravating and mitigating circumstances in order to decide whether to recommend the death penalty. In the penalty phase of Ritter's trial, the jury, having found him guilty of premeditated murder, was required to consider the aggravating circumstances, namely whether his crime was "heinous, atrocious, or cruel." This, as the judge instructed, was a question of whether the crime involved extreme and outrageous depravity as exemplified either by the desire to inflict a high degree of pain, or utter indifference to the suffering of the victim, as well as whether the victim had suffered fear, emotional strain and terror before the murder was completed. The photographs of Helene Varga, which had already been admitted in evidence in the guilt phase, provided gruesome testimony that these criteria had been met. Against this parade of horrors, the only mitigating circumstances in Ritter's favor were his lack of a previous criminal record and his contributions to science and society; but his good character, once put in issue, had been demolished by the introduction of his diary and the infamous magazine article which had become known as the "Raskolnikov interview." The jury was unanimous in finding him not only guilty beyond a reasonable doubt but depraved enough to deserve the death penalty. Why, Charlotte asked herself, should she expect herself to do any better than the jury?

The trial transcript disclosed no obvious signs of prejudice or legal error, except perhaps in the use of photographs of the victim, admitted to show Ritter's motives, intent and deliberation. The prosecution's theory of the case was plausible and supported by the evidence. Helene Varga was a call girl with whom Ritter had been involved for many years, as shown by dozens of photos and receipts she'd kept locked in a safe deposit box in New York. The existence of this stash suggested that she was blackmailing him. According to the state, he lured her to his in-laws' townhouse in North Palm Beach, where he tortured and killed her, partly to stop the blackmail and partly for a sexual thrill, as evidenced by the pictures he took during and after this horrific process. Not having seen the photographs — there were no copies of them with the transcript — Charlotte couldn't judge whether they were so prejudicial that they shouldn't have been admitted. Sol Levy had objected strenuously both to the photographs and to Ritter's diary. He succeeded in keeping the diary out of evidence until the penalty phase, and in general his performance seemed competent enough. After reading the diary and the Raskolnikov interview (which could have been used in cross-examination if he'd testified), she concluded that Sol had been justified in advising him not to testify. The diary was a farrago of nihilistic jottings about the folly of religion and the baselessness of morality, couched in tones of arrogance and megalomania; the Raskolnikov interview was even worse. And then there were the photographs. The coroner testified that the murderer, while torturing his victim to death and afterwards, had arranged her body in a series of sexually explicit poses, as if he was shooting pornography for necrophiliacs. That sickening exercise had led to one of the most telling arguments for Ritter's guilt and the characterization of his actions as heinous, atrocious and cruel. An ordinary killer might have tortured Helene Varga to death, the prosecutor told the jury, but only a monster would document this crime on his digital camera and hide the memory card in the back of a bureau drawer in his in-laws' house so he could come back and look at them again and again.

The only evidence in Ritter's favor was his claim of innocence, which, since he hadn't testified, could not form the basis of an appeal in the absence of newly discovered evidence. Helene Varga's blood and DNA had been found on the garage floor and in the trunk of her rental car. Ritter's DNA, of course, was all over the house. Her body had been too badly decomposed for the time of death to be determined precisely, but Ritter had been placed on the scene, within the probable time frame, by his mother-in-law. In all likelihood he was guilty as charged. Even so, shouldn't Charlotte try to save his life? The Titus Foundation was committed only to protecting the innocent; other groups, which opposed the death penalty as such, would represent Ritter if she withdrew. Yet it was a gut-wrenching certainty that in a couple of weeks, when she read about his execution in the news, she would feel that she was responsible.

Charlotte knew what her mother would say. Jeannine Ambler was a retired Philadelphia public school teacher who had opinions on a wide range of topics and was proud enough not to keep them to herself. No doubt she'd heard of Ritter — he'd become the poster child for both sides of the capital punishment debate. "Aren't there enough black men on death row," Charlotte could hear her mother saying, "poor black men who fell into a system that was rigged against them? Is this why you went to law school? To spend your time trying to save some professor who murdered a whore?"

No, Charlotte thought. I didn't go to law school to cook up legal defenses for a psychopathic killer of women, whether he's white, black or purple. And I didn't sign up with the Titus Foundation to get murders out of jail.

Charlotte had made her decision. She'd call the Titus Foundation and inform them of her conclusion that Ritter was probably guilty. They'd turn the case over to one of the anti-death-penalty groups and then Charlotte could withdraw from the case with as clear a conscience as she was ever likely to have. She'd have to spend a few more days in Florida, conferring with Julie Halkins and the new lawyers, and saying goodbye—that would be the hardest part—to her client. Then she could go home. When she got home to Philadelphia she'd lock herself in her apartment for a few days listening to Nina Simone and try to figure out how she wanted to spend the rest of her life.

5.

Chris Ritter

My ordeal began in a slightly seedy bar on Broadway called Dominick's Tap Room, where one balmy evening near the end of our senior year — it was just twenty-four years ago this month — I sat at a table drinking pitchers of beer with Tim, Doug and Kathryn. There must have been fifty people in the place that night, but I can't picture any of them clearly. I don't know if Craft was there or not. Kathryn, I remember, was fiddling with a throwaway camera she'd brought back from a wedding.

The four of us were chatting about our plans for the future. Tim had landed an internship at an off-Broadway theater, Doug had been accepted into the MBA program at NYU, and Kathryn would be working with troubled teenagers in the Bronx. My own outlook was clouded by an overdue Bursar's bill for $968 in library fines and lab fees which I had no money to pay. I'd been accepted into the Ph.D program in evolutionary zoology and awarded a scholarship known as the Janssen Fellowship, which was being blocked by my overdue bill. That night at Dominick's my thoughts were troubled, almost desperate. How was I going to find the money to pay that bill and keep my future on track?

We were on our fourth pitcher of beer. Tim was teasing Doug, who had recently persuaded a certain Psych major named Alana to sleep with him. Though he'd had his share of casual girlfriends, including (according to him) a sexy receptionist at the office where he worked the summer before, Doug was crazy about Alana, and the feeling was mutual.

"I'll bet the breakthrough came when you told her about all the money you're going to make on Wall Street," Tim suggested.

I knew I'd already had too much to drink, but unfortunately that didn't keep me from opening my mouth. "Hey Doug," I said, "you wouldn't happen to have an extra $968 lying around, would you? I'd sell my soul to get that Janssen Fellowship."

It was just a figure of speech — "I'd sell my soul" — but Doug seemed to take it literally. "For $968? Is that all your soul is worth to you?"

"It'd be worth a lot more if I actually had one," I laughed.

Doug smiled his best salesman's smile, mastered the summer before when he interned for a commercial real estate company. "You wouldn't actually need to have one."

"What do you mean?"

"You could sell it on an as-is, where-is basis, with no representations or warranties. If it doesn't exist, that would be the buyer's problem."

"Is this what they teach you in business school?" Tim laughed.

As far as I was concerned, it was all a big joke. I grabbed one of the paper place mats, turned it over, and wrote out an advertisement on the back: "For Sale: Soul of aspiring biologist. Or should I say 'Immortal soul?'"

Doug shook his head. "No reps or warranties."

"Right." I finished my writing and declaimed: "Soul of aspiring biologist. As is, where is. $1,000 firm. Must have cash by May 13."

"That ought to do it," Doug nodded. "Better add the phone number."

I'm not sure what happened next. Suddenly everybody in the bar seemed to be looking at me. Kathryn's camera flashed as she snapped a picture. Doug picked up the check and pushed me toward the door. "Let's go."

I grabbed the place mat and staggered toward the door behind Tim and Kathryn. On the wall beside the door was a bulletin board, usually devoted to selling used cars and finding roommates. Somehow I found a thumb tack and pinned the place mat to the wall.

Wednesday, May 9, 2012, 1:00 p.m. 17 days to execution.

Charlotte tapped on Sol's office door to inform him of her decision. "Come on in, Charlotte," he smiled, rising to greet her. "Come on in and have a seat."

She cleared a chair and sat down. "I wanted to thank you for all the help you've given me," she hesitated, unsure how Sol would react to her news. "I've read the transcripts and I think you're right. He's lying about everything. The far-fetched story about his life being taken over by some shadowy figure — what was the name?"

"Craft," Sol nodded. "'Far-fetched' would be the most charitable way to describe it. Did he tell you about advertising his soul on a bulletin board in some bar in New York?"

"Advertising his soul?"

"Yes. Claims he wrote out an ad on a place mat and stuck it on the bulletin board. And then this Craft — well, it's beyond far-fetched. It's absurd, delusional, psychopathic."

"Anyway, I've decided I can't take the case."

Sol's blue eyes blazed with icy ferocity. "Can't take the case? What are you talking about?"

"I've been struggling with this—reading the transcript, reading the diary — and I think you're right. I think he killed that woman."

"Of course he did! I told you that."

"Well — I assumed you knew this — the Titus Foundation doesn't represent guilty people. They don't get murderers off on technicalities."

"What kind of a lawyer are you?" Sol glowered as if she were the murderer. "If we didn't represent guilty people, we might as well close up shop."

Charlotte held steady, reminding herself what she'd heard about Sol: that his legendary success in the courtroom had been based on his ability to project moral outrage, even when defending the worst criminals on the most indefensible grounds. "It's not my choice," she said evenly. "If Ritter is guilty, which is what you and I both believe, I have to turn the appeal over to one of the anti-capital-punishment groups. They'll represent him better than I can."

"There's no time for that!" Sol pulled out a handkerchief and swabbed the sweat off his forehead without breaking eye contact with Charlotte. What she saw on his face wasn't anger so much as pain and despair. It was as if his own life were at stake. "In a few months or a year the Supreme Court will abolish capital punishment once and for all," he said, "but it won't do your client any good if he's dead, will it?"

Charlotte stood her ground. "You said yourself he's a sociopath."

"Yes, and he should spend the rest of his life behind bars. But don't toss him into the killing machine."

"Actual innocence is the only argument he's got left. If it succeeds, he'll be out on the street. You can't have it both ways."

"Don't you see, Charlotte?" Sol shook his finger at her like a parent disciplining a child. "This case — every capital case — isn't about guilt or innocence. It's about the death penalty and that's all it's about. A lethal injection isn't a technicality. We've got to stop murdering people in the name of the law."

Charlotte didn't agree with Sol in his unequivocal opposition to capital punishment. She viewed the death penalty with suspicion and disapproved of the erratic and discriminatory way it was applied, yet she thought it was called for in some extreme instances. In any case her views were irrelevant to her obligations as a lawyer, and Sol's self-righteousness was getting on her nerves. She wasn't playing some role in a "killing machine." She was just trying to do the job she'd volunteered to do.

Sol must have sensed her annoyance. He smiled his folksy smile, inviting her back into the friendly fold of Southern hospitality. "You see all these books, Charlotte?" he asked, with a gesture that swept in the shelves behind him and along the walls. "They're all about Hitler and the Holocaust. It's sort of an obsession of mine. Because I'm Jewish, I guess, though I like to think it goes beyond that. I read every book I can get my hands on about the Holocaust. I can't put them down, even though I know how the story ends. The Nazis handed out death sentences to six million people — or twenty or thirty million, depending on how you do the math — basically because they didn't like their names or their faces or their religion. And that wasn't the first genocide or the last. You can add the Tasmanians, the Bosnians, the Rwandans, the Native Americans and the millions of Africans killed by the slave traders. I don't have room on my shelves for all the books it would take to describe those horrors. But I already know what I need to know. We've got to stop the killing."

Charlotte shifted uncomfortably in her chair. "We?"

"The human race. We've used up our death penalties for the next ten thousand years."

Wednesday, May 9, 2012, 10:00 p.m. 17 days to execution.

Charlotte didn't want to waste any of Ritter's precious time pretending to reconsider her decision. Her mind was made up, she told Sol, politely but firmly, and he backed off, politely but clearly disappointed. She spent the rest of the day drafting a memo to the Foundation and locating a pro bono group that would take over Ritter's appeal. Sol left the office for a meeting in Jacksonville. He wouldn't come back, he told Charlotte, so he said his goodbyes and left her with his best wishes, or his second-best wishes, since they were noticeably cooler than before. She finished her work just before five o'clock, packed her briefcase and stopped at Millie's desk to say goodbye. They chatted for a few minutes and Charlotte turned to leave. "Oh, I almost forgot," Millie said, handing her a flat brown envelope with her name printed on the front. "This came for you."

Charlotte dropped the envelope into her briefcase and drove back to her hotel. That night she tried to relax with a nice seafood dinner, a walk along the waterfront and a glass of wine at the hotel bar. It wasn't until she was ready for bed that she remembered the envelope in her briefcase. It was addressed to her with no return address and no evidence of postage. The words "Hand Delivered" were printed across the top. Inside she found a yellowed, folded rectangle of paper which opened into a place mat from Dominick's Taproom in New York, featuring a menu of beer and pizza at prices that hadn't been seen in her lifetime.

She caught her breath as she turned the place mat over and read the words scrawled across the back:

For Sale: Soul of aspiring biologist. As is, where is. $1,000 firm. Must have cash by May 13. 212-565-5215 - Leave a message.

Part II: Heinous, Atrocious and Cruel

"The universe we observe has precisely the properties we should expect if there is, at bottom, no design, no purpose, no evil and no good, nothing but blind, pitiless indifference."

— Richard Dawkins, *River Out of Eden.*

6.

Chris Ritter

I didn't really sell my soul, of course. Not literally, at least, as proposed in the ad on the bulletin board. But I think my friends, by setting up that little prank, were trying to tell me something. It was their response to my becoming an insufferable intellectual snob.

Kathryn was in Social Work, Doug in the business school, and Tim spent four years getting stoned when he wasn't acting in plays. As a student of science, I believed that I was the only one who was acquiring any substantive knowledge. I was the only one who cared how the universe actually worked, as opposed to how somebody hoped it might work. And as a biology major, I was the only one who'd been exposed to the most significant and revolutionary ideas of our time: the recent breakthroughs in evolutionary genetics. In my junior year I read *The Selfish Gene*, by the British zoologist Richard Dawkins. That book changed my life in ways I've only recently begun to understand. Dawkins's argument, in a nutshell, was that evolution is driven by the self-replicating, self-perpetuating chemical complexes we call genes, and that all living things, including humans, are nothing but machines constructed by these genes for the sole purpose of ensuring their — that is, the genes' — own survival.

I never tired of boring my friends with the insights I'd gleaned from *The Selfish Gene*. For me it was like finding out about sex: a discovery that could never be unmade, a fatal taste of original sin which is not the knowledge of good and evil but its opposite, the knowledge that in the universe there is no good or evil but only the pitiless indifference of matter and energy. And there was another consequence of this theory — the materiality of the human soul — that I never stopped expounding to my friends. To me it seemed the ultimate test of the materialism that everyone at the university took for granted. No one believed in God anymore, and everyone assumed that the only thing that really exists is matter and energy. People talked about "spirituality," but nobody believed in immaterial beings or forces of any kind. You couldn't invoke them to account for any actual event or phenomenon unless you were prepared to be laughed at or locked up. But there was a taboo against drawing the ultimate conclusion: that any apparent spiritual experience is the product of brain cells deceiving themselves, and that any other interpretation of the evidence is like praying before you buy a lottery ticket.

The guards — apart from being a corps of slack-jawed, beer-bellied good old boys who would probably put the entire population behind bars if it guaranteed their job security — are all honorable men. On a personal level, they display a healthy camaraderie among themselves and genuinely seem to enjoy each other's company. We often hear them laughing and joking in the hallway. They're quick to come to each other's assistance, even in the face of serious personal risk, when a recalcitrant prisoner needs to be dealt with. They have a common enemy us. They never lose sight of the fact that many of us are soulless psychopaths, including, in their eyes, me. I might look at them the same way, since they're determined to kill me as soon as the law allows them to. But at this stage, for some reason, I don't hold that against them any more than I would an earthquake or a deadly virus. "I don't blame you," I told Billy Bob one day as he strip-searched me after a riot. "You're just doing your job."

"Damn straight I'm doing my job," he agreed. "You got a problem with that?"

Teague faces us as usual through the bars of his cell. In his impenetrable eyes I'm no different from Billy Bob and Bubba, just another enemy, an affront to his unrepentant pride. The sight of him brings back images of a nightmare I've been trying to forget: a silent, ragged group of black people walking toward me over the ocean, their feet lapped by the waves, staring ahead as they sink farther into the water, first to the knees, then to the hips, the chest, the neck, until their faces go under without a struggle and all that's left is the whites of their eyes bobbing like froth on the surface. I reach out to help them but it's too late: looking down, I see them gazing up at me as they sink to the bottom. Teague seems to inhabit the same unblinking silence, his eyes forever open, his words swallowed by the darkness before they are spoken. I can feel the hatred in his stare: he has marked me as his next victim. He wants me out of the way so he can finish his journey to hell.

"Just so you know," Billy Bob says before he steps away. "When the time comes, it won't be one of us."

"What do you mean?" I ask.

"You know, that actually gives you the injection. It'll be somebody from outside, special-hired for the occasion. A private citizen."

"Wearing a mask," Bubba adds. "So nobody can tell who he is."

"Could be anybody," Billy Bob explains. "Could be your next door neighbor."

"Could be your family doctor."

"Or your kid's Sunday School teacher."

"Thing is," Bubba says, "the law says it has to be a person of high moral character."

"That's right," Billy Bob agrees. "Who else would do something like that for a hundred and fifty bucks?" He glances

toward Teague, whose murderous eyes don't register a response.
"You wouldn't kill somebody for such a piddling amount, would
you, Teague?"

"No," Bubba says, answering for Teague. "It's strictly a
volunteer thing. You know, public service."

ChChri

Graduation was three days away and my Bursar's bill remained
unpaid. With just $26 to my name, I had all but given up on the
Janssen Fellowship and graduate school. After a night of wandering
the streets fretting about my future, I stopped at Dominick's for a
beer, as I often did at that hour of the night. As I sidled past the
circular bar I couldn't help noticing a beautiful dark-haired woman
about my own age, dressed in shorts and a halter top, who sat by
herself sipping a tall, tropical drink. I slid onto a barstool across
from her and saw the bartender point in my direction. She finished
her drink and stood up with her purse slung over her shoulder. The
next thing I knew she was wedging herself between me and the
construction worker on the next barstool. I turned halfway around
and peered into her dark, luminous eyes.

"Are you the guy who put the ad on the bulletin board?" she
asked in a low, sexy voice, seemingly dead serious.

I had to laugh, from embarrassment as much as from the
absurdity of the situation. She must have seen the place mat stuck
to the wall and asked the bartender who put it up.

When I acknowledged that I was the one, she pulled an
envelope out of her purse and handed it to me. "Here," she said.
"This is for you."

Before I could say another word, she smiled goodbye and
headed for the door. As she passed the bulletin board, she reached
up and unpinned the place mat, folded it in half, and stuck it in her
purse. Then she disappeared into the night.

Tossing a few dollars on the bar, I ran outside and searched in every direction. The mystery woman was nowhere in sight. I stood on the sidewalk, wondering if what I'd just experienced was a dream. I pulled out the envelope and counted the money. It was real: ten crisp $100 bills, enough to pay my Bursar's bill and ensure my eligibility for the Janssen Fellowship.

So this is how you sell your soul, I laughed to myself. I didn't have one, but I'd take the money. Why the hell not?

Thursday, May 10, 9:00 a.m. 15 days to execution.

Charlotte phoned Sol Levy's office shortly after 9:00 a.m., knowing that Millie would answer. "Millie," she said, "Where did that envelope come from? The one you handed me as I was going out the door?"

"It was hand delivered," Millie said. "I found it stuck inside the door when Mr. Levy left for his meeting."

"Thanks. Could I talk to Mr. Levy, please?"

"Oh, he'll be in Jacksonville all day. You might try to reach him on his cell phone this afternoon."

Charlotte called the prison for an appointment with Ritter and drove out to Raiford, her mind spinning with desperate hopes and stratagems. The place mat might not prove anything — it certainly wouldn't be enough to stop Ritter's execution — but for her it changed everything. It meant there was at least some chance that he was telling the truth and she could handle the appeal, for which she suddenly felt an overpowering responsibility. She felt ashamed of herself for coming so close to abandoning her client.

The day was blazing hot, sweltering with a jungle-like ferocity. In the prison parking lot she found the usual crowd performing for the TV cameras in the blinding sun. Rednecks, ministers, college students, middle-aged women in pants suits: zealots for and against life, guns and capital punishment, including the bald woman with the high-pitched voice, the puffy-haired blonde, who snapped another picture of Charlotte on her phone, and the tortured-looking clergyman they called the Devil's chaplain.

Ritter sat in his usual place, shackled to the steel table in the visitors room under the supervision of two guards who found Charlotte's presence amusing. Billy Bob and Bubba, he called them, but of course those weren't their real names. "They're all alike," he told her. "Used to watch me like hawks. Now they hover like vultures."

"I need to talk to you," Charlotte said simply.

Ritter faked a smile. "I hope you're here to tell me I can go home."

She opened her briefcase and laid the place mat in front of him.

His face turned even paler than usual. "Where did you get this?"

"It was hand delivered to Sol Levy's office in an envelope with no return address. Is this your handwriting?"

"Of course it's my handwriting. Who else's would it be?"

She watched him carefully. "I need to be sure this is genuine."

"There are the ketchup stains I left on it," he said. "There's the hole where I stuck in the thumb tack. It's real."

"You didn't give this to Sol, did you?"

"Sol? Are you kidding? He never believed this thing existed. I haven't seen it since it was on the bulletin board at Dominick's."

"How do I know one of your friends didn't send it?"

"I don't have any friends."

Ritter seemed genuinely distressed — angry, desperate and confused — which is how any normal person would react. But how sure could she be that he was a normal person? The afternoon before she had declared him a psychopathic killer. She could accept his answers but the conclusion they pointed to seemed incredible, almost ridiculous.

"Craft must have sent it," he said.

"So then" — she tried to sound casual — "you think Craft responded to this ad and bought your soul—"

"He didn't literally buy my soul." Ritter blinked at her as if she were crazy.

"But," she hesitated, "was the place mat sent by the person who took it down from the bulletin board?"

"No," Ritter said, shaking his head.

She tried again. "This Craft you keep talking about, this man who got control of your life — was he the one who took down the place mat?"

"No, not directly."

"Who was it then?"

"It was Helene Varga."

Chris Ritter

Now I see that seemingly meaningless transaction at Dominick's as the turning point of my life, the beginning of a series of temptations to which I succumbed, one after the other, in my long trek toward self-destruction. There are some bumps and forks in the road from innocence to degradation; I stumbled often, hesitated, weighed the meaning of every step. But there was never any doubt which path I would follow. Soul searching is child's play if you think you don't have one.

My first temptation was the woman who handed me the envelope, whose name, I later learned, was Helene Varga. She lured me away from Kathryn even before we were married. There were other women — first Greta, for whom I sacrificed my self-respect and the values of my profession, and then a procession of graduate students, secretaries, cocktail waitresses — but it was Helene who held me in her thrall and comforted me as I moved on to greater temptations. It wasn't just about sex, but something much bigger than that, something I had only an inkling of in those early days, an elemental force that led me from sex to vanity, then to spite and envy, rebellion and domination. My first love was always myself. It was my pride, my vanity — the conviction that only I knew the way to the truth — that led me down the path of lies.

I wish I could say it was someone else who did all this. I wish I could say it was Kathryn or Wagner or my parents or Uncle Ed who ruined my life. And yet I can't hide from myself that I'm the only one responsible for what I've done. What about Craft? Craft played on my weaknesses, furnished me with justifications for my betrayals, and I have no doubt that he murdered Helene. But for my actions I take full responsibility. I'd pray for forgiveness if I thought anyone was listening.

But I'm getting ahead of myself. I need to go back to when the temptations began.

I never told Kathryn where I got the thousand dollars I needed for the Janssen Fellowship. As soon as we all graduated, Tim and Doug carried off all the furniture and relocated downtown, leaving me with the answering machine and the unpaid phone bill. Kathryn moved in with some girlfriends on the East Side. I needed to stay near the university, so I found a basement studio around the corner from the De Luxe Luncheonette. The four of us got together for drinks or dinner as often as our busy schedules allowed. As time went on I saw more of Kathryn than the others and gradually we separated ourselves from them, mutating, adapting, recombining, as we evolved from friends into lovers. And when we plunged over that ancient, irreversible line it was as if we'd become a new species, the first of our kind. Like all young lovers, we were quite certain that nothing like this had ever happened before in the history of the human race. If our friends felt left out, we didn't care. I felt a personal triumph over Tim and Doug, who were both in love with Kathryn and insanely jealous of my relationship with her. Especially Doug, who'd taken to wearing Italian suits and yellow power ties, as if he were already rich and famous. His soulmate, Alana, had dumped him a month after graduation in favor of a recent law graduate. When it came to Kathryn, neither he nor Tim could bear the thought of losing the fight for love and glory to a science nerd like me. But they were good sports about it. They teased us mercilessly, drank toasts to our grandchildren, sent us sex toys in plain brown wrappers. When Kathryn and I were married two years later, Doug paid for the rehearsal dinner and Tim served as best man. None of them — least of all Kathryn — had an inkling how false and corrupt I'd already become by the time we exchanged vows.

Academically, my first year of graduate school was a disappointment. My only friend — and I didn't really like him — was an ungainly Nebraskan named Andy Wagner, who'd learned genetics by breeding ferrets in his parents' basement in Omaha. He was introverted, cynical and too clever by half. My advisor, Professor Hirschorn, was an enigma. A world-renowned expert on evolutionary zoology, he seemed almost terrified of the subject. He could talk all night in his Hungarian accent about single-scull rowing or Beethoven's piano sonatas or even the technical details of some chromosomal combination, but if you turned his attention to Darwinian theory his brow would darken and his voice drop to a murmur, as if he had some terrible secret he could not bring himself to share with a student. "Ah yes!" he would whisper, turning his eyes away. "We don't know about that, do we? We just don't know."

By the middle of the spring semester, Kathryn was regularly spending her nights at my apartment. One afternoon I came home early from the zoology lab and was shocked to find a message on the answering machine from a woman who said she was the one who'd given me the money at Dominick's (I still didn't know her name). At first I thought it must be a joke, but no one knew anything about her; no one could have imitated her low, sexy voice or guessed the location of our first encounter, which she mentioned in the message. She asked me to meet her in Central Park, inside the entrance just south of the Metropolitan Museum. When I arrived it was after dusk. The trees stood in deep shadows on either side of the deserted pathway, and when she appeared beside me she seemed almost luminescent, as if she'd dropped from the sky. She wore a shimmering low-cut dress and a gauzy white jacket. Her dark hair hung in curls across her shoulders.

"I don't even know your name," I told her.

"Helene," she said, drawing out the second syllable. We exchanged pleasantries, and she led me to a park bench where we sat facing each other in the moonlight. "It's been almost a year," she said. "How are things going in graduate school?"

The question caught me by surprise. How did she know I was in graduate school? "Listen," I said, "there's something I need to talk to you about. I've got a girlfriend—"

"Kathryn."

"—and I really can't have you leaving messages in your sexy voice asking to meet me in some secluded spot in Central Park."

"We could get on a more regular schedule if you'd like."

I felt my stomach turning over. "How did you know her name?"

"What do you mean?"

"How did you know Kathryn's name?"

Helene gave me her sweetest smile. "People talk, you know. A university's like one big fishbowl. Everyone knows you're practically living with her."

"I can't believe this!" I was on my feet, circling the park bench, light-headed with anger and disbelief. "Why are you stalking me?"

She was still smiling, only a little mischievously now. "You took the money, didn't you?"

I sprang away, trying to catch my breath. "So what if I took the money?"

"What would Professor Hirschorn think," she said, "if he knew where his star Janssen Fellow got the money to enroll in his program?"

"How do you know anything about Professor Hirschorn?"

"And what would Kathryn think?"

I couldn't believe what I was hearing. "You're blackmailing me?"

"No, just trying to make you see the position you've put yourself in."

For a long moment I stood studying her dusky face and her vixen's eyes: they were utterly fearless, shameless, oblivious to the enormity of her situation. "What do you want from me?"

She lowered her voice to a whisper. "Just a little fling. A one night stand, if you want to call it that."

Trembling, I sat back down beside her. "You want me to sleep with you?"

"Is that such a horrible idea?"

"Just one night? Is that all? And then what?"

"Then you'll be free to do as you please."

Helene's sexual blackmail excited me in ways I'd never experienced before. How often does it happen that a beautiful woman demands to have sex with you? Kathryn was a little cold, a little grudging in her affection, while Helene was warm and eager. Even her threats — which I didn't quite take seriously — added to her allure. But I knew I was playing with fire and this was a temptation I had to resist. And so within a few days after the encounter in Central Park, I asked Kathryn to marry me. She accepted and I resolved never to see Helene again.

There were still some unanswered questions. How had Helene found out about my relations with Kathryn and Professor Hirschorn? I suspected my fellow graduate student Andy Wagner, the ferret breeder from Nebraska, a lumbering nerd with inch-thick glasses who could probably be bribed with an ice cream cone.

I found him one day bent over a microscope in the chromosome lab. "Wagner, have you been talking to anyone about me?"

"What?" He lifted his head and goggled at me in confusion. "Not really."

"Any women? Specifically, a girl about our age or a little younger, with a dark complexion, black hair, deep brown eyes?"

"Why are you asking me this?"

"Because I don't like being spied on."

"Whatever," he muttered, and went back to his work.

To head off any unwanted messages, I had my phone disconnected and ordered a new one with a different number. But one day at school I went to check my mail slot and found a small sealed envelope with my name on it. That's all: just my name, no box number or other address. Inside the envelope was a small cardboard folder, the kind they give you at a hotel for your plastic key card. In fact the folder was from the Four Seasons Hotel. It held a plastic card and a note in a feminine hand: *Room 828. Tonight at 8:00.*

I glanced up and saw Wagner squinting at me as he yanked computer catalogs from his mail slot. He smirked and lumbered away. I thought of confronting him but quickly decided against it. Better to keep this secret to myself.

The thought of the key card tortured me all afternoon. It had to be from Helene, but how could she afford the Four Seasons? If she wasn't paying for it, who was? When it was time to go home, I called Kathryn with the usual excuse — I'd be working late at the lab, so she might as well sleep at her place that night—and caught the subway downtown. At the Four Seasons the doorman eyed me with contempt, as if he knew why I was there.

Helene and I spent the night drinking and talking and having sex. I told her about my work, and unlike Kathryn she didn't try to change the subject. I could tell she respected me for what I was doing, and even more so for what I aspired to do. She was Nuyorican, as she put it: born of Puerto Rican parents and raised in New York, trained in dance at the High School of Music and Art. She was a dancer, which explained how she could be so sensuous and so ethereal at the same time.

Helene had the most beautiful eyes I'd ever seen. She kept them open wide as we embraced and bored them into mine as if she'd found some mystical point in my soul. It was so much better than anything I'd experienced with Kathryn, but when it was over I felt ashamed of myself, as if I'd been paying for sex.

"Who are you working for?" I asked her. We were lying on our backs, barely touching as we stared at the light reflected on the ceiling.

"His name is Craft," she said evenly.

"Craft? Who is he?"

"That's all I can tell you."

I sat up. "Is he paying you to do this?"

"Not this," she smiled. "This was my idea."

Before I slipped out of Helene's hotel room that night I told her that this would be the last night we'd spend together. I didn't mention my engagement to Kathryn — it didn't seem right that Helene should be the first to know — but instead mumbled something about the complexities of life. She didn't argue or disagree, though I could see the disappointment in her eyes. Three days later I found a message in my mail slot — "We need to talk" — proposing to meet at an Italian restaurant in the West Village. Fair enough, I decided. Talking was the least I could do.

It was one of those candle-lit grottoes with high-backed booths that seem to exist only for conspiracies and assignations. The headwaiter was a small, furtive man who greeted me with a complicit smile, as if by merely stepping inside I was confessing to something dark and shameful that he would ignore in exchange for a handsome tip. He led me to a corner booth where I expected to find Helene sipping a glass of wine. Instead it was occupied by a heavy-set, balding man with a napkin tucked under his collar like a bib, picking at the broken remains of a lobster with a tiny fork.

An obvious mistake, I assumed, but when I turned around the waiter had melted into the gloom. The man wiped his hands on a napkin and stood up to greet me. He was well over six feet tall and shaped like a barrel, his face framed by a receding hairline and a Van Dyke beard. It was a massive but finely-turned face, built around a long pointed nose and a pair of dark eyes that were set a little too deep and a little too close together. He wore a tweed suit, a spotless white shirt and a woven red tie, and when he spoke it was with the exaggerated precision of a foreigner, possibly from Eastern or Central Europe. I was outraged to realize that somehow I'd been tricked into dining with this impostor instead of Helene.

"Hello, Christopher," he said in a low, resonant voice. "Won't you have a seat?" He extended a huge white hand. "My name is Craft."

Craft. That was the name Helene had given me when I asked who she was working for. "Where's Helene?" I demanded.

"Please sit down! People are listening."

On the other end of the room two waiters loitered beside the pastry cart, rolling their eyes in a pantomime of inattention. I slid into the booth without touching his hand. "Where is she?"

"Helene had another commitment this evening," he replied, keeping his voice low. His mouth moved in a twisted, exaggerated fashion when he spoke. "But I thought it was time that you and I met. I've taken something of an interest in you."

"I came here to see Helene."

His smile had faded to a patronizing smirk. "Just so there's no misunderstanding: Helene works for me. It was my thousand dollars she paid you."

"Listen—"

"Having said that, I can understand why you wanted to see her." He offered me some wine — which I refused — and poured some for himself. "She's a warm-hearted girl, as you've already found out for yourself."

"Maybe you should try minding your own business."

"This is my business, Christopher. Everything that concerns you concerns me."

The waiter appeared beside us and announced the day's specials like a spellbound auctioneer. He poured some wine into my glass and I guzzled it greedily as I swabbed a piece of bread in olive oil and tried to calm down. I considered standing up and walking out, and of course now I realize that's exactly what I should have done. But at the time I had no inkling of the danger I was in. I saw it as an opportunity to question this man who'd paid me a thousand dollars for no apparent reason and to understand what he thought he was doing. And I wanted to know how he was connected to Helene.

"All right," I said. "Let's try to talk about this like rational adults. I'll take you at your word that Helene was working for you when she gave me that money."

"Good." I noticed then, and on many later occasions, that even when he was at his most serious, Craft always seemed to be smirking. Not a humorous or indulgent or disinterested smirk. On the contrary, he gave the impression of being on the verge of an outburst that never came. His eyes, his lips, his hands — they never stopped moving, but their movements seemed checked by some artificial restraint. He was as restless as a wolf in a cage.

"In fact she told me as much."

"She wasn't supposed to mention that."

I shrugged. "And I assume you had your reasons for having her do that."

"Of course."

"But that was a year ago. What do you want from me?"

Craft set down his wine glass and leaned forward, pulling me toward him with his sensuous mouth. "If I may speak candidly, you've been something of a disappointment to me, Christopher. You went to graduate school — that's a good thing, a very good thing. It's what you wanted. But now here it is a year later, as you say, and what are you doing? Still slogging around with your course work, not doing any serious research or making much of a splash in your department. I expected more from you."

"I don't owe you anything."

"Do you need more money? Is that the problem?"

"No, the problem is that you have no right to expect anything from me. I didn't obligate myself to you in any way."

"Well, you posted that ad on the bulletin board, didn't you?"

"That was a joke."

He smiled as if to show that he understood the joke. "Everyone knew that."

"I didn't sell my soul."

"No, of course not. The whole 'soul' thing is just a metaphor. I realize that."

"If I'd thought I had a soul to sell, I would have demanded a lot more for it than money."

"Like what?"

"Like the secrets of the universe," I laughed, glancing around to make sure no one was listening. "At the very least."

His eyes glowed like blue coals in the candlelight. "I was hoping you could discover those by yourself."

"What are you talking about?"

"You're a scientist, aren't you? Isn't that what science is all about: unlocking the secrets of the universe? You don't need me to do that."

I felt confused, aware only of my growing anger. "What do you want from me?"

"I only want to help you succeed on your own terms."

"Help me? How can *you* help me?"

He wiped his hands on his napkin and wriggled out of the booth, dropping a hundred dollar bill on the table. "Unfortunately, right now I have another engagement. We can talk about it in greater depth at our next meeting."

I stood up and started to follow him. "Was Helene working for you when she met me the other night?"

He turned and fixed his smirking eyes on me one last time. "I wasn't paying her to sleep with you, if that's what you mean. That was her idea. But I did chip in on the expenses. The Four Seasons doesn't come cheap, you know."

"Stay out of my life."

"I have only your best interest at heart."

7.

Thursday, May 10, 4:00 p.m. 1̄5 days to execution.

Visiting the prison left Chaīlotte feeling anxious and depressed. Ritter seemed unreal in hiē absurd determination to have the salvation of his choice or none at all. The place mat had shaken him out of his apathy, only to confirm him in his desperation. She doubted that anyone could help him.

As she drove out the prison compound, a red pickup trailed behind her at a distance. Shē noticed it in her rearview mirror but thought nothing of it.

She called Sol on his cell phcne and told him about the place mat. His reaction was skeptical and defensive: obviously it made him uncomfortable to be discovering new evidence at this late date. "This isn't a smoking gun," he told her. "Even if it had been shown to the jury, it wouldn't have changed anything. I still wouldn't have let him take the stand."

"It's been a long day," Charlotte said. "Are you going to be in the office tomorrow?"

"I'll be here in the morning. Why don't you come over around nine?"

She returned to her hotel and spent an hour soaking in the hot tub, trying to float away the anxiety that had been tightening its grip on her.

But there was no respite in inactivity: another day of Ritter's life had ticked by. Luckily she hadn't sent her memo to the Titus Foundation before she fourd the place mat. She changed her clothes and had a quick dinner in the hotel restaurant. Then she headed back to her room, intending to call her mother as she had promised, though she didn't know what she'd say. Would she be returning to Philadelphia or not? Did she have a chance of saving Chris Ritter's life? Her mind wandered idly as she made her way through the winding corridor to her room. Then she saw something that shook her out of dreamy self-questioning with a tingle of fear.

Leaning against her door was another flat brown envelope. She carried it into her room and sat down on the bed. The envelope looked the same as the one she'd received the day before: her name printed on the front, "Hand Delivered" across the top, no return address. Her hands shook as she tore it open. What she found inside turned her stomach: twenty-four glossy color prints of Helene Varga's nude, blood-drenched body twisted into a variety of obscene poses for the benefit of the camera. In some she was still alive, in others unconscious or dead. The effect was so disgusting, so overwhelmingly offensive that Charlotte understood why the jury had convicted Ritter, even though the pictures contained nothing specifically implicating him. The judge should never have let the jury see those pictures over Sol's objection, especially before the penalty phase: that was a prejudicial error which in itself merited reversal on appeal. But it was too late to dwell on "technicalities." The only defense that mattered now was actual innocence, and these pictures — even for Charlotte — challenged that belief. And they loosed a fear that pierced her like a spike: This, they said, is what could happen to you. And whoever sent them knew what room she was in.

She didn't want to touch the pictures or see them lying around. She shoved them back into her briefcase and locked it. Was whoever left them watching her from outside? She bolted the door and snapped off the lights, stepping over to close the curtains.

Through a crack along the side she peered out into the dusk. Palm trees swayed in the squalid summer air as a storm blew in from the south. She could just make out her rented Honda parked between a black SUV and a red pickup. Nothing to be alarmed about, she told herself. She counted nine red pickups in the parking lot. Just about everybody in this part of Florida drove a red pickup.

Friday, May 11, 9:00 a.m. 14 days to execution

The next morning Sol's office looked like a blood-splattered crime scene. The window over Millie's desk had been smashed by a gallon-sized can of red paint, which then splashed all over the reception area. Sol stood beside the desk in his shirt sleeves and a pair of rubber gloves trying to salvage some of his papers. Charlotte's stomach clenched with the fear she'd tried to suppress when she looked at the photographs the night before. She wanted to run back to her rental car and drive as far away as she could go.

"I've seen it before," Sol smiled, trying to reassure her. "My Dad was a highly unpopular lawyer back in the civil rights era."

"Is Millie OK?"

"I sent her home. Someone's coming in to clean up this mess."

Charlotte was alarmed that Sol didn't take the situation more seriously. "Did you call the police?"

He smiled and led her back into his office. "Someone's trying to prove a point," he said as he peeled off his rubber gloves and invited her to sit down. "That point appears to be that Ritter is a monster and we should let justice take its course. Who did it? I don't know. For all I know it could be our friends in the DA's office."

"Are you serious?"

"I'm also a highly unpopular lawyer in certain quarters. But we're not going to let that stop us, are we? Let me take a look at that place mat."

Sitting at his desk, he examined the place mat under a gooseneck lamp like a jeweler appraising a diamond, studying the front, turning it over to look at the back, then scrutinizing both front and back a second time. "Did Ritter say this was the real thing?"

"He's sure of it. And there's something else." She reached in her briefcase for the envelope containing the photographs. "Last night I got another package at my hotel. Whoever left it even knows what room I'm staying in." She handed Sol the envelope and watched his reaction. "I assume these are the pictures the murderer took of Helene Varga after he bludgeoned her to death."

Sol shuffled through the pictures as if they were snapshots she'd taken on her vacation. "During and after," he said. "She wasn't even dead yet when some of these pictures were taken. The police printed them out from the memory card they found in the townhouse and used them as evidence at the trial."

"Along with the memory card," Charlotte said, recalling the transcript.

"These aren't the prints they used at the trial — those were marked as exhibits. This must be a duplicate set."

"Where's the memory card?"

"I assume it's still in the evidence locker. But of course the pictures were probably downloaded onto a computer long ago." Sol held up a photograph showing the victim's naked torso and her battered head, twisted to one side in an unnatural pose. An earring dangled from her ear. "In the penalty phase, they used these pictures to show that the murder was heinous, atrocious and cruel. Can't really disagree with that, can you?"

Charlotte turned away with a new rush of revulsion. "Those pictures are obscene."

"They are, and what doomed Ritter was the fact that he stashed the memory card where he could find it later, in a bureau drawer in his in-laws' bedroom."

She couldn't believe how disinterested, almost cheerful Sol seemed as he flipped through the photographs, and it annoyed her how he'd glided into talking about Ritter's guilt as a fact. "Assuming it was Ritter," she said.

"You still think he's innocent?"

"If I didn't think so, I wouldn't be here."

He blurted out a short, incredulous laugh and flashed his avuncular, Southern-gentlemanly smile, signifying, she supposed, that he was proud of her persistence and loyalty, even if only a fool could believe that Ritter was innocent. "Charlotte," he said in a confidential tone, even though they were alone in the office, "I don't want to discourage you, but what are you going to say about the earrings? You see that earring in her ear?" He held up the photograph they'd been discussing and fished for another one in the envelope. "Now look at this picture that shows the other side of her head. No earring, but a damaged ear lobe where it was torn out."

"I remember the testimony about that in the transcript."

"Neither of those earrings was found on her body or in the townhouse. But when the police went to Ritter's house in New York with a search warrant, they found one of them in the suitcase he'd brought down with him to Florida."

"It could have been planted. Ritter told me about this. He left that suitcase in the townhouse while he was out on the boat. That's what he would have said if he'd been allowed to testify."

"Allowed to testify?" In half a heartbeat Sol's color rose from pasty white to crimson. "Are you joining the chorus of presumptuous, ill-informed, second-guessing, Monday-morning quarterbacks who think I committed malpractice in advising my client not to testify?"

For a moment Charlotte wondered if he was going to challenge her to a fight. "No" — she smiled to remind him that she was a woman — "but there's something wrong here, isn't there? Maybe the prosecutors or the police printed these pictures from the memory card and sent them to me. But you said yourself they didn't even know about the place mat."

"As far as I know," he huffed.

"There's one person who would've had access to both."

"And who would that be?"

"Ritter calls him Craft."

"Craft! Some shadowy figure who goes around giving money to graduate students, taking over their lives, and framing them for murder fifteen years later? Do you understand why I advised Ritter not to testify? Craft doesn't exist."

"The real murderer, then. Whoever he is."

8.

Chris Ritter

Kathryn and I announced our engagement in late October at a dinner party hosted by her parents at a steak house on East 33rd Street. The guests included Doug and Tim, along with Professor Hirschorn and Andy Wagner and a few other graduate students. I didn't really like Wagner but it would have been awkward not to invite him. Kathryn's parents, Bill and Louise O'Donnell, had flown in from Wisconsin to attend an office supplies convention and were staying at the Marriott near Madison Square Garden. Bill was a solid Midwesterner who owned an office furniture business and made no secret of his admiration for Ronald Reagan. Louise talked constantly in a monologue worthy of James Joyce (which neither husband nor daughter seemed to notice), centering on their vacation home in Florida and the goal of retiring there as soon as possible. Both of them were drinking so heavily that I wondered how we were going to get them back to their hotel without calling an ambulance. Kathryn had warned me to avoid certain subjects — politics and religion, and even the weather to the extent that it might have some connection with politics or religion. Unfortunately Wagner had not received this warning. Overcoming his usual reticence, he downed an impressive quantity of champagne and launched into a competing monologue which for a time actually succeeded in silencing Louise, or at least reducing

her stream of consciousness to a conversational trickle. His topic was recent work in evolutionary genetics that focused on sexual selection, mating behavior, bird cuckoldry and the like, viewed through the jaundiced eye of the selfish gene, and his conclusion was that Kathryn and I, the happy couple, were groping around somewhere down on the evolutionary ladder with rutting tadpoles, rhesus monkeys in heat, and the lesser prairie chicken.

Louise had turned purple, unaccustomed to any blockage of her word flow or possibly just gagging on her surf 'n' turf. "Enough!" she exploded. "Is this the kind of thing you talk about at an engagement party?" She downed another mouthful of champagne and struggled to get her monologue flowing again. "I mean, all this stuff about tadpoles and rhesus monkeys, it's sort of sick, it's not Christian, it's not even American, it reminds me of something I read in the *Readers Digest*—"

"Face it, Louise," Wagner pounced, "we're animals. We're animals who got here the same way the other animals did. When it comes to courtship, marriage and fidelity, it's way too late for the Walt Disney version. We need to ask: What would Darwin say?"

Louise pushed her chair back from the table in disgust. "It's people like you who are ruining this country—"

"Who've already ruined it," Bill corrected, nodding gravely.

"— by dumbing morality down to the lowest common denominator. Going on about tadpoles, for heaven's sake, at our daughter's engagement party!"

"For example," Wagner pressed on, smirking in my direction, "why does the male lesser prairie chicken commute between two nests, maintaining both a mate and a mistress, but only has offspring with one of them?"

"That's called adultery," Louise croaked, struggling for breath as she tried to stand up. "In case you haven't heard, it's one of the Ten Commandments: Thou shalt not—"

"Do the Ten Commandments apply to the lesser prairie chicken?"

Professor Hirschorn, who sat next to Louise, seized her wrist and pulled her back into her seat before she could answer. His white hair was plastered back on the sides of his head and for some reason he'd worn a tuxedo. "Pay no attention to these young people," he advised in his thick Hungarian accent. "What do they know? Nothing!"

"It's a question of family values," Louise muttered. "The American way of life!"

"As opposed to Communism," Bill explained.

"Your President Reagan," the Professor nodded, smiling back at Bill, "is a very great man."

"If you happen to be rich," I blurted.

Kathryn gave me a kick under the table but I foolishly went on. "On the other hand, if you're poor or uneducated or underprivileged or black, you might as well stay under a rock because all the family values in the world aren't going to put food on your table."

Bill set his champagne glass down carefully and leaned toward me with an unpleasant smile. "You don't get it, do you? We are the uneducated. If we're not poor, it's only because we've worked hard for what we have. Is that underprivileged enough for you?"

"Dad—"

"Or should I have gone to some fancy college? Maybe studied law so I could figure out new ways to let criminals go free, or business so I could work on sending more jobs overseas?"

"Or biology." Louise squinted at me like a snake. "You could have studied biology."

Kathryn sat with her face buried in her hands, leaving me to deal with her parents on my own. The fate of our relationship hung in the balance, and I did not rise to the occasion. Instead I sat there speechless, paralyzed by the certainty that whatever I said would be wrong, probably disastrous. At that moment Tim, with his flair for theater, started chiming on his glass with a spoon, and when he had everyone's attention he leaped to his feet and delivered a short, humorous speech, which did little to dispel the air of hostility that had settled over the table. When Tim had finished, Professor Hirschorn, as if by pre-arrangement, stood up to propose the toast.

The Professor, in his tuxedo with his white hair slicked back on the sides, looked like Grandpa on "The Munsters" and sounded like Count Chocula. But he spoke with a gravity and sincerity that immediately absolved us of all the missteps and inanities we'd been guilty of that night — and even, by the time he finished, inspired Kathryn to send a tentative smile in my direction.

"As some of you may know, I am a widower," he began. "I was married to my dear wife for thirty-seven years before she passed away, and I can speak on the subject of marriage with some authority because I have seen it through to its conclusion, as I will one day soon see my life to its conclusion. Until then I cannot hold myself out as an authority on life. Whether it has any meaning or purpose, only God knows. We who have seen cruelty and suffering beyond our capacity to understand" — he glanced down at Kathryn's parents, who stared drunkenly ahead as if they knew what he was talking about — "and have sometimes wondered whether this universe was made to delight us or torment us, can only envy these young people in their love for each other, in their hope for the future, and yes, even in their ignorance, as they take this step forward, perhaps — with apologies to you, Wagner, in your erudite idiocy — like a pair of prairie chickens fulfilling their destiny in some grand design that they, and we ourselves, can never hope to understand. Salud!"

Looking back on that engagement party, it seems almost surreal, like a scene from an Eastern European movie. Kathryn's parents loved Professor Hirschorn almost enough to overcome their distaste for me. I was shocked to hear him speaking of God and destiny as if those were meaningful concepts for a scientist. I didn't believe that the universe had any grand design, or any design at all, either to delight or torment. It was brute matter, the result of the Big Bang several billion years ago; but that didn't tell me, I realize now, whether everything that happens is random or predetermined. I made the mistake of thinking I could have the best of both worlds. I thought I could enjoy the delights and avoid the torments.

One afternoon after my appeals had been exhausted and I'd been moved onto death row, Billy Bob and Bubba appeared at my cell and led me in manacles and leg irons down the long hall to the visitors room. That day Billy Bob was tall and lean with a missing front tooth and Bubba was the cocky barrel-chested type. Neither of them said a word, but they gave the impression that what they were doing was particularly distasteful. They strapped me into my seat at the high metal table like an astronaut being prepared for takeoff, then opened the other door and admitted a thin, balding Asian man who wore a badge that said "Chaplain" at the bottom. I had never seen this man before. He was about my age, with a bulbous nose and a blotchy complexion, and although I could tell he wanted to be friendly, he avoided my eyes, ducking and bobbing like a fighter backing away from a dangerous foe. There was something sad, almost tortured in his expression, as if he'd committed some monstrous crime he needed to atone for.

He sat down across from me, laid his clipboard on the table and waited until the guards had left the room. "My name is Paul Young," he said. "I'm one of the chaplains here at the prison. I counsel prisoners on death row who have no religious faith."

"I didn't request any counseling."

"I know that. First let me explain—"

"Guard!" I shouted. "I want to go back to my cell!" I could see Billy Bob and Bubba smirking through the window on the door.

"They won't come," the chaplain said with a bashful smile. "Unless I push this buzzer."

"Push it, then."

"I will if you want me to, but first I'm required to inform you of your rights. Each prisoner scheduled for execution is entitled to twelve hours of spiritual counseling, regardless of religious belief. The program is completely voluntary and non-sectarian, and is not aimed at converting you to any religion or set of beliefs." He spoke in a monotone, as if reciting something he'd repeated a thousand times; I realized I was getting some kind of Miranda warning. "You can choose whether to participate or not, in your sole discretion, and you can discontinue your participation at any time. Nothing you say will be held against you."

That little touch almost made me laugh. "Except that you're going to kill me."

He seemed embarrassed by that comment, ducking to avoid meeting my eyes. "I'm not going to kill you. I don't believe in capital punishment." He glanced at Billy Bob and Bubba, who goggled back at us through the window like fish in an aquarium. "They are, when your time comes."

"Push the buzzer."

He squinted down at his clipboard. "It says here you have no religious affiliation. Do you believe in God?"

I shook my head no.

"Do you believe in the Devil?"

"It's hard not to, when you're living in hell."

For an instant he let his eyes meet mine. "Can I take that as a yes?"

"I don't believe in immaterial or supernatural forces of any kind. But if I were going to believe in any, it would probably be the Devil."

"That's a good first step," he smiled.

Such was my introduction to Chaplain Paul Young. He serves as chaplain to non-believers, of which there are surprisingly few on death row. The place is a hotbed of religious faith and disputation; a preview, perhaps, of my own special place in hell, where the punishment for my atheism will be to spend eternity surrounded by murderers bent on saving my soul. The inmates, especially the worst ones — the sexual predators, the child killers, the sociopaths — treat Paul Young with the hostility and scorn they usually reserve for their defense attorneys. They call him the Devil's chaplain.

At that first meeting he never pushed the buzzer to call the guards. We talked for an hour, until Billy Bob and Bubba burst in to hustle me back to my cell. Chaplain Young told me a little about himself — he was trained as a clinical psychologist and became a prison chaplain after some unspecified crisis — and I gave him the basic outlines of my own career, with which he already seemed familiar. Since then I've spoken to him half a dozen times, shackled to that same metal chair, under the silent scrutiny of the guards who will soon escort me to my death. True to his word, he has never tried to proselytize or convert me. On the contrary (as befits a man who has never been able to look at me directly for more than a few seconds at a time), his method has been simply to ask questions and let me do the talking. I've told him the story of my life from one end to the other, omitting only the most shameful parts. I've told him of my troubled childhood, my ambitions, my betrayals, my decline and my fall; and he has listened sympathetically, without condoning or condemning, just nodding, shaking his head, taking an occasional note. It troubles me, no, it angers me, that he's shown a complete indifference to the whole reason I'm talking to him — the crime I'm supposed to have committed — as if that brutal act, and whether I committed it or not, is of no consequence to him. But I'm hardly in a position to complain: After six sessions I feel guilty because I haven't been completely honest. I still haven't told him about Craft.

"Is this getting us anywhere?" I asked as our session neared its end.

"I don't know," he said. "I do feel that something is missing. Perhaps you're withholding some key piece of information." He flashed a reassuring smile and quickly turned away. "Most inmates do."

I glanced at the door, expecting the guards to burst through at any moment. "You've never asked me about the crime I'm supposed to have committed."

"I figured you'd get to that eventually."

"There's no 'eventually' here."

"I know," he said, peering up from his clipboard with a faint smile. "So perhaps you should hurry up and tell me what's on your mind."

"Don't you even want to know if I'm guilty or innocent?"

"Everyone is innocent," he said, looking away. "And everyone is guilty."

I spent my second year of graduate school — the year before my marriage to Kathryn — trying to cement my relationship with Professor Hirschorn, which had cooled after the fiasco of the engagement party. Our department was divided between woozy old men like Professor Hirschorn and a cadre of ambitious Young Turks openly questioning authority, getting their tickets punched

— and whenever they got the chance, throwing each other under the bus. My nemesis Wagner was one of those who tried to play both sides of the street, combining serious work on evolution with frequent quotations from Albert Einstein about God not playing at dice with the universe. That was pure cynicism; he didn't believe a word of it. I stayed awake at night thinking up ways to discredit him.

Kathryn worried about my increasing obsession with departmental politics and what she called my cynicism. "It's never cynical to tell the truth," I told her. "What's cynical is to peddle an illusion as the truth."

"Sometimes I worry about you," she said. "How are you going to teach our kids the difference between right and wrong when you don't believe in anything but selfishness?"

"You really don't get it, do you?" I was so angry I could have throttled her. "There's no reason I can't be just as ethical as the next man without believing in a pack of lies."

Kathryn wasn't the only one who tried to talk me down from my high horse. Tim, who in college I'd thought of as an amoral playboy, even something of a psycho in his pursuit of exploitative relationships with women, had emerged as a spokesman for spirituality second only to the Dalai Lama. The scion of a wealthy family, he searched for the meaning of life in the Barnum and Bailey world of the theater. He had a brilliant theatrical imagination, but he was too cerebral to be a good actor. He could memorize the lines and go through the motions, but he lacked empathy, the ability to stand in the shoes of the characters and project their emotions. Even the effort to do this in a performance left him depressed and exhausted for days afterward. Sometimes we thought he had a serious mental illness. A year before graduation, he finally got professional help and began taking medications to help smooth out his ups and downs.

One Saturday morning when Tim and I met for coffee at the De Luxe Luncheonette, I mentioned Professor Hirschorn's speech at the engagement party. "I can't believe that my advisor is proposing toasts to God and destiny."

"You really have sold your soul, haven't you?" Tim said.

The question made me flinch. "What are you talking about?"

"This whole materialism thing," he smiled. "You've really bought into it."

"I didn't 'buy into it.' It happens to be true."

"True?" he laughed. "What kind of particles is truth made of?" He pretended to be searching for something on his tray. "Quarks? Neutrinos? Gluons?"

"This may come as a surprise," I said, "but there's such a thing as the real world — as opposed to fantasies and illusions." Tim had just enrolled in a MFA program in theater and intended to pursue a career as a director. "Like the ones you deal with in the theater," I couldn't help adding.

He peered at me over his steaming coffee cup. "My goal in the theater is to create an experience more real than any you could have in the so-called real world. Art isn't about illusion. It operates on a spiritual plane that's way more real than those molecules you look at under your microscope."

Doug, too, had his opinions, which he was only too happy to share with me. In those days I saw Doug as the great pragmatist, who focused on the practicalities of business as I plumbed the mysteries of life and Tim chased the illusions of art. I realize now that he was trading in a different kind of illusion, the illusion of wealth. He joined an investment banking firm that specialized in underwriting junk bonds secured by overvalued collateral. It took almost twenty years for that illusion to play itself out, as his career melted down along with Wall Street and the rest of the economy. By then he was married to Kathryn and I was on death row.

Wagner, Kathryn, Tim and Doug — the people closest to me were generous with their opinions and advice. I should have listened to them. Instead, without understanding what I was doing, I turned my life over to Craft.

Around that time, Oscar Lopez,. the owner of the De Luxe Luncheonette, was killed in an auto accident. His wife Carmen died of leukemia a few months later. I'd met some of their kids, the older ones who sometimes helped out in the luncheonette. There was a boy of fifteen — a smart, good-natured kid who seemed out of place in that neighborhood—and a daughter about a year younger who probably should have been kept under lock and key. When the mother died, the kids had been scattered to the four winds. The two youngest went to an aunt in Washington Heights, the teenage vixen to her grandparents in the Dominican Republic, and the good-natured boy Alex — now fifteen, the same age I was when my father killed himself — landed in a foster home in the Bronx. Luckily there was no Uncle Ed lying in wait for Alex. The foster parents were a truck driver named Fuentes and his wife who had five children of their own. They fed the boy well but mostly left him to his own devices.

One morning at the luncheonette the counter man handed me a napkin with a phone number written on it. The number belonged to Mrs. Fuentes, Alex's foster mother. "Mr. Ritter, I know you're a good man," she said when I called. "Alex always talks about you. You're a smart man, he says. He wants to be like you. Can you talk to him? He's not doing so good."

Apparently Alex had stopped going to school during his mother's illness and never took up the habit again. The social workers were threatening to remove him from the Fuentes home if he didn't return to school. And so, without exactly knowing why, I took on the role of tutor and mentor to this skinny kid with blotchy skin who, I soon learned, had no interest in anything except sex, various kinds of lethal weapons and the New York Yankees. It seems ironic now, twenty years later, in view of what we've each become — myself a convicted murderer, Alex a respected New York police detective — but I have to take much of the credit for his success. I taught him math and English, I showed him how to behave if he wanted adults to take him seriously, and most important I convinced him that if he stayed on his present course he'd end up in prison. That, it turns out, was what I knew the most about.

One windy Saturday in April, I huddled beside Alex on a park bench in Poe Park, near Fordham Road in the Bronx. Mirroring the rows of identical buildings that line the streets in that neighborhood sat rows of identical old ladies, clad in identical black coats and hats and clutching identical black handbags, perched on the park benches like crows — or ravens, perhaps I should say, in honor of the poet who'd inhabited the wooden cottage on one end of the park. There was some undefinable horror in that scene, in those black-clad octogenarians dribbling crumbs to the pigeons strutting and humming around them like wind-up toys: some quality I saw there that led me to venture away from math and English to more philosophical topics. I tried to interest Alex in some reading on evolution, and before long the conversation touched on the subject of good and evil, which in a careless moment I suggested did not exist.

"You been out on the street, you seen evil, man," Alex said, nodding confidently. "It's out there. You been out on the street, you seen it."

"Sure you see it, but —"

"Lot of bad things going down out there."

"But you see, it's just an idea, a judgment — it's real in that sense — but it's not a thing that really exists, not part of the natural world."

Alex was laughing now. "Ask these old ladies who moved here from the Holocaust. They tell you."

"Moved here from the Holocaust?"

"Some of them live in my building," he nodded. "Old Jewish ladies. They moved here from the Holocaust. I don't know where that is but you ask them, they tell you all about it. They been there."

Alex said goodbye and hurried off to Fordham Road to hang out with his friends. I stayed behind to jot down a few notes about his progress and to gather my thoughts about the coming weeks. The wedding was coming up in early May and then Kathryn and I would head to St. Thomas for our honeymoon. I'd tried over and over again to end my relationship with Helene, but neither of us could bring ourselves to do it. As the wedding approached I'd stopped responding to her messages, and that only resulted in more pain, more enticement, more frustration. The thought of her tormented me day and night. I told myself that one more night together wouldn't do any harm. And then what? Obviously this couldn't continue after the wedding. Or could it? It would be easy enough, especially on Saturdays when I was supposed to be with Alex. Sex is no big deal, I told myself. It's not evil; there's no such thing as evil. It's love, in fact. And why can't a man love two women at the same time? My answer to what might charitably be called my conscience was what the bank robber said when he pointed his gun at the teller: Nobody's going to get hurt.

As I closed my notebook the sun sank behind the rooftops. The temperature suddenly dropped and a cold wind whistled through the park, sending a chill through my clothes and rustling the newspaper of the man sitting beside me. I had hardly noticed this man when he sat down. He appeared like everyone else: he wore a long black coat and a black hat, and he kept his face buried in his newspaper. But when the wind almost plucked the newspaper out of his hands, he turned sideways and spoke to me. "If you read Poe," he said in a friendly voice, "you'll find that he thought evil was inherent in the nature of things. So in that sense it is part of the natural world. Or the supernatural world, which amounts to the same thing."

I swiveled in alarm and realized that the man was Craft. "How long have you been sitting here?"

"Pitiful, isn't it, that a kid his age doesn't know what the Holocaust was?"

I was furious but determined not to lose control. "Sit somewhere else or I'll have you arrested for harassment."

"Just trying to stay in touch. Is there something wrong with that?"

"I don't owe you anything."

"That's correct. Whatever you do, you do of your own free will."

"So try minding your own business."

I stood up and tried to escape, but he tagged along beside me as if we were the best of friends. It was three or four blocks to the subway and I was hoping I would see a police officer along the way. "I've told you this before," I said. "When you paid me that thousand dollars, you got nothing in return."

"That's certainly been true so far. Your academic career is going nowhere fast."

I stopped and faced him defiantly. "What are you talking about?"

"You've published a couple of half-decent papers, barely serviceable work. You don't get along with your advisor and you haven't been able to settle on a thesis topic. Word on the street is that you're floundering."

"That's ridiculous. Professor Hirschorn—"

"And your Janssen Fellowship is in jeopardy."

I stepped closer and lowered my voice to make sure no one could overhear. Not that anyone on that street would have been the least bit interested. It was a typical street in the Bronx, teeming with Middle Eastern food vendors and Hispanic teenagers and black women trudging home from work. "Where did you hear that? Have you been talking to Wagner?"

"I sit on a couple of boards," Craft smirked, keeping his voice low. "I hear things."

I felt a little queasy. "What do you want from me?"

"I don't want anything from you, Chris. I just want to help you."

"I don't need your help."

"I can open doors for you. I have friends in high places who can keep the money flowing in."

"I'm not in this for the money."

"I know that."

"If I wanted money, I could have gone to Wall Street and been a millionaire by now."

"I know that. And I'm glad you didn't. I'm glad you're as idealistic as you are, Chris. But don't cut off your nose to spite your face. You can do well by doing good. There's nothing wrong with that."

Now I felt desperate, confused, ashamed that I had somehow let this man insinuate himself into my life. I wanted to run away from him but instead I stood there and begged for his help. "Do you think you could help me keep the Janssen Fellowship?"

"I hope so. I can certainly try. But you've got to do your part, Chris. You can't achieve your goals with wishful thinking. You need to take a more pragmatic approach to your career. A little more calculating, maybe a little more — well, I hate to say it, but maybe a little more like Wagner."

"I hope I never sink that low."

"No, I'm sure you won't. But your first order of business is to find a thesis topic. May I make a suggestion?"

Why not? I'd begged for his help. Why not go all the way and let him tell me how to write my dissertation? I stared ahead blankly.

He went on: "What possible Darwinian explanation can there be for a soldier who throws himself on a hand grenade to save the lives of his comrades? The soldier dies and doesn't reproduce. How can you explain that in terms of the selfish gene?"

"The altruism problem," I mumbled. "There's a lot of work going on in that area."

"Well, why not jump into the fray? 'The evolution of selflessness.' Very cutting edge. And in the meantime, give Helene a call, won't you? You're breaking the poor girl's heart."

The next day I checked on the trustees of the Janssen Fellowship. No one named Craft served on the board, and the departmental secretary had never heard of him. But the incident played out just as Craft had predicted. I met with Professor Hirschorn to discuss my proposed thesis topic — 'Adaptational value of altruistic behavior' — and two weeks later an anonymous donor made a large contribution to the Janssen endowment, stipulating that the funds be used to support my research.

At Professor Hirschorn's suggestion, I wrote a thank you note conveying my heartfelt appreciation to the trustees and the anonymous donor for their selfless generosity. And naturally I called Helene.

The wedding took place in late May after the end of my second year of graduate school, at a pseudo-luxurious country club near the O'Donnells' vacation home in Florida. Avoiding the forms of religion, we were married by a seventy-eight-year-old Southern Baptist police judge to the sound of mosquitos being electrocuted by bug zappers. It was an ice cube's throw from the spot where Helene's body would later be found.

Tim and Doug were there, of course, along with a few other friends from college and graduate school. Professor Hirschorn overcame his aloofness to accept the invitation, and Andy Wagner, who I was hoping would decline, flew down with him from New York. It was supposed to be the happiest day of my life, and in spite of everything I still think it was. Kathryn looked stunning in her bridal dress, girlish no more, her red hair towering over a splendid white neck, her tentative smile finally regal and absolute. She was mine, I was hers, and nothing could tear us apart. When the time came to kiss we held our embrace so long that the old judge cleared his throat and jokingly threatened to hold us in contempt. After we'd stood for what seemed hours in the reception line, Doug opened the first bottle of champagne and delivered a hilarious toast, in which he declared that he himself, along with every other young man at the wedding, was in love with Kathryn and had nothing but envy and spite for the lucky groom.

My last few years of graduate school are distilled in my memory into a single nightmare image: walking, then running, on an accelerating treadmill while a torrent of books and papers crash down on my head. I was working so hard, both on field work and on my theoretical writing, that I scarcely had time for eating or sleeping. For my thesis on the evolution of altruism I studied naked mole rats, vampire bats, male bonnet macaques, barn swallows, gorillas and chimpanzees, not to mention their close cousins, homo sapiens, though instances of true selflessness in that species are exceedingly rare. And that was part of the problem. The more I thought about altruism, the less of it I perceived or experienced. This should not have been surprising, since I was trying to explain selflessness in terms of its opposite. If you receive any benefit from your selfless behavior — even so much as feeling good about yourself — then it's not really selfless behavior, is it? And if the benefit you receive, in terms of survival value, doesn't outweigh the cost, then your penchant for selflessness will die out in a couple of generations. Was I chasing a chimera?

Naturally I began to look at my own emotions and those of the people around me with a jaundiced eye. Wagner, of course, was the poster child for the selfish gene, a man who would have made Machiavelli blush. Tim and Doug were pursuing their careers with a solipsistic abandon that made everyone around them want to run for cover. Even Kathryn, my loving wife, came under my microscope. In light of what was going on in our lives, it wasn't hard to see her in deterministic, biological terms. After a year of marriage we decided to stop using birth control; we assumed she would be pregnant within a month. When nothing happened, she consulted her doctor, who stalled for a year before ordering a fertility workup. With each passing month, Kathryn grew more tense and manipulative — in one tearful moment she intimated that she might divorce me if I was the source of the problem — and I began to see her behavior since the day we met as the expression of her genes. Luckily we were still young: a few hormones, a routine of late-night temperature-taking, and within a few months Kathryn was pregnant with our daughter Casey.

The day Casey was born was the greatest day of my life. When I held her in my arms for the first time I burst into tears with an upsurge of love I'd never felt before. But deep in my heart the damage had been done. I knew why Kathryn had driven herself to such lengths to bring this child into the world, and I knew why I loved her the way I did. We were following a decree that had come down from some muddy burrow where ground shrews bred two hundred million years ago. "You know why babies are cute?" Wagner smirked when I told him the joyous news. "It's so you won't kill them."

The more I observed myself and others, the more my materialism hardened into cynicism. Of course I didn't see it that way at the time; I always objected strenuously when Kathryn called me a cynic. But more and more I began to see morality and idealism as nothing but adaptations to advance the self, which could be dispensed with like any other inappropriate adaptation in a given situation. The whole edifice of religion — increasingly under the sway of right-wing fundamentalists — I condemned as delusory and dangerous, which did not endear me to Kathryn's parents. Of course I still had my personal values, which I clung to more tenaciously than ever. Like all respectable biologists, I had nothing but scorn for the so-called Intelligent Design movement that had begun to attract attention at that time. I threw myself into liberal causes, becoming active on a faculty committee opposing the University's proposal to displace hundreds of poor African-Americans from their homes in order to make room for a new physics lab. Ironically — or presciently, some might say — I became an outspoken opponent of the death penalty, which I denounced as a crime against humanity. I congratulated myself on my high moral principles, but at heart I knew they were as accidental as the color of my eyes. I began keeping a diary in which I blithely recorded the progress of my moral decay.

Yes, that's the diary that became Exhibit A at the penalty phase of my trial. I have Craft to thank for that. I met him every couple of weeks in some out-of-the-way venue, which made it impossible for me to learn anything about him. Later when I tried to tell the police about Craft, it was the random nature of those encounters, as much as anything else, that made my story seem so fantastic and unbelievable. I never knew his address or phone number; when I needed to reach him I'd leave a note on the bulletin board at Dominick's and within a few days I'd receive a call. Why did I keep dancing to his tune? I owed him, even held him in awe, for saving my skin on the Janssen Fellowship. Maybe he really could open doors for me, as he claimed, and ensure the resources I would need for my research. And often I needed his help in finding Helene, who had a habit of disappearing for months at a time. She never seemed to have an apartment of her own: she'd stay with her mother in Queens or some other relative who barely spoke English in a neighborhood where I didn't feel safe, and then she'd just disappear. I should have suspected that she had a drug habit but it never entered my mind. Months would pass, miserable, agonizing months; I couldn't sleep, I couldn't work, until I found her again. I didn't exactly love Helene but I needed her as an antidote to Kathryn's coldness, especially after the fertility rites took over our marriage. Craft could always find Helene and bring her back, and in my gratitude I began to confide in him as if he were my friend. I told him of my disillusionment with Professor Hirschorn, my rivalry with Wagner, even my frustrations with Kathryn — and on a more positive note, the joy I felt at the birth of my daughter. He seemed a sympathetic listener, though I realize now that he was merely collecting my confidences in order to use them against me.

When I suspected Wagner of falsifying data for his dissertation, Craft advised me to expose him with an anonymous note to Professor Hirschorn. I remember it was a wintry day in December, late in the afternoon. We stood on a terrace overlooking the East River a few blocks north of the UN. Craft wore a camel coat with scarf and gloves; I buried my hands in my pockets and tried to face away from the wind. "I wouldn't stoop that low," I said. "No matter how much I hate Wagner."

"Your scruples are admirable," Craft said with a smile. "But don't let them get in your way. Wagner has no such scruples: he'd sell you out in a heartbeat if he got the chance. Why should you be any different?"

"I'm not like Wagner," I said.

"Oh, yes, you are. And the sooner you realize that, the better off you'll be."

He reached in his coat pocket and pulled out a small leather-bound book. "This is for you," he said, pushing it toward me.

I took a step back. "What is it?"

"What does it look like? It's a blank book. You should start keeping a diary."

"Why?"

"You need to write down your arguments with yourself so that eventually you'll come out the winner."

He flipped through the book as if he were shuffling a deck of cards. "The pages are all blank. You see that? They're all blank. You can make your life whatever you want it to be."

9.

Charlotte felt much better after lunch. Sol called out for sandwiches and a large order of tropical fruit salad — pineapple, grapefruit, melon chunks and mango — which he served on the conference table along with a couple of Cokes. They sat across from each other, strictly avoiding the discussion of "business" — as Sol termed their last-ditch efforts to save Ritter — in favor of sports, geography and local history. A clean-up crew had done its worst with the red paint, leaving a toxic cloud of solvents that gave Charlotte a headache. She was sure now that she would represent Ritter. Even Sol had agreed to accept the hypothesis of a "Craft" if that's what it took to keep her on the case. "Whatever you want to believe," he said with the friendly condescension she found so annoying. "You might already have enough to ask for a stay if Ritter will let you." Still she had to resist the urge to run away. She was almost six feet tall but had always felt smaller, despite the confident way she carried herself. When she met someone new, the first thing they noticed (though rarely commented on) was how high and small her voice was as compared to her body; the second was how deep her mind was as compared to her voice. Of course there was a little girl in there, as there is in every woman, but she knew her own strength and could use it when needed. She had struggled with depression, especially since college. Her mother said it was all in her head, but it didn't seem that way. Sometimes she felt as if she'd awoken on a larger planet, where the gravity was so strong she could hardly lift her arm or get out of bed. When she played the piano, especially Mozart, it was like landing on Mercury;

her fingers felt as if they might fly away. She still wasn't sure if the law was a planet she could survive on.

She had emailed her memo to the Titus Foundation detailing her conclusion that Ritter deserved their support, but in her private thoughts she found nothing but doubt. She didn't trust Ritter, but she trusted the system that had stuck him on death row even less, especially in its Southern dispensation, a Billy Bob and Bubba contraption just a few Playboy calendars away from lynch mobs and chain gangs. And now something strange and troubling had made its appearance in the case, something she felt compelled to combat as if her own life depended on it: she couldn't allow herself to ignore the sickness she saw in those photographs. "These are evil," she said, pushing the pictures away for what she hoped would be the last time.

Sol stared back with the usual twinkle in his eye, as if even that statement fell within the purview of his superior intelligence. "Do you believe in God?" he asked, surprisingly.

"Yes, I do," she said.

"I count myself as an agnostic on that issue. But on the subject of evil I've reached some definite conclusions."

Charlotte smiled involuntarily — and inappropriately, she realized, mirroring Sol, whose affable tone would have been better suited to discussing the merits of the fruit salad. "You don't think these pictures are evil?"

He speared a chunk of melon with a toothpick and it vanished into his mouth. "My dad was in the Army during the war," he smiled. "He was a photographer attached to Eisenhower's staff and he toured the death camps after they were liberated, taking pictures of the heaps of human hair and the emaciated bodies dumped into pits. I was brought up to share the anger he brought home from that experience. I think he named me Solomon in the hope that I'd acquire the wisdom to answer the question he was always asking: If there's such evil in the world, how could God exist?"

"A lot of people have asked that question."

"I've spent my life agonizing over it. I've read all these books on Hitler and the Holocaust, and quite a few others, and I've come to the conclusion that it's a false question. Evil is a dangerous superstition."

Charlotte's breath faltered, as it always did when she was trying to keep from showing her anger. Her throat was suddenly dry. "There's such a thing as evil," she said, gulping the last of her Coke. "Slavery was evil. The Holocaust was evil. That's not a superstition."

"Evil doesn't exist apart from us humans and our actions. We create it, but we talk about it as if it's a supernatural force, as if we were actors in a drama imposed on us from outside. We don't want to acknowledge that we're the ones writing the script." He chomped down on the last bite of his sandwich and stood up. Then he picked his way around the table, reaching out occasionally to pluck a book from the shelf and slip it back in its place.

"There are evil people, people who have no values or ideals," Charlotte said, trying not to choke on the words as they rattled in her throat.

"Hitler was a failed artist who thought of himself as an idealist," Sol said. He disappeared through the door to his office, where he continued his search of the bookshelves, again returning empty-handed. "If he'd had a little more talent and training, he might have become a successful painter. Or if he'd been really lucky, he might have been an actor or a director — that's where his true talent lay. He was a theatrical genius, stage-managing the rise and fall of the Third Reich right up to the flaming *Götterdämmerung* in Berlin."

Sol waved his hand dismissively toward the bookshelves. "I have a book around here somewhere — I can't seem to find it right now — that shows how much of what Hitler did was copied straight out of the Ibsen plays he admired in his youth. Ibsen, the humanist! The truth about Hitler has been ignored by the world. People want to believe he was evil, or at the very least a madman. They don't want to believe that with a few lucky breaks he might have turned out just like them, or like one of the celebrities they love so much. That would be the true banality of evil, wouldn't it?"

Chris Ritter

Wagner seemed to be following me like a family curse. Professor Hirschorn asked us both to stay on as research fellows and within a year we received junior faculty appointments. I had no use for Wagner — he was a clever charlatan who would do anything to advance his career — but I still had my principles, which forbade me to engage in the kind of backstabbing he was so adept at. Instead I focused on my research, through which I'd achieved a new level of intellectual excitement. My only regret was that I had been born too late to write *The Selfish Gene*. Had I been twenty years younger, I might have *been* Richard Dawkins: I would have had the same powerful ideas and expressed them with the same brilliance, probably in a book with the same captivating title, and his phenomenal success would have been mine. At least that was my fantasy.

"The man knows how to turn a phrase," Craft said when I mentioned Dawkins. "In fact, as I read his books, sometimes I feel that I must have been whispering into his ear as he wrote them."

We sat at the counter of a coffee shop in the Port Authority Bus Terminal, sipping bad coffee from paper cups one rainy day in

March. "But when he strays outside of biology"—Craft took a bite of his cinnamon coffee cake, the second piece he'd ordered since we sat down — "he doesn't follow his ideas to their logical conclusion."

"You're saying Dawkins doesn't go far enough?"

"He says there's no good or evil in the universe, only pitiless indifference. But then he talks about fairness and decency as if they were written in the stars. 'Don't get me wrong,' he says. 'I'm a good man — I vote Labour.' You see the problem? If good and evil are nothing but fantasies, where did fairness and decency came from?"

Craft was poaching on my turf: the evolution of altruism, which I'd been studying and writing about for years. There was an answer, but it was a complicated one which not even all biologists could agree on. I tried the simplistic approach. "Our moral sense has evolved," I said, "just like any other instinct. It's just like sex or aggression or looking after your children."

"I almost forgot," he laughed. "You're an expert on morality!"

He shoveled the last few crumbs of coffee cake into his mouth and washed them down with what was left of his coffee. "You don't mind taking care of this, do you? I'm a little strapped for cash."

He took a step toward the waiting room, where a large group of Asian tourists marched in single file behind a tour guide waving a red banner. "Let me leave you with this question," he said with a predatory smile. "If my instinctual drive to dominate or take advantage of my fellow creatures—and maybe to inflict pain on them, or even kill them—is stronger than my instinct to treat them fairly and decently, then which instinct should I follow?"

He disappeared into the crowd just as the waitress arrived with our check.

That wasn't the only time Craft stuck me with the check. His instinct to cheat his fellow humans (myself, at any rate) was much stronger than his instinct to treat them fairly and decently. But in terms of career advancement, the meals I bought him were worth every penny. He taught me that science is the equivalent of the medieval Church, a bastion of power that aims at domination by claiming a monopoly on truth. It comforts the faithful with the illusion of a coherent, understandable universe, which however is subject to radical change at any time upon the revelation of new data. All this is typical of our species, reflecting our drive for survival and evolutionary advantage through the exercise of intelligence. We know this, yet somehow we imagine that the future will be different, that we will not only survive but progress. We can't bear to believe in pitiless indifference, no matter how hard we try. We must believe in Providence. We must believe in salvation.

"But as a member of the priesthood," Craft told me one day as we rode in a taxicab to Penn Station, where I had to catch a train to Washington, "you can't indulge in any naïve self-delusions. You have a responsibility."

I was on my way to deliver a talk on "The Promise of Evolutionary Biology" to an audience of government officials, and Craft wanted to make sure I said nothing to shake their faith in science. "If anyone expresses skepticism about where biology is headed," he said, "talk about the miracle of modern science— antibiotics, cancer vaccines, organ transplants and the like. But be sure to leave some room for mystery. People need to feel some awe about life, some mystery; they don't want to think they're just a bunch of proteins and junk DNA that'll soon be headed for the compost heap. You've got to let them feel that awe, but don't overdo it or you'll lose your power over them. Miracle and mystery aside, they need to think you know exactly what you're talking about. These are the people who dole out the research dollars, don't forget. They need to see you as an authority figure."

The taxi edged into the jumble of traffic in front of Madison Square Garden. I paid the driver and climbed out ahead of Craft, and as we parted — we never shook hands, not once in the whole time I knew him — I registered my usual protest, probably for the last time: "Whatever happened to science as the quest for truth?"

He burst into laughter. "We've looked at that model and found it needed some correction. I've just given you everything you need: miracle, mystery and authority. You can forget the rest. Now you'd better hurry or you'll miss your train."

I resisted Craft's blandishments for over two years. Wagner plagiarized research from the internet, falsified data, lied to the senior faculty whenever it would advance his career. I kept my head down and concentrated on my work, confident that sooner or later my rival would meet his downfall. Instead his career took off while mine foundered in the starting gate. Yet in spite of almost overwhelming temptation I was too proud to call him out, too proud to engage in the kind of dirty tricks it would have taken to bring him down.

Until Greta arrived in the department.

The affair with Helene continued but I was never obsessed with her the way I became obsessed with Greta. It was mainly sex and a little excitement, to counterbalance Kathryn's coldness and our increasingly loveless marriage. I never considered leaving Kathryn after Casey was born. My whole world revolved around that little girl. I spent every spare minute with her, cuddling her in my arms as I read her a book, carrying her on my shoulders to the playground, showing her how to build a tower with her blocks. When my son Liam — if he was really my son — was born six years later, shortly before my arrest, I wanted to find a place for him in that special world I'd created with Casey but I never really had the chance. Nothing that's happened or could happen, including my impending execution, will ever be as painful as losing those kids. I lost them the day I was arrested. In Kathryn's eyes I was a murderer — worse, the murderer of a drug-addicted prostitute in her parents' house — and unfit to spend another minute with my children.

Of course at the time (no one believes this) I didn't know that Helene was a prostitute, and I had no inkling of her drug habit. That only came out later, when the police brought in witnesses to identify her body. In retrospect I should have known that Craft was orchestrating and financing our relationship right from the start. We always met at some unlikely venue and she always had a story to tell — she had just moved in, it was her sister's apartment, her cousin worked at the hotel — that explained what we were doing there. I had my suspicions but no conceivable explanation to support them, so you might say I looked the other way. She was a warm, loving woman and I was grateful for every minute I spent with her. In my vanity I imagined that she loved me.

On weekends I concealed my trysts with Helene under the camouflage of trips to the Bronx to tutor Alex Lopez. Alex was one of the brightest students I've ever taught at any level. When I wasn't spending the afternoon in bed with Helene, I was teaching Alex what he needed to know to graduate from high school. Apart from English, math and science, I taught him how to use his brain. I disabused him of the superstitions his parents and teachers had instilled in him and taught him that rational thought is the source of all true understanding. When he finally graduated, I expected him to go to college, possibly to follow in my footsteps in biology.

Imagine my disappointment when he informed me that he had enlisted in the Marines, with the goal of becoming a police officer.

Then he asked me to look after his two younger sisters while he was away, providing the same services I had provided to him. Of course I agreed, but he could sense my hesitation.

"I know you'll help my little sisters," he pleaded. "You helped me a lot."

"I know, but—"

"You're a good man."

"Don't worry, Alex. You can depend on me."

But that turned out to be a lie. After he left for the Marines, I stopped returning calls from his sisters and soon lost touch with the family. It was one of the betrayals I can't forgive myself for — the youngest sister ended up dead of an overdose and maybe I could have prevented it. But I had a family of my own and had to give the highest priority to my career. I'd done a lot for Alex, as he acknowledged, but my generosity had its limits. I'd taught him scientific reasoning, attention to detail and dogged perseverance in the application of logic to facts. Years later, after Helene had been killed, I would have occasion to regret the thoroughness of his education.

Monday, May 14, 9:00 a.m. 12 days to execution

I sit across from the Devil's chaplain, shackled to my chair, desperately trying to make him believe in Craft.

I've told him my story from the beginning, from a cow-patch in the Southern Appalachians to a successful career in biology as I pursued my dream of knowledge. Told him about Helene: Helene the lover, Helene the dancer, the actress, the prostitute, the drug addict and finally Helene dead and rotting in a ditch. Told him about Kathryn and Wagner and Greta and the mastermind of it all: Craft the tempter, Craft the author of all my woe. I was powerless to resist him in any of his guises. Like a great actor, he could take on any role: the therapist, the thinker, the thug. All this and more I tell Paul Young, the Devil's chaplain, who can explain nothing about the world. He too is a therapist, or tries to be. He gives the impression that he doesn't believe a word I've said.

"You don't believe in Craft, do you?" I ask him.

"Of course I believe in him."

"Do you think he's real?"

"Absolutely. I even know who he is."

I can't help laughing. "Have you got his phone number? You could save the state a lot of trouble if you'd just call and ask him to confess."

His face is serious, though as always his eyes dart away. "I read your article in Nature about the evolution of the human brain."

"I'm sure that's badly out of date by now."

"But it's still extremely interesting." He flashes a quick smile and stares down at his clipboard. "You pointed out that the brain — where all our thoughts and behaviors originate — has evolved like every other organ of the body. And so to those who deny the genetic origins of human behavior, you would argue—"

"It's nonsensical to say there's nothing genetic about our thoughts and behavior."

"Exactly."

"Go on. I know what I wrote."

"The point I took away was this," he says, eyes still on his clipboard. "If you look at humans as animals, it's extremely unlikely that most of our thoughts and actions aren't conditioned by evolution, and yet you say that 'subjective Darwinism' is practically nonexistent." His eyes finally met mine. "I'm not exactly sure what you meant by that."

"People aren't aware as they go through the day that they're thinking and acting to maximize their Darwinian fitness. Every single one of their thoughts and actions might be — and undoubtedly is — determined by a hard-wired Darwinian calculus, but they're completely unaware of it. If asked, they would deny it."

Billy Bob and Bubba, both of them fat and simian today, peer in at me through the window. Our time is almost up. "It's one of the oddities of the human brain," I add, with a quick nod toward the guards. "You take a troop of baboons, whose every action is aimed at surviving long enough to replicate their genes, give them a haircut and add a centimeter of cerebral cortex, and before you know it they're building cities and spouting Greek philosophy. And they'll tell you that their philosophy has nothing to do with all that scrounging on the savanna to make a living."

"Our subjective mind is like a dog on a leash, I think you said. Held by a Darwinian master who never shows his face. The Other."

I can feel the anger prickling up inside me. "Is that who you think Craft is? The Other?"

"In my world — I'm the chaplain for non-believers, remember — everyone gets to create his own devil. You choose your evils and create a devil to tempt you with them. If you succumb, you have someone to blame. If you resist, you can feel virtuous, superior even to yourself."

"Superior to yourself?"

"Because that's who the tempter is. Call him Craft, call him Satan or Mephistopheles. He's you, that part of yourself that you don't want to know about. The Darwinian master who holds you like a dog on a leash. The Other."

"Craft is real," I insist, straining at my shackles.

"Of course he's real." The chaplain stops darting his eyes around and for a long moment bores them into mine, and what I see looking back at me is a different person, no longer sensitive and shy but servile, contemptuous, sneering. If there's an Other, this is what it looks like. "He's part of you."

Now I'm furious, knocking my head backwards against the chair. "No, Craft is real. I've seen him, talked to him. I've touched him."

"Did he touch you back?"

"You're not a chaplain," I yell. "You're just some kind of frustrated psychologist. Push that buzzer! I want to go back to my cell."

He keeps his voice down. "Of course, if that's what you want. But before you go, there's something I want to ask you. Is there any proof of this Darwinian master theory? Any hard evidence?"

"Of course there is. There are some people who don't seem to have a Darwinian master guiding them through their lives. For some reason — it could be a lesion in one of the frontal lobes — they lack the ability to sustain a Darwinian strategy. They're intelligent enough, but they always try to game the system. They think the rules don't apply to them. They lie, they cheat, sometimes they kill, and they usually get caught. They usually end up in prison. Look around."

"And do they have a name, these people?"

"Sure they have a name. They're called sociopaths."

10.

Charlotte had spent the weekend lounging around the hotel pool with a mystery novel, catching up on her emails, and talking to her mom on the phone. Other than that, she didn't speak to anyone, do anything or go anywhere. If her weekend was boring, that was just what the doctor ordered.

At Sol's office on Monday morning, she spent two hours on the phone with Julie Halkins, who agreed — provided that Charlotte did all the work — to be available for consultation and court filings if Charlotte could find a legitimate basis for appeal. They agreed that the place mat and the photographs weren't enough. Charlotte needed to find evidence that the real murderer was still out there somewhere. Craft — that's what it boiled down to: she had to find Craft. She stuck the place mat and photos in her briefcase (Millie had made copies for Sol) and booked a flight to New York for the next morning, hoping that Ritter's ex-wife and ex-friends could lead her to Craft.

That left time to drive down to Ritter's in-laws' house that afternoon. Sol had been unable to reach the in-laws, but she'd take a chance on finding them at home so she could see the scene of the crime before she left Florida. It was a three-and-a-half hour drive down the interstate to North Palm Beach. At the insistence of her GPS, she skipped the exits for Cocoa Beach and Vero Beach and all the other places where people might be having fun. At last the GPS ordered her off the interstate into a privileged landscape of gated subdivisions, golf courses and cul-de-sacs lined with townhouses backing on boat slips, where she was informed that she had reached her destination. It was just after five o'clock.

The man who opened the door was wrinkled, blotchy and bald. He looked as if he'd spent the last half of his seventy-odd years hiding under a rock. He held a cocktail glass in his hand that was either half full or half empty, depending on your opinion of the human race. Something in his bloodshot eyes told Charlotte it was half empty.

"Mr. O'Donnell?"

The man nodded warily. "Why are you here? Isn't Thursday your day?"

A woman's voice creaked behind him: "Who is it?"

"It's the cleaning girl, but I don't know what she's—"

"I'm not the cleaning girl." Charlotte stopped him before he made her even angrier. "Are you Mr. O'Donnell?"

"Yes, I am. How can I help you?"

His wife sidled up beside him, a slight, sun-tanned woman with an absurd hairdo. She held a glass that had a long way to go before her hopes would be dashed. "How can we help you?"

"My name is Charlotte Ambler," Charlotte smiled. "I'm an attorney representing Christopher Ritter." They backed away, almost closing the door. "Your former son in law."

"We know who he is," Mr. O'Donnell said. "But what are you doing here?"

"May I come in?"

Mr. O'Donnell held the door open just wide enough to allow Charlotte through, making it clear that he was willing to let her in but that was all, in case anyone else lurked on the doorstep. In the living room, Mrs. O'Donnell watched her closely in case she tried to run off with the TV. "I'm Louise," she said. "And this is Bill."

"Nice to meet you," Charlotte nodded, accepting the invitation to sit on an uncomfortable chair.

Louise offered her a drink — a choice of ice tea or lemonade, not what they were drinking — and sat across from her on the sofa. "So," she said, "you're trying to get Chris off and you want us to help you?"

"I'm just trying to keep him from being executed."

"I just hope you're not being paid with the taxpayers' money," Bill said, his outlook darkening as he reached the bottom of his drink.

"I'm not being paid at all," Charlotte said. "I'm a volunteer with the Titus Foundation."

"Some kind of do-gooder group, is it? Thinks it's a public service to set murderers free?"

"Actually, no. We only represent innocent people."

The O'Donnells stared back at her as if she'd just dropped down from the sky. "Innocent?" Louise stammered. "You think Chris is innocent? Even his own lawyer admits he's guilty."

"Mr. Levy?"

"Yes, Sol Levy. He told us that after the trial."

"You were there?"

"Sure we were there. I had to testify."

"We were also paying his attorney's fees," Bill grumbled.

"Well, I'm Chris's lawyer now," Charlotte said. "And I think he's innocent."

Bill glided into the kitchen to mix himself another cocktail. "You're trying to stall it off, right?" he said, his spirits fortified by the new drink. "Tie it up in appeals until some liberal governor will let him go?"

Louise, rattling the ice cubes in her empty glass, gave way to anger and despair. "How do you people live with yourselves?" she yelled at Charlotte. She stood up and marched into the kitchen, returning with another drink, which she quickly began to drain. "It's ironic, that's all I can say, that you'd come here to try to convince us that he's innocent. Don't you realize he killed that woman right here in our house? Right over there?" She pointed to a place on the carpet about six feet from where Charlotte sat. "There's nothing to see. The police ripped up the carpets and we had to have them replaced."

"Cost about two thousand dollars," Bill mumbled, deep in his new drink.

"That was when he'd brought her here the umpteenth time to have sex with her. *In our bed* — we had to get rid of that, too — right in front of the pictures of his wife and kids. He didn't even try to deny that. Do you seriously think we're going to help you?"

"I can understand that you don't like Chris Ritter," Charlotte said, "that you'd like to see him executed—"

"We do *not* want to see him executed," Louise insisted. "Capital punishment is against the teaching of our church. But if that's what it takes to keep him away from our grandchildren, then we'll have to accept it."

"I'm flying to New York tomorrow," Charlotte said, "and I hope to be able to talk to your daughter and her husband."

"Not the kids. Leave them out of it."

"I will. Could you give me Kathryn's phone number?"

Louise jotted down a number and handed it to Charlotte. "I think this is the right number. Let me have yours and I'll call you if I find out it's been changed."

She wrote down Charlotte's number and collapsed into a tearful monologue. "When I think back on the happy times we had with Chris! We loved him, we were so proud to have him as our son in law. When they got engaged we took them out to dinner with his professor — Professor Hirschorn, what a wonderful man! — and some of his friends, Tim and Doug of course, we loved them too. Doug was Chris's best friend, now he's married to Kathryn — I guess you knew that — and there isn't a nicer man in the world, he's been such a good father to the kids. And Tim, you know, always coming to the rescue when things got tense between Bill and Chris. I won't deny it, there were times when Bill and Chris almost came to blows, it was always about politics or some stupid thing. The only friend of Chris's we didn't like was a guy named Wagner — I don't remember his first name — he was totally snide and disrespectful, always intent on embarrassing everybody whenever he could."

"Is it true that Doug paid Chris's legal fees?" Charlotte asked.

"Well, we all chipped in," Louise said. "Didn't we, Bill?"

"Were you here when it happened?" Charlotte pressed Louise. "The murder, I mean?"

"You know we weren't," she bristled. "We got here the next night, a couple days earlier than Chris expected. It's our house, isn't it? He was here by himself, acting like we snuck in on him. Then he beat it out of here like the fox who got caught in the henhouse."

"But how did you know Chris was here the day of the murder? Isn't that what you testified?"

"Well, he was supposed to be here. That's what I said at the trial, isn't it? He'd asked if he could stay here, if he could use the boat, if we were going to be around—"

"But didn't he tell you he was going out to the island?"

"That's what he told us. But how could I know if it was true?"

Charlotte forced a smile. "I still don't see how you could testify that he was staying here the day of the murder."

"What was I supposed to say? Was I supposed to help him get off so he could murder my daughter and our grandchildren?"

"Did Chris ever mention a man named Craft?"

"Craft? No, I've never heard that one. Have you, Bill?"

Bill had finished his cocktail and sat scowling into his empty glass. "Chris had a chance to tell his story at the trial and he didn't take it," Bill said. "Why would he do that if it was halfway believable? That story he told Kathryn about seeing the Haitians, I read about that in the paper the same time he did. That doesn't prove anything."

"Was he here when you arrived?"

"No, he was out somewhere, probably dumping that poor woman's body in the swamp. He came back in the middle of the night after we'd gone to bed."

"Was Helene still here when you arrived?"

"No, of course not. What are you implying?"

"Nothing. Just asking a question apparently nobody ever asked you before."

11.

Chris Ritter

I come now to the part of my story I'm ashamed to tell anyone, even here on death row, where my neighbors are serial killers, hit men and child molesters. Charlotte will never hear this part of the story, but I'm going to try and remember what really happened. At least in my own mind I'm not going to rewrite history to make myself look better. If anyone were listening, all I'd ask of them is: be patient, be tolerant, don't judge me until you've heard the whole thing. There's worse to come.

Andy Wagner had become the bane of my existence. His career as a charlatan prospered as my own honest research attracted little attention. Even his dissertation was a fraud. I had occasion to observe his techniques when I accompanied him to Montauk Point on the tip of Long Island to collect field data on the sex life of the speckled sandpiper. He paid scant attention to the sandpipers — those colorless creatures were left to fend for themselves as he concentrated on his own surprisingly abundant sex life. He spent the whole time in the hotel bar picking up women and taking them back to the room we were supposed to be sharing.

When Greta arrived as a new post-doctoral fellow, every man in the department fell in love with her. She was a slender Filipina beauty who'd just graduated from Berkeley: soft-spoken and brilliant, with more fresh ideas in one hour than most of us — especially Wagner — could have hoped for in a year; intellectual but down to earth, sophisticated in science yet traditional, a devout Catholic. Wagner moved in on her like a hawk. Within a week they were dating and within a month they were living together in the spacious apartment he'd found for her. Greta didn't seem to notice that he was sponging off her, using her to do his scut work, disparaging and then stealing her ideas. My sense of justice was outraged but I won't pretend to any noble motivations. I was crazy about her and I was jealous — powerfully and vindictively jealous. Wagner had crossed the line.

Late one night, after everyone else had left the zoology lab, I rifled through Wagner's file cabinets until I found the bound field notebooks where he'd recorded his original data for the sandpiper study. I stuck them in my backpack and dropped them into a dumpster behind the lab. Then I planted anonymous rumors on the internet that Wagner's dissertation research had been falsified. In a few weeks the senior faculty initiated an investigation, beginning with a request to review his field notes. Professor Hirschorn was shocked when Wagner informed him that the notebooks were missing.

Wagner was summoned to appear before the Ethics Committee, and the night before the meeting he asked me to speak on his behalf. We met on the library steps, shivering in the March wind like a pair of Cold War spies. He huddled beside me, his face florid, murmuring his desperate hope that I could save his career. If only I'd explain that I'd accompanied him on one of the trips to Montauk Point when he recorded his observations in the lost notebooks....

"I can't say I remember anything that could help you," I told him.

"What are you talking about? We drove out to Long Island and stayed at some hotel, and in the morning you went to the sand dunes with me and—"

"All I remember is that you spent most of your time picking up women in the hotel bar."

"I don't believe this. You're having a memory lapse? My career's on the line."

"Why should I get sucked into your problems?" I asked him. "It can't do me any good to be associated with a cheating scandal."

He stared at me with the shock of betrayal in his eyes. "This is... unbelievable."

As I headed across the quadrangle I planted the germ of an idea in his mind. "Say hi to Greta for me."

Greta appeared at my office the next morning to plead Wagner's case. She looked more beautiful than ever, and obviously embarrassed to be there. She wore a dark red turtleneck and a plaid woolen skirt, radiating a girlish glow that contrasted demurely with the gray light seeping in through the window.

"Unfortunately my mind is a blank about that trip," I told her. "But I'd love to be able to help, especially since you're asking me, Greta."

She smiled and glanced outside at the morning drizzle.

"I could imagine my memory reviving under the right conditions," I said.

"Conditions?"

"Sometimes, to jog your memory, you need a little something out of the ordinary, a little special attention. That's something you might be able to provide, Greta."

Her incredulous eyes finally met mine. "Are you talking about sex?"

"I'd like to take you out to dinner, that's all."

"You're married." Her voice dripped with disgust.

"It's a chance to save Andy's career. Isn't that why he sent you?"

Disgust gave way to anger. "You've got the wrong idea. Andy would never do that. He'd rather get thrown out of here than agree to anything like that."

"I doubt it."

"You don't know Andy.'

"Oh, I know Andy. You talk to him. See what he says."

I can only imagine the scene that must have ensued when Greta told Wagner I'd offered to help him if she'd sleep with me. Initially she was shocked at his reaction, I'm sure. But the next morning — after what I assume was a night of resistance, recrimination, pleading, bullying and tears — she left me a note asking if we could get together that night. The timing was critical because the Ethics Committee would be meeting the next afternoon. I made up some excuse for Kathryn and met Greta for dinner at the same Italian restaurant where I'd first met Craft. She came in a faded sweatshirt, her dark hair pulled back like a boy's, with no makeup to cover the indignities of a sleepless night. She looked deflated, as if the spirit had been sucked out of her.

"I'm not going to hurt you," I said.

She kept her eyes down. 'Do we have to talk?"

"Of course we have to talk. Isn't that the whole point of having dinner?"

"Everything's changed for me in the past twenty-four hours," she said, looking up. "I don't care what happens now. So let's just go wherever we're going and get it over with."

Without answering, I summoned the waiter and ordered the rack of lamb for two, plus a nice bottle of Chianti.

"You say everything's changed," I said after the waiter had brought our food. "What did Wagner tell you? That if sex can be used to further a good cause, then it's nothing to be ashamed of?"

"What he said was way worse than that."

As we ate in silence she grew more and more agitated, casting her eyes about the room as if searching for an escape route. Finally, when I signaled for the check, she reached behind her head with both hands and unfastened a necklace that had been hidden under her sweatshirt. It was a silver chain with a cross pendant I'd often noticed her wearing. As we stood up to leave she let the pendant slip off the chain and onto the table, where it came to rest under the edge of a plate.

"What are you doing?"

"I can't wear this anymore," she said. "Especially tonight."

"Come on. I'll take you home."

"No, not at my place. I can't—"

"It's all right," I said. "I'm just taking you home."

I never intended to sleep with Greta. Not because of any moral scruples so much as out of male pride in not paying for sex. I had become obsessed with her, but my machinations were all aimed at Wagner. I wanted to open her eyes to him, to make her see him for the despicable worm he really was. And to that extent I succeeded. She left him the next day with two black eyes and an uncertain future, with Wagner no longer able to steal her ideas or pimp her out to advance his career. But my deceptions had other, terrible consequences that I should have foreseen. Greta's relationship with Wagner and the way it ended broke her spirit and changed her life forever. She was through with men, she told her friends, and would never marry. She was equally disillusioned with science and religion. Before the end of the semester she dropped out of the program and found a job with an insurance company. When I called and tried to talk to her she said she never wanted to hear from me again. But she didn't seem to blame me for the disaster I'd set in motion; in fact she thanked me for sparing her the consequences of Wagner's betrayal — something, she said, that

most men would not have done. I took a certain vain pride in that
compliment. But now I realize that what I did was far worse than
exploiting her for sex. I robbed her of her innocence, her faith, her
career, her capacity for love, for all of which — until the
executioner finishes his work — I will never forgive myself.

My own innocence was lost and gone forever. I knew that, but I
deluded myself that I was the only one who noticed. Though
Kathryn had never joined in my self-deceptions, I imagined that
she retained some faith in the basic goodness I could no longer
find in my heart. That was another self-deception. Tim remained
skeptical of what I called rationality and he called soulless
materialism; Doug humored me in whatever folly I pursued, for
reasons I began to understand only later. But none of us, myself
included,   really grasped how far I'd gone down the road to
nihilism. As my career blossomed and I found myself turning into a
celebrity, the milestones began to blend into the landscape.
Cheating on Kathryn, exploiting Helene, destroying Wagner and
Greta — with those behind me it was a short journey to the point
of no return. To some people it must have seemed obvious.
Professor Hirschorn saw where I was headed, even before I
betrayed him; he punched my ticket and sent me on my way.

And then there was Craft. I could hide nothing from Craft —
even, or perhaps especially, those parts of myself that I should have
been most ashamed of. I never lied to him. On the afternoon of
my dinner with Greta, I had met him in the food concourse in the
basement of Grand Central Station. We sat on a high-backed
wooden bench that resembled a church pew, side by side like
strangers waiting for a train. Craft sipped Diet Coke through a
straw from a large paper cup as I confessed my plot to discredit
Wagner and undermine his relationship with Greta.

"Why be ashamed of yourself?" he asked when I had finished. "You're one of the few who can look the truth in the eye and not blink. You have the right to do what you need to do."

"Greta's just an innocent bystander."

"Is she really so innocent? Her innocence is sort of a come on, isn't it?"

"No, that's not right." The idea appalled me. "Not at all."

"Why else would you be so attracted to her?"

He stood up and shoved his empty cup into the trash can. "The tempter or the tempted," he chuckled, facing me for the first time. "Who sins most?"

I don't want to paint myself in a positive light just because I didn't carry my corruption of Greta to its logical extreme. At the time I prided myself not on my decency or compassion but on my clear-eyed command of the situation. In my diary I recorded what Craft had told me: I was one of the few who could look the truth in the eye and not blink. I had the right to do what I needed to do.

In my testimony to the Ethics Committee, I honored the letter if not the spirit of my agreement with Greta. I testified that the field notebooks existed and that I'd seen Wagner record data in them. But I hinted — by disputing charges that had never been made — that he had destroyed the notebooks rather than submit them to Ethics Committee review. And because I'd heard that Professor Hirschorn planned to offer a tenured position to Wagner in preference to me, I had no choice but to suggest a broader conspiracy. There could be nothing wrong with Wagner's data, I argued, since Professor Hirschorn had personally reviewed and approved it. When I left the hearing I felt like a soiled rug that needed to be beaten and hung out to dry. But I knew I had the right to do what I needed to do.

Though Wagner was cleared, it was obvious that he could never get tenure. He left at the end of the semester and took a job teaching at a high school in New Jersey. Professor Hirschorn sank into a deep depression and spent the afternoons drinking in his office. Rumors swirled that he would soon be forced to retire. And that tenured appointment that had been earmarked for Wagner? Naturally it went to me.

Suddenly my career was on a fast track. With Wagner out of the way, I focused my research on the marine beach habitats where he had carved his niche. Kathryn's parents owned a townhouse in North Palm Beach, Florida, where we spent our family vacations after Casey was born. Docked on the lagoon they kept a 20-foot Grady inboard, which I was welcome to use whenever I wanted. I took up the study of a species of sea turtle that inhabited some isolated islands between Florida and the Bahamas. Each morning at sunrise I would cruise out to the islands, sixty miles off shore, to collect data on the reproductive strategy of the turtles. The environment was exceedingly delicate: the slightest human scent would be enough to spoil the breeding ground for years to come. So I stayed in the boat — it was big enough to sleep in — and wore special rubber boots and gloves when I went ashore. This research gave me back the solitude I needed and led to some publications that added to my growing stature in zoology.

But it was my work on the evolution of altruism that put me on the cover of *Time* magazine and led to my interviews on NPR and public television. The "Intelligent Design" movement was taking off and I quickly emerged as a spokesman for the Darwinian cause. The creationists were busy planting the idea, even in some university science departments, that there was something called "irreducible complexity" which blew away the whole theory of natural selection. Of course that was rubbish, but it could only be debunked by an expert biologist. I wrote countless articles, reviews and op-ed pieces and participated in dozens of debates at universities and think tanks. By and large the Intelligent Design crowd were serious and intelligent men (they all seemed to be men) and I enjoyed rolling up my sleeves to debate them. I even enjoyed debating the evangelical Christians, though I found their arguments childish and easy to refute; for the most part they were regular folk, the kind I grew up with in southwestern Virginia. Ironically, my bitterest opponents were the leftist professors who seemed to think that finding the roots of human behavior in evolution and genetics was the last stop before Nazi death camps.

It was after one of the more publicized Intelligent Design debates that a reporter for some magazine I'd never heard of — an astonishingly attractive blonde from Houston named Amy Pierce — walked up to me and started asking questions with a sweet smile and a soft Southern accent that reminded me of home. We chatted a few minutes and her smile seemed sweeter still; her blue eyes shined back at me like a hard, gemlike flame. By coincidence we were staying at the same hotel. At dinner we talked about a lot of things before we found our way back to her room, and then, when we were done having sex, we talked some more. I didn't realize it was an interview.

We lay stretched across her queen-size bed, enjoying drinks from the mini-bar as I recalled one of the highlights of the day's debate, when a philosophy professor from the University of Chicago had accused me of "physicalism."

"What he was calling physicalism—the idea that the universe consists of physical matter and energy — isn't some crackpot notion I just dreamed up. It's the whole basis of modern science, though no one wants to admit it. The physical universe. There isn't anything else."

"That's pretty stark," Amy said, running her fingertips over my chest.

"No God, no spirit, no soul, not even any morality or general principles unless you want to go the way of Plato."

"That's *very* stark."

"I'm one of the few who can look the truth in the eye and not blink," I boasted, quoting Craft. Obviously I'd had a little too much to drink.

"No good or evil?"

I shook my head. "Just the physical universe."

"So then you could do anything, couldn't you?" She hoisted herself up on one elbow and stared back at me with a conspiratorial gleam in her eyes. "You could lie and cheat and steal and it wouldn't make any difference."

I felt uncomfortable. Though we lay stretched naked across her bed, our limbs entangled, surrendered into each other's power as only two lovers can be, I realized I didn't really know this woman; I didn't know her at all. "Theoretically, yes," I admitted. "If you wanted to."

"You could get some stranger in a hotel room," she smiled, reaching her free hand across my shoulder. "Get them drunk, tie them up. Maybe rough them up a little. Couldn't you?"

Was she threatening me or tempting me? Or just playing a kinky mind game? I stared into her glistening blue eyes and found no answer.

A defiant smirk tugged at her smile. "You could even kill them."

I rolled off the bed and bent over to pick up my clothes, avoiding her eyes.

"It wouldn't make any difference, would it?"

"Who knows?" I answered without thinking. My only thought was to escape from that room alive and fully clothed.

"You're asking the same question as Raskolnikov in *Crime and Punishment*, aren't you?"

"I'm not asking anything," I said. The last thing I wanted to do was talk about some crazy Russian novel I read in college.

"Why shouldn't you murder someone if you have a good enough reason?"

For a long moment my dignity hung in the balance, as I stood tottering in the peculiarly vulnerable position of a man pulling on his pants. I knew the game would be up if I had to hop more than once on the same foot.

Her smile had disappeared. "From a purely philosophical point of view?"

"Well" — I got both legs into my pants and slipped my shirt on with only minor resistance — "I don't approve of chopping up women with an axe, if that's what you're wondering. But from a purely philosophical point of view, I think Raskolnikov was probably asking the right question."

I leaned over and kissed her chastely on the forehead, as if she were what she in fact was, a woman I hardly knew. "Now I have to say good night," I murmured. "I've got an early flight."

I can quote that interview verbatim — an interview is what it turned out to be — since it was posted on about a hundred websites. As it happened, the voluptuous Amy Pierce worked for a right-wing magazine dedicated to discrediting every idea conceived since St. Thomas Aquinas. What she wrote wasn't exactly what I'd said, but it was close enough to cause a national scandal. *"Was Raskolnikov Asking The Right Question?"* ran the headline. *"Atheist Professor Says Yes!"* She left out the kinky sex and surrounded her incendiary misquotations — "It's perfectly all right to murder someone if you have a good reason" — with statements I'd actually made: "There's no such thing as good and evil. There's no God, no spirit, no soul, not even any general principles. I'm one of the few who can look the truth in the eye and not blink."

I had my fifteen minutes of fame — on the radio talk shows Dostoevsky's axe-murderer came across as a hero compared to me — until the public moved on to new sensations. The Academic Dean ordered me to apologize (exactly to whom, I wasn't sure), but I refused. I would not ask forgiveness for saying what I knew to be true. Thus began my career as a heretic within the University establishment. Atheism and egotism they accepted without a second thought; murder they could condone if it was committed in a good cause; good and evil they viewed as relative terms. What they couldn't abide — unless it was camouflaged in arcane theoretical jargon borrowed from French philosophers — was my claim that there are no general principles.

My career had shifted into high gear. The negative publicity from what became known as the Raskolnikov interview resulted in more publications, more speaking invitations, and ironically, even more prestigious committee assignments at the University and a position in the administration. But as my career advanced, the situation with Kathryn continued to deteriorate. Her New Age spirituality, her faith in social improvement, and most of all her dismissive attitude toward my ideas — all of these combined to set the stage for many a late-night argument. She accused me of being aloof and unloving, too tied up in my work, not sympathetic enough to her and what she cared about. But of course she had her own silent, inexorable agenda. By the time Casey was five years old, we were having sex infrequently but, I noticed, with clockwork regularity: exactly once a month, on the date she'd chosen to conceive her next child. Or so I assumed. As it happened there was a little more to it than that.

We still got together with Tim and Doug on a regular basis. I remember one Saturday night at Doug's apartment on the East Side. He wanted to impress us with how much money he was making, so he pulled out all the stops. Roast duck, grilled salmon, homemade pasta with clam sauce, hot and sour soup from Chinatown, cannoli's from Little Italy. It was a feast and we had a great time — at least I thought we were having a great time — carrying on like we were in college again. Finally we settled back for an array of after-dinner drinks, each in its proper glass, offered by Doug with an air of proprietorial self-importance. I chose ruby port, Tim a single-malt scotch; Doug poured himself some Courvoisier in a brandy snifter the size of a goldfish bowl.

As I sipped my port I recounted the incredible hostility I'd encountered in the Intelligent Design debates, not so much from the evangelical Christians as from the academics who ought to have known better. "What it comes down to is this," I said, raising my glass as if proposing a toast. "No one wants to admit that humans are animals, just a few mutations ahead of gorillas and chimpanzees. Our entire civilization is an attempt to deny that fact."

Kathryn glared at me. "Chris, do we have to get into this?"

"That's what we are," I persisted foolishly. "Animals."

"Yeah," Tim said. "Look at Darwin and his beagle. Sometimes you can hardly tell them apart."

"The social sciences get everything wrong because they don't take evolution into account. They're like astronomers still pretending the earth revolves around the sun." I peered at Tim over the rim of my glass. "The humanists are even worse. They profess to be agnostics — which is a polite way of saying atheists — but they're afraid to give up their illusions, all their myths and bogus principles, which they know don't exist outside of their heads."

Tim leaped to the humanists' defense, as he always did, and his defense was moving and eloquent if you overlooked the fact that it was nonsense. "There's a spiritual dimension to the universe that your mechanistic calculations will never be able to explain," he declared, downing his single-malt scotch in one gulp. "Whether it's supernatural, or just another aspect of nature, I don't know. Is it God? the life force? the Tao? Who am I to say? But I do know this: the real world — the one we actually live in — is made up of beauty and poetry and music, not electrons and quarks, and it's driven by emotions and values and metaphors, not mathematical laws. And someday you'll realize that, Chris."

I was about to riposte with some of the zingers I'd rehearsed in the debates, but Kathryn, slurping her way through a generous dose of Grand Marnier, quickly brought the argument down to the personal level. "Chris, I hate to say this" — when someone begins that way, especially your wife, you know she's loving every minute of it — "but I'm not sure your world view leaves much room for love."

"Of course it does," I protested, taken aback.

"Or compassion or sympathy or anything else that makes life worth living." She set her glass down hard on the table.

"Of course it does, Kathryn." My eyes told her not to go any farther with this argument in public. "You know that better than anyone."

Tim jumped back into the fray without missing a beat. "So what is love like in this mechanistic universe? Not to get too much into the details of married life " We all laughed, Kathryn a little too sharply, I thought.

"Seriously," he pursued, "what's it like? Sort of like one computer talking to another through the USB port?"

"You really want to know?" Kathryn asked.

"It's more a question for Chris," he said, turning to me. "To have love, don't you need some concept of goodness as part of human nature? I mean, why would you love someone if you didn't think they had some kernel of goodness in them? And in a mechanistic universe—"

"I never said goodness isn't part of human nature," I snapped. "In fact, I wrote my dissertation on the evolution of altruism."

Doug peered over the top of his brandy snifter like a dog guarding a bone. "But where does this goodness come from? Is it in our genes?"

"Where else would it be?"

"It just sort of evolved," Kathryn mocked. "He thinks everything just sort of evolved."

"Listen," I said, trying to put the discussion back on an intellectual plane. "Visualize a group of Ice Age hunters surrounding a woolly mammoth and trying to kill it. Each hunter has to risk his life for the group. He can't let the others take all the risk or he won't get his share of the meat. That means he has to have something like altruism."

Tim and Doug exchanged glances as if altruism wasn't one of their vocabulary words.

"Selflessness, if you will. The willingness to do something for others which gives the hunter no immediate benefit and exposes himself to risk. But of course it's not really selfless, is it? If he doesn't take his share of the risk, his children will starve and his genes will disappear from the gene pool."

Doug gestured toward Tim with his thumb. "You over there with the sloping forehead! Out of the pool!"

Tim laughed but came right back to the argument. "All right," he said quietly. "Let's fast-forward to the modern world. It's wartime and a group of soldiers have been sent on a nasty mission.

The same virtues would apply, wouldn't they? Cooperation, altruism, self-sacrifice? Group solidarity?"

"Of course."

"Congratulations!" He raised his empty glass as if proposing a toast. "You've just explained the camaraderie of the guards at Auschwitz."

12.

Charlotte had never liked New York City. It always gave her the feeling that she was an extra in a disaster movie, with an asteroid or an alien invasion scripted to arrive in the next scene. By the time her taxi reached Manhattan, she had a splitting headache and wished she could just lie down. Instead the driver dropped her off at Kathryn and Doug Leipzig's apartment on the East Side.

Kathryn had pretended to be surprised when Charlotte called her. She and Doug would be home that afternoon, she said, if Charlotte really needed to talk to them. They lived in a spacious multi-story apartment with an interior staircase and picture windows framing the East River. They offered Charlotte a chair that was as soft as a kid glove and sat down across from her on a white leather couch. She introduced herself and explained the mission of the Titus Foundation. They seemed embarrassed when Charlotte said she thought Ritter was innocent. Doug looked out the window and smoothed the crease in his pants, glancing discreetly at the phone he'd placed on the arm of the couch. He was apparently something big on Wall Street, big enough that he assumed Charlotte had heard of him. He had the relaxed manners of a man who was richer than anyone ever needed to be. A friendly, sincere man, with a thin coating of modesty over what was undoubtedly an enormous ego. Likeable, as he'd always been, a little overweight, with graying hair and clear brown eyes that neither begged nor cajoled. He flattered Charlotte by saying he'd heard of her firm and asking where she went to law school, which he wouldn't have asked unless he already knew the answer. The room — the living room, apparently, though it seemed more like a lobby — was decorated with wooden sculptures that might have come from Africa or Oceania, each on its own pedestal. There was also a portrait of Kathryn, illuminated with hidden spotlights, as if she were already dead. She was still attractive in the mannered style of a rich man's wife. Tanned, thin, accustomed to getting her way. Her default emotion seemed to be embarrassment. When the daughter came home from school — she looked about fifteen going on twenty-four, dressed like a junior dominatrix with an expression to match — Kathryn whisked her up the stairs without introducing her to Charlotte. The boy who was supposed to resemble Doug — he would be twelve by now — was nowhere in sight.

"So what's this all about?" Doug asked pleasantly, as if he didn't know.

"The execution is scheduled for next week," Charlotte said.

Kathryn lowered her eyes. "I didn't know that."

"The clock has finally run out," Doug said. "Believe me, we did everything we could."

"I understand that," Charlotte said. "I'm working with Sol Levy. He says you've both been more than generous."

Doug leaned forward earnestly. "Then what is it we can help you with now?"

"Chris has told me his version of events, which involves a man named Craft who he believes framed him for the murder."

"I've heard all that before," Kathryn said. "When Chris was arrested, he told me that story."

"Do you believe it?"

"No, I'm afraid not. Chris lied to me about everything."

"You don't know who Craft is?"

"I don't think he ever existed."

"Same here," said Doug. "Chris never mentioned anybody like that to me."

Charlotte was starting to feel ridiculous, as if they were humoring her. Was she the only one foolish enough to fall for such a tale? "He's tall, over six feet, pretty heavy, with dark wavy hair and a European accent. Sometimes he wore a beard or a goatee."

Describing him only made her sound more ridiculous. Kathryn and Doug pretended to think the question over and shook their heads.

"Do either of you remember an incident in a bar called Dominick's when Chris offered to sell his soul for a thousand dollars?"

"It's been a long time," Doug smiled.

"That was part of the crazy story he told me," Kathryn said, "but he didn't use it in the court case."

"No," Charlotte said. "Sol advised him not to. It doesn't mean the story is false."

Doug seemed to be losing his patience. "Let me get this straight. This Craft guy is supposed to be the one who answered that ad?"

"Exactly." Charlotte opened her briefcase and pulled out a copy she'd made of the place mat. "Do you recognize this?"

The two of them stared at the place mat — Charlotte had copied it front and back — as if history was coming alive before them. Doug snatched the place mat and turned it over to read the back. "Where'd you get this?"

"Do you recognize it?"

"It looks like the place mat Chris wrote out his offer on. I told him to use this language, *As is, where is.*"

"It was delivered to Sol's office a couple days ago. It's what made me think Chris has been telling the truth."

"It's the real thing, all right," Doug said. "Only this is a photocopy."

"That whole incident was so stupid," Kathryn said, "and so exaggerated in Chris's mind. He claimed he needed the money to graduate. I think he got it from his uncle. Nobody bought his soul."

"But people saw the ad on the bulletin board," Charlotte said. "Craft might have been there. Do you remember anyone who looked like him? Tall, heavy-set, with a beard?"

Doug laughed. "A lot of guys in bars look like that."

"I might have a picture somewhere," Kathryn said.

Charlotte could hardly believe what she'd heard. "A picture?"

Kathryn looked more embarrassed than before. "I had a little throwaway camera I got at a wedding. I snapped some pictures of Chris holding up the place mat. I remember looking at the prints with him when they were developed."

"Do you still have them?"

"I might. Let me take a look." She excused herself and disappeared up the stairs.

"She never throws anything away," Doug smiled.

"How long have you been married?" Charlotte asked.

"About nine years, I guess. How long has Chris been on death row?"

"About ten."

"Sounds about right."

Kathryn must have known exactly where to look. In five minutes she returned with a couple of blurry snapshots that must have been taken twenty-four years before. There was Doug, recognizable though decades younger, and a boyish-looking Chris Ritter, who hadn't aged as well, and another young man with longish dark hair and glasses (who turned out to be Tim Salis), the three friends grinning and clowning around as Chris held up the place mat with his ad written on it. There were the waiter and the bartender, red-eyed from the flash. In the background, around the bar, were tall men, fat men, bearded men, but none who fit Ritter's description of Craft.

"Do you know any of these people?" Charlotte asked.

Kathryn and Doug both shook their heads. Doug's eyes strayed to his phone, which must have been alerting him to more important issues. He reached for the phone and stood up, waiting for Charlotte to do the same. "I don't know how to put this," he said. "We don't want Chris to die, but we don't want him out on the street either. Because he wouldn't be out on the street, he'd be up here stalking us and our kids."

"Or something a lot worse," Kathryn said.

"Aren't they his kids?"

Doug ignored Charlotte's provocation. "He was my best friend in college but after that he went off the rails. He started thinking there was no such thing as right and wrong, no morality, he could do as he pleased. I work on Wall Street, which is supposed to be a den of iniquity, and I've never known anybody who comes close to believing the kinds of things Chris wrote in that diary. I don't know if he killed anybody, but I do know I don't want him around the kids."

"He's a psycho," Kathryn said, staring down at her fingers. "He cheated on me the whole time we were married. He slept with prostitutes in my parents' bed, under pictures of me and our kids. And he talked about the kids as if they were robots or something. He's sick." She raised her eyes and gave Charlotte a woman-to-woman look. "You've met him. What do you think of him?"

Charlotte smiled but deflected the question. "Can I take these pictures with me?"

"Sure," Kathryn said. "I don't know why not. They're not going to save him."

Later that afternoon Doug found Kathryn sobbing on the white leather couch, as motionless as the statues hovering on the pedestals around her. He sat down beside her and touched her hand. "We shouldn't have let her in," he said.

"My mother warned me it wasn't going to be pleasant."

"It'll be over soon."

Kathryn felt like a spectator to some one else's emotions. It was so long since she had loved Chris that the self who cried for him now seemed a stranger to her. The girl who fell in love with the laughing student in the picture, the young woman who married the promising scientist, the wife who suffered betrayal and humiliation and finally horror at what he became — that was the self who sobbed inside her. And that self was sobbing for another stranger: the boyish-looking student, the gentle lover, the excited new father. That self was innocent of what ten years on death row had done to Chris.

Doug's phone buzzed. "I have to go back to the office," he said.

Another stranger, Kathryn thought. "Go ahead," she said. "I'll be okay."

Chris Ritter
Tuesday, May 15, 3:30 p.m. 10 days to execution.

I feel bad about the way I've been treating Charlotte. I'm harsh with her because I don't want her to like me. Losing the case will be bad enough without losing a friend. She certainly doesn't need a friend like me. She's a lovely woman: attractive and smart without being a show-off. In another lifetime I could see myself falling in love with her.

I'll spare both of us that ordeal. That's a lifetime I'll never see.

Billy Bob and Bubba don't have such an elevated opinion of Charlotte. They're polite to her face, but then call her a whore and tell dirty jokes about her all the way back to my cell. "Don't be offended, Ritter," Billy Bob says when I give him a look. "All lawyers are whores. What's she like, compared to the one you killed?"

"She's trying to save my life," I tell him.

"How much is she charging you for that?"

"Nothing."

"Well, I sure hope you get your money's worth."

One afternoon Professor Hirschorn asked me to stop by his office. He'd been diminished by the Wagner controversy and the jealousies and suspicions it aroused. His mood was dark, brooding, sardonic, the way it had been after his wife died. In his eyes there was a vast emptiness.

I tapped on the door and was invited inside. Professor Hirschorn huddled in front of the window in his usual brown suit, staring across the quadrangle at the empty sky. "Einstein said the most incomprehensible thing about the universe is that it's comprehensible," he said without turning around. "But is it really? Is it comprehensible at all?"

"I don't know," I answered. "When you're doing science—"

"You torture tiny bits of the universe into patterns and declare that you've unlocked its secrets. But your most cherished discoveries will be debunked by the next generation of graduate students. You know that." He turned to face me with an ironic smile. "And why not? The laws of nature don't exist outside of the human mind. Matter and energy exist — whatever they may turn out to be — but there's no separate order of existence for the laws they follow. All that exists is tiny bits of matter and energy behaving in certain ways."

"But in biology—"

"Biology is an illusion, a human construct." He pronounced that judgment with the authority of a self-evident truth, challenging me with his empty eyes to prove him wrong. "Why should life be different from the rest of the universe? I can tell you: there's no such thing as a species. Just a bunch of similar protein complexes — call them plants or animals, the classifications are arbitrary — that perpetuate themselves with a high degree of regularity."

I wanted to say something, anything, to make him stop. It was like listening to my father's drunken maunderings after my mother died. I wanted to run out into the woods to make it stop.

"Unless," he added sarcastically, "unless you believe in some shadowy world of forms or principles that this world is striving to fulfill."

"No, I don't believe in anything like that."

"Then let me ask you a question which my late wife, God rest her soul, forbade me ever to ask in her presence, after the first time I made the mistake of mentioning it over fifty years ago, before we came to this country: If there are no laws and no forms or principles, how can there be any such thing as goodness or morality? How can there be any such thing as justice? It's all an illusion, isn't it?"

"No," I stammered, though I knew he was right, "that can't be true."

He laughed. "What is truth?"

I backed toward the door, but my instinct for self-advancement made me stay and hear him out. I sensed that this was some kind of test. After staring at me for a minute or more, he invited me to sit down. We chatted aimlessly for a few minutes; then he informed me that he had decided to retire, effective immediately, and move to a farm in New Hampshire. He intended to name me Acting Chair of the Department.

"Now you'll have to learn how to act like a chair," he smiled. "It's not hard. You get down on all fours and let everyone push you around."

By the time my son Liam was born I imagined that I had freed myself of all the illusions Kathryn and the others taunted me with. In fact I'd arrived at the philosophy I had instinctively tried to shelter Professor Hirschorn from, the ultimate heresy his wife had forbidden him to utter: If there are no laws of nature outside of nature itself, and no forms or principles in the universe, how can there be any such thing as goodness or morality? How can there be any such thing as justice? How can there be any such thing as truth? When I asked myself those questions I felt as if an enormous weight had been lifted off my shoulders. I felt that I had found something even greater than truth: I had found freedom. That freedom would be my law, my justice, my truth.

I was still seeing Helene as often as I could. Sometimes she called herself an actress, sometimes a dancer; I didn't really care as long as she was there when I needed her. To camouflage my activities with Helene, my lies to Kathryn became ever more elaborate, usually involving late night committee meetings and travel to conferences at distant universities. Field research also afforded an excellent opportunity for deception. A couple of months after Liam arrived I took Helene with me to Florida to continue my research on the island sea turtles, charging the whole trip to my department. We stayed a week at my in-laws' townhouse while they were in California visiting Kathryn's sister. Each morning at sunrise we would cruise out to Baxter Island in the Grady, Helene sunning herself and reading fashion magazines while I collected data on the turtles. It was on one of those visits to the island that I first noticed footprints in the sand, which both frightened and infuriated me. I'd heard about drug smugglers from the Bahamas who sometimes landed at isolated islands and murdered anyone they found there. But it was the damage to the habitat that most worried me. The turtles would not lay their eggs on a beach that was disturbed by humans. I bought a deer rifle like the one I used to hunt with back in Virginia. I wasn't sure what I intended to do with it — protection, I told Helene; just in case. I stashed it with the fishing gear I carried with me on the boat.

Helene was a lot more troubled than I was about what we were doing down there. Dining at the University's expense, chilling our drinks with my mother-in-law's ice cubes, having sex under pictures of my wife and kids. "I want to stay someplace else," she said one evening as we sipped margaritas on the balcony. "It's not right."

"What's not right?"

"All these kinds of things. Staying here. Spending all this money that's not ours."

"What's wrong with it?" I teased her. "You going moral on me all of a sudden?"

"You could call it that. It's not the way I was brought up."

I laughed. "Like everyone else, you were brought up to believe in a bunch of nonsense."

"You don't believe in anything, do you?"

"Not really," I said. "I'm a free man."

My freedom was not to last long. Not much longer than Helene's
life, as it turned out. We enjoyed our little fling in Florida and when
we flew home I sensed that she was different, that she had stepped
across some line from which she would never step back. I felt
different too. I was nervous and ill-tempered and met each day
with a deepening sense of alienation. I could hardly talk to Kathryn
and I had a hard time relating to my infant son Liam. He was
wrinkly and colicky and bore no resemblance to me.

One morning I had a message from Craft. He wanted to meet me
at the Tombs, that complex of dungeons adjoining the law courts
in lower Manhattan where the unlucky are dispatched into the New
York prison system. We met under the pedestrian overpass that
Craft called the Bridge of Sighs and walked around the block to a
small Italian café with red and white checkered tablecloths. The
waiter seated us at a booth and disappeared into the kitchen.

"I've heard about some of the things you've been saying,"
Craft frowned, shaking his head.

"You talked to Helene."

He nodded. "I've also read that interview."

"The Raskolnikov interview? You had to be there. That
woman actually—"

"You shouldn't go around saying such things." He scowled at
me in a way I'd never seen before.

"Why not? You're the one who told me I could look the truth
in the eye and not blink."

"And the truth you discovered was that truth doesn't exist," he
mocked. "How could you be looking at it in the eye?"

The question infuriated me. Wasn't this the man who'd been
stripping away my values, tempting me with selfishness and
nihilism, for the past dozen years?

"I had values once," I said.

"Yes, and you traded them for the power to explain the universe in material terms. That's what selling your soul meant. Don't you get it? And now you think you don't even have a self beyond the illusory excitation of a few brain cells. It's not surprising that you've turned into a monster."

"You did this to me."

He stood up and glared at me with contempt. "You're exactly where you wanted to be. All the kingdoms of the earth are at your feet."

I grabbed a salt shaker from the table and threw it at him with all my might. "Get out of here!"

The salt shaker bounced off his shoulder and fell to the floor. Still laughing, he turned and headed for the door.

"Get out!" I called after him. "I'm done with you!"

I've never seen Craft again. For a long time I expected to find a note in my mailbox, an email in my inbox, a message on my answering machine, summoning me to another session with this intruder who seemed to hold me in his sway. I imagined what I'd say to him, how I'd ignore him, defy him, spit in his face. In my fantasies I was always prepared for our next meeting. But the call never came. Weeks went by, then months, and I felt disappointed, almost offended, not to have heard from him. We'd been through a lot together, the two of us. Wasn't I worth at least a follow up call?

But all I heard was silence. Craft was done with me. He'd been a protector of sorts, my dark conscience, my guardian demon. And now I was on my own.

In the late 1990s the excitement in biology was about Dolly, the cloned sheep, and whether cloning could be expanded to even higher forms of life, including humans. President Clinton came out against it, as did the Vatican and many others who warned that science was playing God and would end up creating a Frankenstein. But in the scientific world we scorned those who based their opposition on such notions; we were quite confident of our ability to deal with any ethical issues that might arise. I felt honored when I was asked to sign a "Declaration in Defense of Cloning and the Integrity of Scientific Research" along with some of the giants of biology including Richard Dawkins, Francis Crick and E.O. Wilson. It seemed clear that the cloning of humans was the next logical step in technology and only an ignorant Luddite would attempt to stop it. Unfortunately I hadn't reckoned on the explosive reaction the cloning declaration would trigger in my own home.

Kathryn came charging into my study waving the New York Times, where the declaration had been published. "I can't believe you signed your name to this," she said. "You've sunk to a new low."

"It's pretty high-minded, I thought. All that stuff about moral issues, ethical dilemmas—"

"You don't think there's any dignity in human life, do you? Well, that's certainly true in your case." She threw the newspaper down on my desk. "All I can say is I hope Casey doesn't hear about this at school."

"It won't hurt her to get a little glimpse of the truth occasionally."

"The truth? That people are just elaborate forms of pond scum with souped-up electrochemical brain processes? Is that what you want your kids to believe? Or even worse: Is that what you think they are?"

Tears streamed from her eyes, whether of pain or anger or frustration, I couldn't quite tell. I stood up to comfort her but she stepped back as if she was afraid to let me touch her. She sat down and buried her face in her hands. I waited.

"Chris," she finally said, looking up at me. "How likely is it that some random molecules would have evolved into brains like ours that can build computers and fly to the moon and back? Do you think all this came about by chance?"

"Not by chance. Genetic evolution is a highly predictable process."

"Did they come from outer space? Did these molecules come from outer space?"

"They might have. There's some evidence—"

"OK, that's enough!" She shook her head. "I feel like I'm talking to one of my clients."

"Your clients? You mean your patients?"

"I think you should get some help."

"What are you talking about?"

"Chris, you have issues, mental health issues—"

"Spare me the social worker routine."

"OK, I'll be blunt. You're sick. You have some sort of borderline autistic or sociopathic disorder. You need help and I don't know if that's going to be enough. I'm worried about Casey."

"Casey? You think I'm going to hurt her?"

"You may already have hurt her. It might be hereditary, Chris. Whatever you have might be hereditary. I want to find out."

I couldn't believe my ears. She thought I was genetically defective for believing in evolution. "You think it's in my genes?"

"Anything's possible," she shrugged. "It certainly isn't what I bargained for."

"What's that supposed to mean?"

"When I married you I assumed — I guess I imagined that our kids would be superior because you're so smart, because you had such good genes. It isn't working out the way I thought it would."

I would never admit it to Kathryn, but even I had begun to doubt my sanity. I did what most men did, said what most men said, but I didn't feel what most men felt. I lived detached from others in a way that frightened me. I found myself watching people, studying them — even my own children — as if they were ants building a nest, trying to understand their behavior in mechanistic, evolutionary terms. I found it hard to imagine that other people had the same thoughts and feelings as I had. And what if they did? What was so special about my own mental life? Wasn't it just the delusion of an elaborate, self-conscious insect with a rich repertoire of thoughts, feelings, aspirations and hopes? Yes, there were some gems in that repertoire — selflessness, generosity, compassion, love — which I experienced every day. But weren't they just the adaptations of a social animal, like the heroism of the ants or the camaraderie of the guards at Auschwitz? It was the opposite emotions — egotism, pride, envy, lust for power and pleasure — that seemed to be taking over my life. I told myself that I was beyond good and evil, but even that was a moral judgment, an attempt at a general principle which did not — could not — exist, except as an illusion, in a material universe.

In my diary I probed my sanity and pushed my speculations to their limits. Alone, late at night, I filled its pages with the madness I could not show the world. And then I buried it in a file drawer where I was certain no one would ever find it.

13.

Tuesday, May 15, 4:00 p.m. 10 days, 2 hours to execution.

The phone calls started as soon as Charlotte left the Leipzigs' building. In the cab on the way to her hotel she could feel the phone buzzing in her purse. When she answered, the caller stayed on the line a few seconds and the phone went dead. The number was an unfamiliar one, with an area code she'd never seen before. After she stopped answering, the caller — it was a man — left voice messages: obscene, threatening messages that made her want to throw her phone out the window. By the time she checked into her hotel, a Marriott near Times Square, her hand was shaking. The desk clerk asked, "Is everything OK?" and she tried to smile back. "Yes, everything's fine."

"OK," the clerk said. "Just let us know if you need anything."

In her room she locked and chained the door and drew the curtains. She felt a panic attack coming on, but she knew she had to ignore it. This is ridiculous, she told herself. She turned her phone back on and dialed Alex Lopez of the NYPD in hopes of seeing him the next day. He wasn't answering either. She left a message suggesting a 2:00 o'clock meeting; then she changed her clothes and went outside for a walk. In Times Square there were so many crazy people that they cancelled each other out; she felt safer among them than alone in her room. She walked east on 42nd Street until she came to Fifth Avenue, where a poster at the entrance to the New York Public Library announced an exhibition of surrealist books: it showed a picture of a book with the caption, *This is not a book*. Surreal. That summed up the way everything looked to her that afternoon.

She dialed the number Kathryn had given her for Tim Salis. Tim was the founder and artistic director of GlobeSpace, a highly regarded off-off-Broadway theater located in the meat packing district south of 14th Street. He was friendly and open to seeing her; obviously he'd been expecting her call, just as Kathryn had been. He invited her to stop by the theater later that day, with the caveat that he'd be busy with try-outs until five o'clock. She stood at the curb and raised her hand: a thousand yellow taxicabs teemed in the streets like hungry carp, but none of them seemed to notice her. After ten minutes she walked back to her hotel and asked the doorman to call her a cab. He blew his whistle and a dozen of them crowded the curb.

At GlobeSpace, she found the outside door unlocked and let herself in. The lobby was dark but she could hear voices, which she followed down a long hallway into the theater. The hallway was decorated with framed posters and photographs from various productions; she'd never heard of the actors or even most of the plays. The performance area had no stage, just an open floor with risers and seats that could be arranged around them. She found a seat near the wall to watch the last of the try-outs. A young actor in jeans and a T-shirt was reading for a role in an upcoming play, which sounded like something by Shakespeare. Sweat poured off his forehead, his lips were pale, his voice dry and faltering. Watching him at some distance was an older man who must have been Tim Salis, slouched on a folding chair and fanning himself with the script. Slight of build with thinning hair and lively dark eyes, he wore an eager, impatient expression, as if he could hardly resist reciting the actor's lines for him. Charlotte had toughed her way through the panic attack in her hotel room, but she felt a quiver of fear when, just as she sat down, the actor launched into a halting lament about the horror and injustice of death:

"Ay, but to die and go we know not where,
To lie in cold obstruction and to rot,
This sensible warm motion to become
A kneaded clod—"

"That's enough!" Tim called out. "Thank you. You'll hear from us if we can use you."

The actor could hardly thank Tim enough for the opportunity to humiliate himself. Tim dismissed him with a few patronizing words and he fled. When Charlotte stepped forward, Tim greeted her with a warmth she hadn't felt from anyone else she'd met on this case, except possibly Sol when he wasn't being condescending. She wasn't a warm person herself — she felt warm enough inside, though she didn't project it: people said she was aloof — but she appreciated it in others, especially men. For a few minutes she avoided mentioning the reason she was there, and so did Tim: they chatted and joked like old friends. He loved directing, he said, and couldn't wait to be finished with the try-outs. "That was supposed to be Claudio's famous speech on death in *Measure for Measure*," he laughed. "Frankly, I'd prefer a gruesome death over listening to that again."

He led Charlotte to his office on the second floor, a cave-like sanctuary enlivened only by an air conditioner rattling in the window. Every surface — his desk and several shelves and tables — was cluttered with books and papers and odd stage properties: masks, wooden swords, oversized puppets. "Pardon my mess," he said. "It never seems to improve. Would you like a glass of wine? It's after five o'clock."

"Sure."

He opened a small refrigerator behind his desk and found a bottle of San Geminiano. It was cool and delicious. Charlotte felt calm for the first time that afternoon, as if all she'd needed, as her

mother often told her, was to sit down and relax. Of course that
wasn't what she was there for. She and Tim both knew that. They
sipped their wine and looked at each other expectantly. It was time
to come to the point of their meeting.

"I just talked to Kathryn and Doug," she said. "They're totally
convinced that Chris Ritter is guilty. They say they don't want him
to be executed, but they won't do anything to stop it."

"Well, I will," Tim said, holding up his glass. "Whatever help
you need, Charlotte, just ask me."

"Thank you."

He emptied his glass and filled it again. "More wine?"

"No, thanks."

"Unlike Kathryn and Doug," he said, "I believe in giving
people another chance, even criminals. I believe in forgiveness,
which is why I don't believe in capital punishment. People can
change, they can see where they went wrong, and ask forgiveness,
at least in their hearts. You can't do that after you're dead."

"No one is beyond redemption," Charlotte said, without being
sure she believed it.

"Ironically, these are some of the things Chris and I used to
argue about. Well, not argue, exactly, but it was a running
discussion over the years. He was a hard-liner. A strict materialist
the way my grandfather was a strict Calvinist. No forgiveness, no
compassion, no salvation. You're just a bunch of molecules and
nothing's going to change that. It was the scientific truth as far as
Chris was concerned. He saw no value in the humanities, no value
in anything when you come right down to it."

"That's still his world view, as far as I can tell."

"Where's the room for values in such a world? I used to ask
him. Why not just pursue your own selfish interests and say to hell
with everybody else?"

Charlotte took a sip of wine and set her glass down on the desk. "What's the story on Kathryn and Doug?" she asked. "Were they an item before Chris was arrested?"

Tim shrugged and tilted his head with a half-smile. "How would I know?"

"Chris thinks so. He thinks the boy is Doug's child."

"Anything's possible, isn't it? All I can say is, they've been my friends for a long time."

"Kathryn started divorce proceedings against Chris a week after he was arrested, didn't she? And married Doug the minute the divorce became final?"

Tim tried to turn the obvious inference into a joke: "Frailty, thy name is woman!"

Charlotte didn't crack a smile: she hadn't finished her cross-examination. "Is there anything to Chris's theory that the two of them bribed Sol Levy to lose the case?"

He reacted with incredulous surprise — "No, that's ridiculous!" — though she reminded herself that he was an actor, undoubtedly a better one than the hack she'd seen performing downstairs. His face was flushed. Could he fake that? It might have been from the wine, or because she had so easily backed him into a corner. "Kathryn's parents might have done that," he said. "They're a piece of work. A couple of Republicans from the Midwest. What else do you need to know about them?"

He reached over to refill her glass, but she put her hand over it and shook her head. Wine was one of the many things that gave her a headache. She opened her purse and pulled out Kathryn's snapshots, which Tim had never seen before, and the copy of the place mat. Tim's account of the night at Dominick's was about the same as Kathryn's and Doug's. He didn't recognize anyone there or remember anyone who stood out from the crowd. They were mostly a bunch of construction workers, he said, rowdy and aggressive but not all that interested in Ritter or his soul. If there was any response to the ad, he'd never heard about it. In fact he'd forgotten the entire incident until Ritter brought it up after his arrest, blowing it up into a big event although it was nothing at the time.

"Why do you think he blew it up like that?" Charlotte asked.

"I guess it was part of his alibi."

"Do you think he's guilty?"

"To be honest, I don't know. I went to the trial. The evidence was pretty overwhelming. Chris didn't testify, but I don't know what he could have said that would have made any difference."

"Did he ever talk to you about Craft."

"He talked to everybody about Craft. After he was arrested. Before that he never mentioned him."

"You think he's lying about Craft?"

"Let me put it this way." Tim seemed to be struggling to find some way to explain Chris's behavior without accusing him. "Maybe Craft is just Chris's bit of theater. You know, an illusion he wants you to accept because it explains things you really want an explanation for."

"I'm not a big theater person," Charlotte said. "I prefer reality to illusion. And I think Craft is real."

Tim smiled back at her and shook his head. "Ritter has gotten to you, hasn't he? He can be a real charmer when he wants to be."

"No, that's not it at all. I don't even like him. It's a moral and ethical issue for me."

"Lawyer ethics? Some people would say that's an oxymoron."

She could feel her hackles rising. "Well, in this case it's not."

"'First thing we do, let's kill all the lawyers.' Shakespeare said that."

She hated that quotation. "I'm not a big Shakespeare fan, either."

"You ought to be. Shakespeare knows everything. Ask him any question and he'll give you the answer."

"OK. Where's Craft? Can he answer that one?"

After a promising start, the conversation had taken a bad turn, tipping into suspicion and hostility when neither wanted it. "I'm sorry," Tim said. "I guess I'm feeling a little too cross-examined."

"My fault," she smiled. "I'm pretty tense about this case."

"I've got an idea. Have you been up on the High Line yet?"

"What's the High Line?"

"It's an elevated pedestrian park built on an old railroad viaduct that starts about a block from here. It's fantastic — you'll love it. Spectacular views of the Hudson River and midtown Manhattan. Even a spectacular view of New Jersey, if you can imagine such a thing."

"Another oxymoron!" she laughed.

Charlotte followed Tim out to the street, around the block and up a long set of steps to the structure he called the High Line. On a beautiful spring evening it was teeming with people, so many, in fact, that they found it hard to navigate through the crowd. The viaduct passed right through the Standard Hotel and skirted the riverfront past a futuristic Frank Gehry creation that was all glass and no right angles. There were gardens and sculptures and places to sit to enjoy the views. Tim pointed out all the familiar sites, which looked unfamiliar, almost unreal, from this angle. After a ten minute walk they stepped out of the crowd into a small amphitheater that invited them to view the cityscape through a frame as if it were a work of art.

He was eager to talk about his new production of *Measure for Measure*, which he was taking up to the Berkshires in the summer. "It's a fascinating play," he said. "Have you ever seen it?"

"No, I don't think so. I'm sure I haven't."

They stepped up to a guard rail and stood next to each other gazing at the Empire State Building, which seemed strangely larger than life. "It's built around some themes you'd probably be interested in," Tim said. "Morality and ethics and how they relate to politics. The dangers of puritanism, which was just getting going in those days. Hypocrisy, which always goes hand in hand with puritanism. The problem of authority and how it corrupts those in power. And an issue that's always timely: When is it acceptable to do evil in order to prevent greater evils?"

"Rarely if ever, in my opinion."

He glanced toward her as if watching for her reaction. "Capital punishment, for example."

"That's an evil that doesn't prevent other evils," she said. "All the studies show that it has little or no deterrent effect."

"Would you do something evil to stop it?"

"What do you mean?"

"Let me put it a little differently." His voice was low and serious, as if he was finally talking about something that mattered to him. "How far would you go to save the life of a condemned man? That's what the plot of *Measure for Measure* hinges on. Lord Angelo is put in charge of the government in Vienna. He begins to enforce the death penalty for the crime of fornication, which has been on the books but never enforced. He sentences a young man named Claudio to death, and Claudio's sister, Isabella — a virtuous maiden who's about to enter a convent — comes to plead for his life. Angelo tells her: I'll spare your brother if you'll sleep with me. She refuses, even after her brother urges her to give in to Angelo's lust. What's her justification? She makes the argument you just made: she doesn't want to prevent an evil by committing another one."

"She's willing to sacrifice her brother's life just to preserve her virginity?"

"In Shakespeare's day, that would have been a closer call."

Charlotte turned toward him, expecting to see him smiling. He stared back with a friendly but serious expression, as if she were an actor and he wanted to hear how she delivered her lines. "You called her virtuous," she said self-consciously. "I'd call her selfish, heartless, puritanical — as much of a moral monster as Angelo."

"Maybe 'virtuous' isn't the right word for Isabella," he said. "That sort of stacks the deck, doesn't it? Shakespeare is asking us to think about what 'virtuous' means. It might be better to say Isabella is *innocent*. She's assumed to be virtuous, but what she really is is innocent, and part of her innocence is that she doesn't realize that virtue sometimes demands a compromise with evil. Sometimes it may require a person to commit an evil in order to prevent a greater one."

Charlotte had the uncomfortable feeling that Tim knew her better than she knew herself. She had never thought of herself as especially 'virtuous' — or moral or whatever it would be called today — but now she realized that she did believe in her own innocence. And in the death penalty case she was involved in, it was her innocence, as much as Ritter's, that was being tested. How far would she go to stop Ritter's execution? And what difference did it make if he was innocent or not?

For a moment she felt close to Tim, as if they were both part of the same unfolding drama. Then without a word she turned away and plunged into the slow-motion crowd of couples, families and sightseers that drifted down the walkway, gawking at the skyline that gleamed in the distance as if it had been built for their enjoyment.

14

Chris Ritter

Teague stares at me day and night. I wake up from my latest nightmare and feel him following me in the half-darkness — it's never completely dark here — as I stand up to use the toilet. He never speaks, but is he trying to tell me something with his relentless stare? Is he trying to bore his way into my cell, into my life, into my head? This nightmare was a variant of the other one. The ragged people who slowly sank beyond my grasp are washed up on the beach like seaweed: a mother with her drowned children lashed around her waist with a rope, a man with his face half chewed off, a young girl with hermit crabs crawling out of her hollow eye sockets. Still, somehow, even in death, even with no eyes, they are staring at me, reaching out to entangle me. I can feel my uncle's deathly hand and Craft's cunning smirk and Teague's murderous gaze that never blinks, all tugging me down into the heap of human seaweed on the beach. An elemental power whirls these forces together and jolts me awake: I'm relieved to be alive and well on death row. That power resonates from Teague, I realize. The guards call him a devil and maybe they're right. Some night they're going to let him into my cell and he's going to kill me.

As my execution nears, Billy Bob and Bubba seem more understanding and solicitous, as if they want our relationship to end on a positive note. Instead of shouting commands or insults, they offer me something to read or ask if I'd like to see the chaplain. I hear whispering in the corridor, and the next thing I know Billy Bob is outside my cell with a notepad and a pencil, poised to take the order for my last meal. "You're allowed to request a last meal," he says. "Provided you place your order ten days in advance."

"Are there any specials?"

It's my first joke in ten years and it falls flat.

"A lot of guys opt for shrimp or lobster," Billy Bob says. "Something you don't get every day."

"No alcoholic beverages," Bubba adds.

"OK," I tell them, "I'll have Tibetan yak steak, Chilean sea urchins—"

"Not to rain on your picnic," Billy Bob cuts me off, "but the total cost can't exceed $40, and all food must be purchased locally."

"Forget it, then. If I can't have what I want, forget it."

Another whispered conference and they try again. It's becoming clear that their hospitality, like everything else in this place, is mandatory. "We've got a tradition here at the prison," Billy Bob says in a more authoritative tone. "On the night of your execution, the warden and his staff will eat the same meal as you. Kind of a Last Supper type of thing."

"Just for them, though," Bubba says. "You've got to eat in your cell."

"All right," I tell them. "I'll have three chicken-fried steaks with lard gravy and fried onions, a triple bacon cheeseburger with home fries, a cheddar cheese omelet with onions and jalapeños, ten ripe figs, a dozen raw oysters, a pound of steamed mussels, eight pork fajitas with sour cream, a sausage and pepperoni pizza, a half-gallon of Ben & Jerry's Death by Chocolate ice cream, three pieces of pecan pie—"

"You gonna eat all that?" Bubba interrupts.

"Sure, why not? If it's my last meal, it might as well be the warden's too."

I haven't painted a pretty picture of myself, I know that. I've been trying to be honest, painful as it's been, but I still haven't come to the worst part: the truth about my last trip to Florida with Helene. That's the part of the story I'll never tell anyone. That's the truth I'm taking to my grave.

I needed to make one last trip to complete my research on the sea turtles. Life with Kathryn had become unbearable. I'd finally begun to suspect what should have been obvious for years: that she and my best friend Doug were having an affair. The signs were all there — I knew how to play that game — and on one level I didn't mind all that much. But there was one aspect of it that tormented me: my growing conviction that little Liam wasn't my son but Doug's. In that argument with Kathryn when she questioned my sanity and the suitability of my genes, didn't she say she was worried about Casey, without even mentioning Liam? The baby had never looked anything like me, and as he got older he began to take on Doug's appearance. And Doug, who was still a bachelor, doted on him like a puppy and always seemed to be hanging around our apartment. To make matters worse, Helene had been avoiding me and the more she avoided me the more I wanted her. Since I planned to be in Florida for several days, at a time when Kathryn's parents would be in California, it was an ideal opportunity for Helene and me to patch up our differences. We could stay at my in-laws' townhouse, where we'd stayed several times before.

For all her moral scruples, Helene leaped at the chance for another free trip to Florida. There was something she needed to discuss with me, she said, and this would be a perfect time to do it. I met her for lunch at a little Greek place on Broadway and we made our arrangements. I'd fly down on Tuesday, hoping to finish my work on the island before she arrived. She was to fly down on Wednesday, pick up a rental car and meet me at the townhouse when I returned from the island on Thursday. I gave her a key and my remote control for the garage door. All she had to do was type in the code and drive into the garage before the neighbors had a chance to notice who she was. From the garage you can go upstairs into the house. We'd used this method before with no one being any the wiser.

At first everything went according to plan. Arriving late Tuesday night, I parked my car on a street about two blocks from the townhouse, let myself in through the back door and took the Grady out early, before the neighbors were up and about. It was a hot, breezeless day, 95 degrees by ten o'clock, the sea a shimmering mirror under the cloudless sky. I made good time to the island, anchored the boat and spent the afternoon making observations and checking my data points. When the sun finally set I stretched out in my hammock and listened to the radio until I fell asleep.

At dawn I awoke to the screech of the gulls swooping and circling over the Grady. The sea was choppy now as a new weather system moved in from the south behind a gusty wind and a wall of towering white clouds. The tide was running out and wouldn't be high again for six hours, which gave me just enough time, weather permitting, to collect the data I needed to complete my research. I slipped on my special boots and gloves and lowered myself off the stern, wading toward the shore but taking care not step on the beach. After about an hour I became aware of a commotion behind me, a babble of voices jangling over the surf and the screeching gulls. I peered over the waves and glimpsed a makeshift wooden boat cresting toward the island, half-submerged, crammed with men and women, all of them black, wearing white clothes and surrounded by naked, wide-eyed children. They seemed to be walking on the water, glistening in the patchy sunlight as if they'd drifted down from a cloud. They called out to me in some foreign language and as they came closer I realized it was French. They must have been Haitians, refugees bound for the Florida coast who intended to land on the island to look for food and water. I couldn't let them do that. There was no water on the island and no food other than the turtle eggs I was trying to protect. Five minutes on that beach would foul it forever and destroy my work for the past three years.

I yelled at them in French and tried to wave them away but they cried out louder and lowered their oars to push themselves closer to shore. I hurried to my boat and climbed aboard. In my fishing case I kept the deer rifle I'd bought when I discovered the footprints on the beach. Without thinking, I took it out and loaded it and waved it over my head. The Haitians bobbed on the water, chattering and rowing closer as if they couldn't believe what they saw. I waved the rifle again, gesturing away from the island with my free hand, and this time I pulled the trigger.

The gun roared and the gulls took off screeching across the water. The chattering stopped and the ocean's vast silence smothered the wind. Then one of the women raised an infant over her head and the clamor rose again as keening and scolding and scorn. The men stared back at me in murderous disbelief. There was no going back. I waved the rifle over my head and yelled through the wind that there were plenty of other islands and sandbars and some of them had water and coconuts and tidal ponds where you could catch fish. But they couldn't hear me or understand me or they were too desperate to listen. The sun beat down on me without mercy and the surf pounded and the women screamed and I fired another shot. Then I leveled the gun at them and made it clear that the next bullet wouldn't be wasted.

The commotion died down as the men turned the boat around and rowed away from the island. For a few minutes the chattering subsided into singing and then the singing tapered off and the Haitians floated away as they'd arrived, the soles of their feet skimming the water. I watched from the deck of the Grady clutching my rifle until they were safely out of sight. I felt sorry for them but I was sure that if I'd let them land they would have killed me. If they didn't find another island they'd be picked up by the Coast Guard and enjoy a few nights in a good hotel before being flown back to Haiti. I knew that was callous but I had other things to worry about. I'd wasted half the morning on this diversion and now I had only a couple of hours to work before the tide ran back in. The clouds were thickening and the wind was pushing harder against the hull, tightening the anchor line hard, and I expected a rough passage back to the mainland.

It was almost dusk by the time I docked the Grady at the boat slip behind my in-laws' townhouse. I'd tried calling Helene as soon as I came within range but she didn't pick up. There was no sign that she'd been at the house, only a slight smell of bleach or disinfectant, as if my mother-in-law, scheduled to return in a few days, was already there. I called the airport and confirmed that Helene's flight had landed on time the night before. The airline clerk wouldn't say whether or not she was on it.

I felt angry, edgy, defensive. Where was Helene? Why had she stood me up? Apparently this was her way of saying good-bye. All she'd wanted was a free ticket to Florida. I thought about going to bed early, but I knew I wouldn't be able to sleep. I was restless, keyed up by what I'd been through that day. Sitting around the townhouse by myself was not an option. I drove to a pick-up joint in West Palm Beach, where it didn't take long to find someone who'd let me buy her a drink. Her name was Lisa and she was from Alabama, a bottle blonde with a pair of blue eyes that were set just a little too close together. She was drinking margaritas and they brought out the party animal in her, she said, which meant she talked loud and laughed about things that weren't funny. She was just old enough to be desperate about meeting men and I was selfish and cynical enough not to care. I gave her a fake name and before long we were on our way to her apartment in a seedy motel-like complex where you could hear country music twanging through paper-thin walls. But she had a nice queen size bed and a generous notion of Southern hospitality. She made me feel a lot more at home than I would have felt at home.

After Lisa fell asleep I switched on the TV to watch the news and my whole life turned upside down. Two dozen bodies, believed to be Haitian refugees, had washed up on the beach south of Palm Beach with the remnants of a makeshift boat. The Coast Guard speculated that the boat had capsized and the refugees drowned as they clung to the wreckage. Among the victims were several children, including a baby and three toddlers tied to their mother with a rope.

That news report literally made me sick. I lurched into the bathroom where I retched into the toilet. After a while I stood up and stumbled back out to the bedroom where Lisa was sleeping. I couldn't face her, I couldn't face anyone. I poured myself a glass of tequila and disappeared from her life without a note or a parting kiss.

After a sleepless night at the townhouse I booked an early flight to New York. My in-laws had arrived unexpectedly while I was out — they were already asleep when I got back — and I couldn't bear talking to them as if everything was normal. At home I locked myself in my study and spent a week compulsively reading accounts of the Haitian refugee tragedy on the internet, not breathing a word about what happened to anyone, including Kathryn. Especially Kathryn. She thought I was angry at her for some reason and I let her think that. I woke up each morning with a palpable sense of the torture my conscience was going to inflict on me that day, as if some tiny fanged creature had been implanted in my brain and was eating me from the inside. What had I done? I had murdered two dozen people in the name of science and my own ego and thoughtless convenience, and I'd done it so cavalierly I didn't even deserve the name of murderer. One afternoon I tried to shake off my depression and even mustered a smile for Kathryn. She turned away in disgust. I had reached the low point of my life. There was no question of reaching out to Helene. After what she'd done to me, that relationship was over.

The next day — it was about ten days after I'd returned home from Florida — the police appeared at my door. There were three officers, and one of them was Alex Lopez, whom I hadn't seen since he joined the NYPD. He stood to one side as if he didn't recognize me while an older man, a detective named Lombardo, handled the introductions. I invited them in and we sat in the living room, Lombardo in the middle of the couch with the others flanking him like bodyguards. I tried to act relaxed, but the guilt must have been splashed all over my face. Lombardo recognized it with a sly smile, the way you might smile at a child you know is lying. I smiled back, too stunned to dissemble. How could they know? How could anyone know what went on at that island?

I must have sighed with relief when Detective Lombardo reached in his jacket pocket and pulled out a picture of Helene. It was a police photo, not flattering — she looked disoriented, bullied, defiant — but it was Helene.

"Do you know this woman?" Lombardo asked me.

"I don't know. I might know her from somewhere. Who is she?"

"You don't know her?"

"No, I told you. She looks familiar but I don't know who she is."

"Her name is Helene Varga."

"Would you mind telling me what this is about?"

Lombardo nodded and glanced at the others, as if my question had proved something. "A couple weeks ago you spent some time at a townhouse in Florida that's owned by William and Louise O'Donnell. I believe they're your in-laws."

"Yes. That's right."

"You were there on the twelfth?"

"I don't know. I flew down on a Tuesday. The next morning I went out to an island about sixty miles off shore where I'm doing some research — I'm a biologist — and slept on the boat. I came back on Thursday. Was that the twelfth?"

"Thursday was the thirteenth."

"Then I wasn't there on the twelfth, except very early in the morning."

Lombardo checked a notebook he'd removed from his pocket along with the picture of Helene. "This woman, Helene Varga, flew from New York to Ft. Lauderdale on Wednesday the twelfth. She rented a car at the airport and gave your townhouse as her local address."

"I don't have a townhouse."

"Your in-laws' townhouse."

"I can't explain that. It must be a mistake."

"The local police talked to your in-laws. They said you were staying there at that time."

"I told you, I was out in the boat. I was sixty miles off shore on the twelfth."

"Did you see anybody out there?"

I could feel my heart racing. "No, there's nobody out there. I never see anybody out there." I tried to change the subject. "You still haven't told me what this is about."

"What it's about is that Mrs. O'Donnell, your mother-in-law, told the police you were at the townhouse on the night of the twelfth."

"Well, she's wrong. And you still haven't told me what's going on. I think I have a right to know why you're asking me these questions."

"You don't know Helene Varga?"

"I told you, I might know her from somewhere but not by name."

Lombardo smirked. "What name do you know her by?"

"No name. I don't know her by any name."

"Just another prostitute?"

"What are you talking about?"

"Helene Varga was a call girl. She flew down to Florida to see you."

"That's ridiculous."

"Her DNA was found in the townhouse."

"Her DNA? What happened to her?"

"We thought you might know."

"Well, I don't, I don't know anything about Helene Varga and her DNA."

Lombardo let his eyes wander around the room, taking in the TV and the stereo and the pile of newspapers on the coffee table as if they were evidence of something. I was just glad he wasn't looking at me. "Her DNA was on the carpet in the living room and it was on the floor of the garage," he said, facing me again. "And it was in the trunk of her car."

I could feel my throat tightening. "In the trunk of her car?"

"The rental car. Remember, that's why she gave your address."

"Is she dead?"

"Yes, Mr. Ritter. Her body was found in a swamp near the townhouse."

I felt sick but I had to pretend I wasn't upset. "Well, unfortunately I don't know anything about it. I was out at the island. I went out there the morning after I arrived and came back two days later."

"What island would that be?"

"Baxter Island. I'm doing a research project out there."

"Anybody see you there?"

"No, I told you. It's uninhabited except by turtles. Nobody ever sees me there. And I don't see anybody." I lurched to my feet, desperate to put this torture to an end. "Is there anything else you wanted to ask me?"

Lombardo stood up and we walked to the door, followed by the others. Alex never once looked me in the eye.

"Did you take the pictures?" Lombardo asked.

"What pictures?"

"You don't know about the pictures?"

"No, I don't know about any pictures."

"All right, Mr. Ritter." He shook my hand and smiled. "Thanks for your cooperation. You'll probably be hearing from us again."

I sat in my study in a daze until it was almost time for Kathryn to come home and then I walked the streets agonizing about Helene and rehearsing every detail of that encounter with the police until my brain was ready to explode. Was Lombardo accusing me of murdering Helene — was Helene even really dead? — or was he trying to trick me into some admission about what happened at the island? Whatever it was, Craft was behind it, I was sure of that. If Helene was dead, Craft had killed her and was trying to frame me for the crime. I wolfed down some fish and chips in an Irish bar on Third Avenue and called Alex at home from the pay phone. "Alex, this is Chris Ritter. What the hell is going on?"

"I can't talk to you about this," he said in a hushed voice.

"Yes, you can. Just tell me what's going on."

"OK, but you never talked to me, right?

"Right."

"This call girl was murdered in Florida and they think you did it."

"Why? Why do they think I did it? "

"Because it happened in your in-laws' house while you were staying there. Your mother-in-law ratted you out."

"I don't believe this! Listen, Alex, you've got to help me. This is a set up, I'm being framed."

"You think your mother-in-law is trying to frame you?"

"No, not her. It's this guy named Craft who's been stalking me for years, I don't know why."

There was a long silence, or what passes for silence in New York. I could hear sirens wailing in the background and the TV blaring and a baby crying as if its life depended on it.

"Did you know this Helene Varga?" Alex finally asked.

"Only slightly."

He waited for me to elaborate, and I didn't. "It was sort of a ... casual relationship, then?"

"It was a long time ago," I said. "Craft set it up. And now he killed her down there and made it look like I did it. You've got to help me, Alex."

Lombardo came back two days later with a search warrant and three new henchmen, not including Alex. They confiscated my computer and the suitcase I'd taken with me to Florida. Then they took me to the police station where they sat me in a windowless room and read me my Miranda rights. I told them I wanted to talk to Alex. I didn't need a lawyer; the whole thing was a big mistake.

I sat there by myself for a couple of hours before Alex appeared. "You make me sick," he said when he walked in.

"What happened?"

He squinted at me as if he were examining an insect. "We opened this safe deposit box Helene Varga had. There was a lot of stuff in it about you. In fact everything in there was about you."

"About me?"

"Pictures of you and her in bed together. Pictures taken at restaurants, hotels, sitting at sidewalk cafes."

"Alex, this is all part of the frame-up. Can't you see that? Craft set this up."

He frowned at me in disgust. "There's hotel receipts, handwritten notes from you to her. And you know what? There's even some pictures taken at your in-laws' house in Florida. She was there with you, wasn't she?"

"A couple of other times. But I didn't see her that week."

"You were lying when you said you didn't know her."

"I didn't say I didn't know her. I said I might have known her slightly."

"You lied to me."

"I didn't know what was going on. I still don't."

Alex stood up to leave. "Was she blackmailing you?"

"No. She never said anything like that."

"They found her suitcase in the swamp about a hundred feet from where they found her body. The key to the safe deposit box was stashed in the suitcase. She must have kept it there so the police would know where to look if anything bad happened to her."

"She was afraid of Craft."

"They also found a camera memory card in the townhouse that has the pictures you took while you were murdering her. Or was it Craft that took those pictures?"

"Alex—"

"Forget it, Chris. You killed her."

"Alex, you've got to help me."

"I can't help you, Chris. You're on your own."

From that point on everything happened in slow motion, the inexorable working out of my fate as I became enmeshed in the pitiless machinery of the criminal justice system. There was an air of destiny about the whole thing, even of déjà vu, like a pre-packaged nightmare. Craft had done his planning well.

Kathryn assumed I was guilty and refused to talk to me or let me see the kids. Tim and Doug tried to be supportive but it was obvious they also thought I was guilty. Doug came to the rescue financially. He hired a lawyer who charged $25,000 to waive extradition and send me to Florida, and in Florida he retained Sol Levy, said to be the savviest defense attorney in the state. I liked Sol at first, but he seemed to have more loyalty to his cronies in the local court system than to me. After the trial, when Kathryn married Doug, I wondered if I got exactly the representation Doug had paid for.

I tried to tell Sol about Craft and his machinations. "You tell that story to a jury," Sol said, chuckling in his folksy way as if I'd told an amusing anecdote around the cracker barrel, "and I guarantee you'll win a free ticket to death row." We argued back and forth for months but in the end he wouldn't let me take the stand. The jury never learned about Craft and of course I got my ticket anyway. My guilt was established by Helene's earring, which the police supposedly found in my suitcase in New York, and the contents of the safe deposit box, which not only showed my connection with Helene but suggested blackmail as a motive for killing her. I should also give credit to my dear mother-in-law, whose testimony placed me in the townhouse at the time Helene was murdered. In the guilt phase, the jury was also shown a sheaf of photographs of Helene being tortured to death, along with some taken after she was dead, artfully posed pornography that turned my stomach and everyone else's. They found the memory chip for those photographs in the townhouse.

In the penalty phase, the most damning piece of evidence was my diary, which Craft had urged me to fill with nihilistic fantasies over a period of years. In one respect I'll admit that Sol was right in keeping me off the witness stand. By doing so he was able to keep the jury from hearing the testimony of the court-appointed psychiatrist, Dr. Claire Simon, based on an examination she'd conducted at a time when I intended to testify.

I remember that occasion well. The psychiatrist got me talking about my views on science and religion and morality as reflected in my diary and my public pronouncements over the years. I gave her my views — and I must say, the views of most of my professional colleagues in their candid moments — about the nature of the universe and human life. I described the Big Bang and the formation of the earth and the evolution of life, culminating in Mozart and Einstein and where we are today. All pretty standard stuff that could be parroted by any undergraduate who bothered to read the assignments.

"Is there nothing beyond that?" she asked.

"No. I'm quite sure there isn't."

"Then is there any reason not to kill someone?"

I chose my words carefully. "There are some very good reasons."

"Apart from the fear of punishment, I mean. Is there any reason you shouldn't walk over here — assuming you weren't shackled to your seat — and knock my brains out?"

"I'd be depriving you of the only period of consciousness you're ever going to have."

"But once I was dead, that wouldn't matter anymore, would it?"

"Not to you. There isn't any 'you' other than some electrical loops in the brain I'd be knocking out."

"What about my family?"

"It would matter to them."

"But it wouldn't matter to you very much, would it?"

The whole line questioning had infuriated me. The psychiatrist was making me out to be some kind of monster without any emotions. "I wouldn't kill anyone," I said. "It would make me feel too guilty."

"Why?"

"Like everyone else, I've been programmed to feel guilt in certain situations."

Dr. Simon smiled as if I'd given her the answer she wanted. "Then that's the reason you wouldn't kill me? Because you've been programmed to feel guilty? Not because it's wrong?"

"Of course it's wrong," I said. "But that term — 'wrong' — doesn't have any scientific meaning. It's just a way of describing the things that make you feel guilty if you're responsible for them."

The psychiatrist smiled again. "If someone died and you didn't feel responsible, would you feel guilty?"

"No, probably not."

"Would you feel some other emotion?"

"I might feel sad or upset, depending on who it was."

Her next question came out of the blue. "Is your mother still living?"

"No, she died when I was fourteen."

"Did you cry at her funeral?"

Dr. Simon didn't testify but evidently she gave some off-the-record advice to the prosecutors. In the penalty phase, they brought in Uncle Ed and asked him if I cried at my mother's funeral. The diary and the Raskolnikov interview were admitted in evidence and the prosecutor beat them to death. He argued that I was a sociopath (or a psychopath, if you prefer), incapable of moral reasoning yet not insane by any legal definition. I knew the difference between right and wrong, he said, but I attached no significance to the distinction. Legally I was in the same category as Ted Bundy and Jeffrey Dahmer: a soulless monster, a freak of nature, perfectly qualified to be tried and executed for my crimes.

The jury agreed.

Tuesday, May 15, 6:00 p.m. 10 days to execution.

And so I came to Raiford for my penance and death. I was guilty not as charged but far beyond what was charged, a murderer more culpable, a heart more depraved, than the State of Florida ever imagined. Here I met Billy Bob and Bubba in their many incarnations, sometimes fat, sometimes lean, sometimes white, sometimes black, sometimes sadistic and spiteful and sometimes — no, almost always — just following orders, just doing their jobs. Theirs is the work of corrections, the work of effacement and excoriation, and they do it well. Theirs is the work of stripping away the accidents of selfhood until nothing is left, no substance or substrate, no illusion, ironically, of any continuous moral actor who could be held responsible for a crime. That's my only salvation: this dissolution of self, this flight from past, present and future, this return to the dust. "The self is a prison where you're a lifer without the possibility of parole," the chaplain told me one afternoon. "You can't escape and you can't get out for good behavior. You've got to serve the term you were sentenced to — it's the only life you'll ever have. And you're going to spend it in solitary, where you'll have to live with everything you hate, everything evil and sick, because that's where it is, in your cell with you."

I started to object that I was innocent.

"Don't tell the guards you're innocent," the chaplain smiled, keeping his eyes low as he always did. "They know it's a lie. When you finally admit you're no better than the killer in the next cell, they might start to believe you. But they won't let you out, because by then you'll have admitted your guilt."

I shouldn't complain: it's where I started, and now I've come full circle. I began in innocence, thirsting only to free myself from every illusion. I can see now that in my innocence was my destruction. Behind the veil of illusion I discovered an insatiable appetite — a soul, though not my own, that knew no restraint, no faith, and no fear—which could be propitiated only by a monstrous ego. In ten days that ego will cease to exist; the appetite in me will be extinguished, if not satisfied. All the creatures of the earth are creatures of desire. In the other animals, this force — the will of the selfish gene to persist and reproduce — displays itself shamelessly as instinct, but in us it is diabolical in its cunning. It holds us at a distance, like dogs on a leash, allowing us to conceal our instincts in our intellects, our pleasures, our moralities, our egos. On death row these vanities are stripped away. First the ego and then the instincts are obliterated; the will to live moves on to the next cell. The law in its wisdom allows ample time for this process to run its course. The prisoner is guaranteed a decade or more of self-flagellation, false hopes, apologies and appeals, at the end of which, if the system is working, there is nothing left of him. Then he is ready to die.

Listen to me, spinning out my tale with philosophy and fancy phrases as if talking or thinking or explaining could change anything. When in fact the more tricked out in logic and eloquence I make my sentences (as if someone might actually be listening), the more self-deceiving they are sure to be. I ought to know that by now. There's only one sentence that matters here. The rest are just another diversionary tactic, another vanity.

"I feel like I'm losing my mind."

In manacles and leg irons, I'm stumbling back to my cell from the visitors room, where I just spent an hour with the chaplain. Billy Bob and Bubba drag me forward by the elbows, trying to measure their pace against mine. I catch a glimpse of Billy Bob's face as it twists toward me: his lips seem unusually protuberant, his eyes glinty and pink, his smile a hideous leer. Spinning toward Bubba, I'm repulsed by his glistening eyes and huge, fanglike teeth. I lurch to a halt, causing both of them to stumble, convinced, for a terrifying instant, that they embody some demonic force that has seized control of my life.

"What's the matter?" Billy Bob asks. His face looks completely normal now.

"I feel like I'm losing my mind."

"Counseling is available," he says.

"Sometimes you just need somebody to talk to," Bubba adds in a soothing voice.

"That can be a big help," Billy Bob agrees.

"It's OK to feel anxious at a time like this."

I'm touched by their concern, which helps bring me back to my senses. As bad as my situation is, it's still explicable as part of the human condition. At least I haven't started believing in demonic forces.

"It's our job," Billy Bob explains as we resume our march, "to make sure you stay sane enough to execute."

15.

Charlotte walked all the way through Chelsea and the garment district toward her hotel. The city seemed more overcrowded and frenzied than ever. Pedestrians spilled from the sidewalks into the streets, taxis flew along in yellow waves, busses raced from corner to corner without ever getting ahead of the crowd. She found a cheap cafeteria called Tad's Steaks, where she waited in line for a grilled steak and a baked potato and sat down to catch up on her messages. She'd apologized to Tim for the way she suddenly turned away from him on the High Line. It was a fear of heights, she told him; she needed to be closer to the ground. He was nice about it, walking her down the long staircase to the street, where they said goodbye. She called his number from the restaurant and left a message thanking him for meeting with her. Her mailbox was filled again with insults and threats and a string of text messages on similar themes, sent from a different number. Reading these messages made her angry, enough that she felt short of breath and her hands began to tremble. But she felt grateful for her anger: it was a good substitute for fear.

At the hotel she tipped a bellman to escort her to her room on the pretext of needing another blanket. Once he'd left, she bolted the door and got ready for bed, even though she still had plenty of work to do. Work, she'd learned, was another good substitute for fear. Opening her laptop, she confirmed the appointment with Alex Lopez, found Andy Wagner on the internet and arranged for a rental car to be delivered the next morning. Then, in response to an urgent email message, she called Sol Levy at home on his cell phone. "You need to come back to Florida tomorrow," he told her. "You're wasting precious time up there."

"I feel like I'm getting close to something," she said. "I've talked to Ritter's ex-wife and his two best friends. They're all stonewalling."

"Charlotte, there's not much time left. Believe me, I've been through this drill before. You've got to file a slew of emergency motions, and they'd better be good ones. As a last resort you'll have to go to the Governor, who's probably out fishing somewhere—"

"Julie Halkins said she would help."

"She's not going to lift a finger, Charlotte. I can do a little work on this, but I don't have much time, and to be honest, I'm not sure I understand your argument. If it's based on new evidence, I hope you have some."

Charlotte hesitated. "I was planning to go down to Philadelphia tomorrow night to see my mom."

"There's no time for that, Charlotte."

Reluctantly she was coming to the same conclusion. "I'll fly back tomorrow."

"Now that we've got that settled," Sol continued, "there's something I need to tell you about. Another piece of new evidence, if you want to call it that, or a new twist on old evidence."

"What is it?"

"It's the photographs you found at your hotel the other day. Millie made copies for me, and I tried to match them to the photos that were used at the trial. They're not the same."

"What do you mean? They show Helene Varga being tortured and killed—"

"Yes, they do, but they're not exactly the same shots. Even though they must have been taken at almost the same time."

"Craft must have used two different cameras," Charlotte said.

"Assuming there is a Craft, why would he have done that?"

"He took one set of pictures knowing he'd leave the memory card in the townhouse to incriminate Ritter. The other set he kept for his own sick enjoyment."

"Well," Sol said, "that's one possible theory."

"It bolsters our argument that the photographs are new evidence that must be taken into account."

"All the more reason why you need to get back down here."

Wednesday, May 16, 6:00 a.m., 9 days, 12 hours to execution.

Charlotte wasn't a morning person; in fact, before 8:00 a.m. she was hardly a person at all. More like a zombie or an automaton, and on a rainy Wednesday when she had to drive from midtown Manhattan to New Jersey at rush hour in a rental car, she could only wonder what she was trying to accomplish. Finding Andy Wagner, that was it: the former professor who probably had more reason to hate Ritter than anyone else. He was a high school biology teacher in Nutley, New Jersey, a suburb about ten miles from the city. Charlotte had found his picture on the internet; her plan was to arrive before school started and intercept him in the parking lot. She spent thirty nerve-wracking minutes in the Lincoln Tunnel and another forty-five navigating the foggy wasteland beyond it, as she listened to the astounding news, repeated on the radio at five-minute intervals, that there were traffic jams all over the area. That's what amazed and horrified her about New York. Every day it comes as a complete surprise to eight million people that living there is impossible and will never get any better. Their only consolation is knowing that they'll be surprised about the same thing tomorrow.

The years hadn't been kind to Andy Wagner. He was taller than Charlotte had pictured him, but bent over like an old man, and so heavy that he had difficulty extracting himself from his Honda Civic. His face was wrinkled and lopsided, and he sported a small, pointy beard like the one she pictured on Craft. In fact, she was struck by how closely Wagner resembled Ritter's description of Craft. She recalled the notes left in Ritter's mailbox, Helene's familiarity with his personal life, and Craft's inexplicable insight into his career. Wagner and Craft couldn't be the same man, since Ritter knew both of them, but could they have been so intertwined that over time they'd taken on a similar appearance?

"Mr. Wagner?" Charlotte said, gliding up beside his car.

He stared at her for a brief moment and then shuffled past her toward the school building. His eyes looked devious and mean.

"My name is Charlotte Ambler," she said, following along beside him. "I'm an attorney representing Chris Ritter."

"I've got nothing to say to you."

"Please. Just a minute of your time."

He squeezed himself between two parked cars to keep her behind him. She walked through an open space and came out in front of him. "Was Craft working for you?"

"Get out of my way."

"Did you kill Helene Varga?

"Get out of my way, I said."

"Or were you working with someone else on that? Craft, for instance? What about Greta? Was Greta involved?"

He stopped and turned an ugly look in her direction. "Get out of my way or I am going to kill somebody and it just might be you."

Now we're getting somewhere, Charlotte thought.

He lurched forward, forcing her to take a step back. "You know, I almost hope you get Ritter off, so I can kill him myself.

What he deserves is a lot more cruel and unusual than what he's
going to get."

She followed him another dozen yards to the entrance, which
looked like an airport security gate. The school had more guards
and security barriers than the Florida death house. As Wagner
slouched through the checkpoint, he nodded to a guard who
stepped in front of Charlotte to block her way. "You have a
badge?" the guard asked. A sign informed her that all visitors must
register at the office and obtain a badge.

"No," she improvised. "I'm on my way to the office to get
one."

"The office doesn't open until ten. You'll have to wait in your
car."

Wagner loitered just inside the building, gesturing toward
Charlotte as he conferred with another guard, a middle-aged
woman whose ample waist was girdled with an assortment of
phones, radios, first aid kits, tasers and tear gas canisters. The
woman fixed Charlotte in her sights and lumbered toward her.
"Can I see some ID, please," she said.

"ID? For what?"

"If you don't show me some ID, I'll have to call the police."

Charlotte dug in her purse for her driver's license and handed
it to the guard. "I guess I need to get a visitor badge. Could you
take me to the office?"

"Come with me, please," the guard said.

Charlotte assumed they were on their way to the office. Instead
the guard escorted her back to the parking lot. "Where's your car?"
she demanded. "Now, if you don't get in it and drive off the school
property, I'll have to call the police."

Charlotte's brush with the law at Nutley High School left her in a
perfect mood for the NYPD's 46th Precinct station in the Bronx.

It was in a rough neighborhood, reminiscent of some she'd visited when she interned at the DA's office in Philadelphia. She parked her car around the block on Valentine Avenue, expecting never to see it again. Inside the station she followed a uniformed officer to Detective Alex Lopez's desk, in a crowded roomful of other desks. Lopez greeted her without bothering to stand up. He looked like a man who used to be in good shape, back before his chin had met his neck. He was sharp-eyed and moderately dark, with a smile that was more cynical than friendly. His desk was taken up mostly by empty coffee cups, framed pictures of his wife and kids, and a huge bobble-head doll of Alex Rodriguez in a New York Yankees uniform.

"Why Alex Rodriguez?" Charlotte asked. "Is he Dominican?"

Lopez nodded. "And his name is Alex."

"Isn't he sort of a disreputable figure for a police officer to have on his desk? Why not Pedro Martinez or David Ortiz?"

"I wouldn't own a doll of any man who ever played for the Red Sox." He leaned forward with a smirk. "Except to stick pins in."

They both laughed, a little nervously, as if they wondered whether jokes were appropriate in the circumstances. "I guess you know why I'm here," Charlotte said. "Chris Ritter's scheduled to die in nine days."

"I'll mark my calendar," Lopez said without smiling.

"He says he didn't do it and I believe him."

"That makes one of us."

"He says he helped your family out."

Lopez flicked the Alex Rodriguez bobble head with his fingertip and watched it jiggle. "He tutored me a little in high school. He didn't help out anybody else in my family, even though I asked him to. And when all this started, he lied to me. I believed him and it almost cost me my job. Why do you think I'm up here in the Bronx? In case you haven't heard, it's a zoo."

"Ritter feels bad about lying to you."

"How touching." He glanced up at the clock. "Look, I'd love to help but I've got about ten minutes. What can I do for you?"

Charlotte tried a small deception. "The evidence you sent down to Florida has been very helpful—"

"What evidence?"

"You know, the place mat and all."

"What are you talking about? I didn't send anything down there."

"Somebody from the NYPD did. I assumed it was you."

He looked at her the way he must have looked at murder suspects when they played games with him. "Any evidence we had," he said carefully — "and all I can remember is the stuff in the safe deposit box — was sent down to Florida long ago. A place mat? What are you talking about? Did Ritter eat a Happy Meal while he was beating Helene Varga's brains out?"

"There was also the diary and the earring you found in his suitcase," Charlotte said.

"Right. I forgot about those. They would have been carried down there by a police evidence courier, under chain of custody rules. You know the drill."

"Was there a list of the items in the safe deposit box?"

"Sure there was. I inventoried the box myself. The inventory might still be around somewhere. I haven't seen it in years."

"Didn't you testify about it?"

"I testified about the contents of the box, not the inventory. They said, did you open this safe deposit box in the course of your duties? Did you inspect all the items in it? Is this one of the items you found there? It's all in the record." He seemed ready to call an end to the interrogation.

"I've read the transcript," Charlotte said. "I'm just trying to figure out if that place mat was in the safe deposit box."

"I don't know anything about a place mat. Is that what you came for?"

"No. I'm sorry this is taking so long. I wanted to ask you about Craft."

Lopez let out a deep sigh, as if they'd come to the part he hoped to avoid. "OK, I can give you about two more minutes." He started piling up the papers on his desk and shoving them into a drawer. "When this happened — when Ritter was arrested and charged with the murder — I didn't believe he could do anything like that. He told me this story about some guy named Craft who was following him around messing with his life. We checked out the story and it was a pile of mierda. Pardon my French."

Charlotte had to laugh. "That's Spanish, isn't it?"

"No shit? Pardon my English. Anyway, I followed every lead that could have exonerated him, even after he was arrested. Everybody had an alibi."

"Everybody? Who do you mean?"

"Ritter's wife — she was at work in New York every day of the week Helene Varga was killed in Florida. Her boyfriend, the wizard of Wall Street, was flying around in China, Thailand and Singapore. Ritter's other best friend, I forget his name—"

"Tim Salis?"

"Yeah. The actor. He was putting on a play downtown."

"What about Wagner?"

"The teacher?" Lopez seemed surprised that she would even ask about Wagner. "To tell you the truth, his alibi didn't stand up. He claimed he was at work every day and that didn't turn out to be true. But we had nothing to link him to the crime. He lived in New Jersey and there was no evidence that he'd ever gone to Florida."

"Except that he was lying."

"He might have been lying for some other reason. People do that, more often than you'd think. Usually because they're cheating on their wife." Lopez stood up and tossed Charlotte a smile. "Speaking of which, I've got to run — unless you'd like to go out for a drink."

She wondered if he really had another appointment. He adjusted his tie, slipped on his jacket and slipped his gun into its holster, and she followed him past the desk officer and out to the street. "What about his girlfriend, Greta Ramos?"

"I don't remember her. Did she have some connection to Ritter? We checked Wagner out, that's all I remember." He opened the door of a police cruiser and wedged himself inside. "Can I give you a ride somewhere?"

She shook her head. "I never accept rides from strange men."

"Am I that strange?" He laughed and started the engine.

"What about his wife's parents?" She positioned herself so he couldn't shut the car door.

"Give me a break. A couple of seniors living on Social Security? They didn't kill anybody."

"It happened in their house."

He motioned her away from the door. "The local cops questioned them. They were out in California when it happened."

"Did you check that story out? Which plane they came in on and all that?"

He slammed the door and pushed the button to roll down the window. "The local police probably did all that," he said. "I don't remember. You've got to understand, all this questioning up here was strictly my idea, and it didn't do my career any good. I wanted to see if there was anything to the Craft story. The Florida police had already made their arrest. They weren't running around like I was, trying to prove the murderer was a character from a fairy tale."

There was a bitter edge to his voice when he said that. He seemed determined to escape, even if he had no place he needed to be. "If you'll excuse me," he said, reaching out to shake Charlotte's hand. "I've got to go."

She walked around the corner and found her rental car where she'd parked it, with a curt love letter from the Parking Authority tucked under the wiper. She tore it up and dropped the pieces in the gutter.

Charlotte ate a solitary dinner at a restaurant famous for serving steaks so large that no one could finish them. Jolly groups of businessmen laughed and shouted while whole herds of cattle were slaughtered to provide them with meat to throw in the garbage. The waiter scowled when she ordered only an appetizer. To placate him, she made the mistake of drinking red wine, which always left her feeling clammy and depressed. In that frame of mind she returned to her room to call her mother. "Mom, how are you? Are you taking care of yourself?"

Jeannine disliked answering questions about her medical condition. "Haven't heard from you for a few days," she said.

"A lot's been happening," Charlotte said. "I'm in New York working on that death penalty case I told you about."

"I thought that was down in Florida."

"It is. I'm up here talking to witnesses."

"Uh huh." Which meant: Why are you wasting your time on that murderer?

"I've changed my mind," Charlotte explained. "I think Ritter's innocent."

"Uh huh."

"Somebody's started sending us stuff about the case." She didn't mention Craft and she certainly wasn't going to say anything about the threatening calls. 'Photographs that were used at the trial."

"*Uh huh.*"

This third "Uh huh," deeply intoned so soon after the first two, should have alerted Charlotte that her mother's patience had reached its limits. "It's like they know something we don't," she went on, "and they're playing with us to see if we can figure out how to save his life."

"Sounds like a whole lot of nothing to me."

Thursday, May 17, 1:00 p.m. 8 days, 5 hours to execution.

Charlotte dreamed of swimming upstream through a landscape shrouded in fog. The fog followed her all the way to Florida, hovering in her head even after the plane had landed. She called Sol from her rental car and found him as discouraging as ever. "I hope you found some new evidence," he said. "The way things stand now you can't even ask for a delay."

"I know that," she said. "I'm driving over to see Ritter tomorrow. I don't know what I'm going to tell him."

But by the time she arrived at Sol's office something incredibly important had happened. Millie returned from lunch and found another hand-delivered envelope stuck in the door, addressed to Charlotte. When she arrived Sol sat across from her at the conference table, unclasping the envelope and peeling it open as if he were defusing a bomb. Inside he found another, smaller envelope, and inside that a puff of cotton containing a small metal object.

"My God." He walked to the window and squinted at the object in the light. "It's the other earring."

Charlotte felt her face flushing, her breath quickening. "The other earring?"

"You remember, the police found one of Helene Varga's earrings in Ritter's suitcase in New York. The other one—"

"I know. Is this it?"

"Let's check the photographs."

Millie brought the file and handed Charlotte the prints that had been left at her hotel a few days before. Sol pulled out a folder of photocopies he'd made before the trial. They compared the newly-found earring with the one that had been photographed in Helene Varga's ear. The two looked identical.

"Where's the other one?" Charlotte asked.

"It was used as evidence at the trial. It might still be in some evidence locker, or it might have been lost or destroyed. In fact," he shrugged, "for all we know, this might be that one."

"What do you mean?"

"This might be the one that was used at the trial. Unless you have both, it doesn't prove a thing. Or it could be a fake, copied from the photograph. You'd have to have both and do a chemical analysis."

Charlotte felt a flash of anger at Sol's dogged skepticism. But he was right, of course: that's why he was a legendary trial lawyer. He didn't make any assumptions. "All right," she said, trying to stay calm. "Let's say you do that analysis and they're a matching pair. This is the proof we need, isn't it? Who else could have sent the missing earring but the murderer?"

"I don't know about proof," Sol smiled, folding the earring back into the cotton puff. "But I do think you've got something here that'll make the judge sit up and listen." He slid the cotton back into the envelope and fastened the clasp to close it. "If you can get him off the golf course."

16.

The two-lane blacktop out to Raiford sizzled in the late morning sun. Charlotte could see the heat welling up from the pavement and baking the dirt roads that branched off into the woods. She stopped at a gas station for a Coke but changed her mind as soon as she opened the car door. It was like opening the door to an oven. The attendant eyed her warily from under a red John Deere hat as she snapped the door shut and sped back onto the highway. It was a deserted, monotonous route through scrubby terrain. Mirages appeared and vanished from the pavement as she considered the arguments she'd try to muster for Ritter's appeal. The new evidence, even the earring, didn't give her much to go on. It was circumstantial, speculative, useful mostly for delay, which Ritter wouldn't tolerate. The clock was ticking faster and louder with each passing day. After two hours she drove under an enormous sign — "Florida State Prison" — that arched over the road as if it marked the entrance to an amusement park. In the distance she could make out the crowd of protestors and death row groupies between the parking lot and the prison entrance. Her stomach churned as she imagined the perp walk she'd have to endure as soon as she parked her car. A cloud of dust scoured across the road from the sweltering desert that surrounded the prison complex. It looked strange and out of place after the near-tropical forest she'd been driving through. She realized that it was there for a reason, to thwart escape attempts. Nothing could live in that heat.

Ritter waited in the visitors room, shackled to the steel table under the surveillance of two black guards. "Do you still call them Billy Bob and Bubba when they're black?" Charlotte asked him.

"It's one of my many flaws," he said with a forced smile. "I'm insensitive to the cultural differences among people who are trying to kill me."

"How about people who are trying to save you?"

"Them too. No offense."

Reaching in her briefcase, she pulled out the photographs of Helene Varga that were left at her hotel. Getting them into the prison had taken over an hour of negotiation with a lawyer from the warden's office who came out to the guard station. They don't allow pictures like this in the prison, he told her: no pictures of victims, no slasher images, no obscenity. She insisted on her right to confer with her client about his appeal and threatened to go to the Florida Supreme Court if she wasn't allowed to bring the pictures inside. Finally the pictures were inventoried and the guards were instructed to keep her under surveillance to make sure she didn't leave any of them behind.

"Somebody dropped these off at my hotel," she told Ritter. "Probably the same person who sent the place mat."

Ritter didn't flinch at the sight of the photographs. "I've seen these before," he said. "They were used at the trial."

"Why would somebody be sending them to us now?"

He shook his head. "You'd have to ask Craft."

"It doesn't make a whole lot of sense, does it? First he leaves the place mat, and then these?"

"The place mat was to show you I wasn't just making him up. The pictures — I don't know. Maybe he's proud of his work."

She opened a small envelope containing the cotton puff and showed Ritter the earring. "What do you make of this?"

He strained at his shackles, his face pale and distorted. It was the first time she'd seen him display an emotion other than hostility, though she wasn't sure what it was. "He sent you this too?"

"You know what it is?"

"Sure I know what it is. I bought them for her. Is that the one they supposedly found in my suitcase?"

"I don't know. What if it's the other one? Why would Craft be sending it now?"

Sweat dripped off Ritter's forehead and streamed down his cheeks like tears. He opened his mouth to speak but said nothing.

Charlotte asked, "Do you think he's trying to save you after all these years?"

"It would be just like him. One of his metaphors."

Glancing up, she met the gaze of Billy Bob — the new black Billy Bob, looking just as mean and stupid as his predecessors — who peered in through the observation window. He gestured with a mock salute, signaling that nothing between her and Ritter had gone unnoticed. She wondered if there were hidden microphones as well. "Are you ready to let me file a motion?" she asked Ritter.

"None of this stuff proves I'm innocent," he said.

"No, but it helps. It should get us a delay."

"I'm not interested in a delay."

"I know that. But the only way this earring could have any value as evidence — assuming it's not the one that was used at the trial — is if we can find the other one and have them tested to see if they're a pair. That could take a while."

To her relief, Ritter seemed to accept that some delay might be necessary. She took his silence as agreement to file the motion. "Here's the argument we have to make," she said. "There's newly discovered evidence — the place mat, the photographs, the earring — and all these things taken together support your version of events, pointing at Craft. But at the trial you didn't testify because there was no corroborating evidence for your story and the jury wouldn't have believed it. Now, based on this new evidence, you should be able to revisit that decision. You should be able to get a stay of execution while we have the earrings tested. If they turn out to be a pair, we'll request a further stay while we pursue our motion to vacate the judgment. At the hearing on that we'll be able to put all the evidence, including your testimony, in front of the court."

"Would that argument work?"

"It's a sound argument." She was exaggerating, maybe even lying, and she sensed that he knew it. "There's no reason not to file the motion."

Again she interpreted his silence as assent. Bubba tapped on the window with the five-minute warning. "There's one other thing," she said as she stood up. "I dug out the newspaper articles about the Haitian refugees you saw on the island. Sol never paid any attention to that because he doesn't think you really saw them."

"I saw them."

"I believe you. And here's the thing: a couple of survivors who landed on the beach were sent to a refugee center. It's possible they're still in the country. Maybe we could—"

"No. Leave that alone." His eyes warned her to stop. "No one would remember me."

"But don't you see—"

He raised his voice, something he hadn't done in a long time. "Leave it alone, I said!"

The anger, the hostility, the unmistakable tremor of menace frightened Charlotte: for the first time he sounded like a murderer. She waved to Billy Bob to open the door before she changed her mind about representing him.

"If you look for those Haitians," Ritter warned her, "I'll confess to the murder on national TV. Guards! Get me out of here!"

The crowd sprang into action when Charlotte emerged from the guard station, cameramen rolling out of their air-conditioned vans onto the broiling asphalt, protesters grabbing their placards from their pickup trucks, autograph hunters rushing forward with copies of *People* magazine. They blocked her path, reaching out to touch her clothes, peppering her with taunts and questions. She noticed the usual suspects, who apparently never went home — the Devil's chaplain, the puffy-haired blonde and her beer-bellied protector, the bald soprano in her Take Back the Night T-shirt — and a few new arrivals at the circus, notably the coiffed and botoxed reporter she'd seen on TV the night before (whose name was something like "Jenniphr Rousso") and her entourage, pushing their way through the mob with the assurance of a victorious army.

"Save a life! God bless you!" one man shouted.

"You ought to be ashamed of yourself!" yelled the puffy-haired blonde.

"What's the next step?" asked Jenniphr Rousso, shoving a microphone into her face. "Are you going to file an appeal?"

"Yes," said Charlotte, her voice faltering. "We'll be filing a motion tomorrow."

"How can you defend a man who did that to a woman?" yelled the bald soprano.

"Do you believe the death penalty is unconstitutional?" the reported asked.

"What I believe is irrelevant. My job is to provide the legal representation the defendant is entitled to."

"Aren't you just trying to buy time by exploiting some technicality?"

"No, not at all. Our motion will be based on newly discovered evidence. Ritter did not commit the murder."

On the drive back to St. Augustine, Charlotte was tailed by the same pickup truck that followed her the first time she left the prison. There were two people in the truck but their faces were blocked by the sun visor. The driver sped close behind her, almost bumping her car, then swerved to the side and tried to force her off the road. Already rattled by her encounter with the prison mob, she felt herself starting to panic. Her body shook as she tightened her grip on the wheel; she had to struggle for every breath. But the idea of letting herself be stopped on this isolated road terrified her more than the danger of crashing her car. She stepped on the gas and tried to race ahead but the truck stayed right behind her, dodging in and out of the oncoming traffic as it tried to push her aside. As a sharp curve approached, she tapped her brakes and after a couple of seconds hit them hard and sped up again, sending the truck into a skid as the driver fought to stay in control. In her mirror she saw the truck come to rest on the sandy shoulder before speeding off on one of the dirt roads that cut into the woods.

By the time she reached Sol's office — it was almost 4:00 o'clock on Friday afternoon — her whole body ached from the tension and her clothes were drenched in sweat. Her head was throbbing and all she wanted to do was lie down. Sol sat her in his most comfortable chair and did everything in his power to comfort her. They both knew that the motion for stay, to have any chance of success, would have to be filed on Monday, together with a motion to vacate the judgment; the research and drafting would take all weekend, working fifteen hours a day. "You're welcome to come over here and work if that would help," he told her.

She smiled and shook her head. "I think I can get more done at my hotel."

"Just holler if you need anything."

She gathered the files she needed and carried them out to her car with Millie's help. The sky had darkened as a late-afternoon thunderstorm moved up the coast. Back inside, she called Julie Halkins and told her to watch for the documents in her email on Monday. "Let's hope she doesn't have any last-minute scruples about signing them," Sol said. "That's been known to happen with these lead counsel. You do all the work and then when your client has about two hours to live, they want to go over everything with a fine-toothed comb."

"Julie says if the court turns us down, she knows somebody in the Governor's office."

"You can forget about the Governor. He'll be out fishing or collecting donations for his next campaign."

Charlotte carried her last armful of files out to the car and stepped back inside to say goodbye to Sol. She'd been wanting to ask him about the portrait that loomed over his desk since the first time she went in there. It depicted a smiling, strong-willed woman of about fifty, whose dark eyes surveyed the room with bemused toleration. "Is that your wife?"

He glanced at the portrait and smiled. "She passed away five years ago. But as you can see, she's still keeping an eye on me."

Charlotte smiled back sympathetically. "Do you have any kids?"

"We had a son," he said, nodding toward one of the photographs behind his desk. "He also passed."

"I'm so sorry."

"That was many years go. A boating accident out on the bay."

He walked her to the door and they stood staring at the menacing sky. The heavy, humid air seeped around them like fumes from a smoldering fire. Charlotte noticed a man watching them from a parked car — at least it wasn't a pickup truck — on the other side of the street. He slouched down when he saw her watching him: she was sure he was planning to follow her to the hotel. Seagulls wheeled over the swaying palm trees, crying out as lightning flashed along the coast.

"This city was named after a saint who taught that God knows everything that's ever going to happen," Sol said. "Do you believe that?"

"No."

"Neither do I. I don't see any evidence that anyone's even paying attention."

She reached in her purse and handed him the earring, still wrapped in the cotton puff. "Here," she told Sol. "You'd better put this in a safe place. It's not safe with me."

Sol laughed and shoved it into his pocket. "Don't worry about those good old boys in the pickup truck," he said. "Down here the first thing you learn is, you can't let the rednecks bother you. They're like the mosquitoes. You've just got to get used to them."

"How do I know they're not still following me?"

"A redneck can't follow a straight line past a beer joint. And believe me, there's enough beer joints between here and Raiford to keep those old boys busy for a long time."

"You realize they're probably the ones who threw the paint can through your window."

"They've had their fun, then. What are they going to do next? Burn the place down?"

Chris Ritter
Friday, May 18, 3:00 p.m. 7 days, 4 hours to execution.

All day I've been trying to recover from Charlotte's visit this morning. I don't think I've been as upset in years as I was when she pulled out that earring and started talking about the Haitians. The whole nightmare came back — Helene, the murder, the Haitians on the boat — like a siren going off in my head. Now it's 3:00 in the afternoon and I'm face down on my bunk trying to ignore the worst headache I've ever had. Sometimes lately I feel shaky, almost feverish, as if my body is finally starting to understand what my mind has known all along. I'm wondering if I can keep my sanity long enough to die with any shred of dignity.

A jangle of keys alerts me to the presence of my keepers. There's been a changing of the guard since this morning: Billy Bob is now an overweight redhead with freckles and a lazy eye. Bubba looks like his evil twin. "Wake up, Ritter," Billy Bob says. "Got to take your sorry ass down to the dispensary."

"I've never felt better in my life," I lied.

"Routine physical," Bubba explains.

The doctor is an Indian man of kindly appearance who avoids eye contact. While Billy Bob and Bubba hold me down, he takes my blood pressure, listens to my heart, shines his flashlight in my eyes. They call it a physical but it's not the kind of physical you get when you apply for life insurance. They're measuring me for my lethal injection.

"Your blood pressure is way too high," the doctor says. He jots something on his prescription pad. "I'm putting you on a blood thinner."

"I've only got a week to live," I tell him.

"I understand," he says, patting my arm. "In the meantime, try to avoid stress."

The noise in the cell block dies down as I'm led back to my cell. The prisoners know I'm scheduled to die in a week. Some nod respectfully, some turn away; most stare back like cattle in a pen. When we reach my cell, Bubba hands me a plastic bag and waits for me to open it.

"Here, son" — he calls me "son" even though I'm old enough to be his father — "We got a little present for you."

"Something to keep in your cell," Billy Bob adds. "Help you pass the time."

It's a plastic hourglass about five inches high. "You turn it over like this, and then like this," Bubba explains. "Until the sand runs out. Then you turn it over again. See that?"

Billy Bob nods eagerly. "It lasts just exactly one hour."

"Don't try breaking it to use as a weapon. It's soft plastic, won't do any good."

They seem to be stalling for time, as if they expect me to thank them for the gift. Across the hall I can see Teague glaring with more than usual hostility.

"Thanks," I tell the guards, turning the hourglass over and setting it on the floor beside my bunk. The cell door clanks shut.

"What do you think, Billy Bob?" Bubba asks as they walk away. "How many times you think he'll be able to do that between now and when he checks out of here?"

Monday, May 21, 9:00 a.m. 4 days, 9 hours to execution.

Charlotte spent the entire weekend researching and drafting the motions and supporting documents. On Monday morning, after three hours' sleep and a cold breakfast, she drove to Sol's office, where she printed out the documents for Sol's review. He read them over carefully and suggested a number of changes, some of which she didn't agree with. She spent an hour making revisions and another hour hashing them out with Sol. Then she emailed the documents to Julie Halkins and called her office to make sure she'd received them. Julie was at lunch, her secretary said, and not expected to return until after 2:00. Charlotte called again at 2:05 and was told that Julie was on another call. Finally at 2:30 she reached Julie, who agreed to review the documents immediately. An hour later she sent them back with dozens of revisions that would have to be made before she could sign off on the motions. Charlotte had no choice but to accept every one of the required changes, including the addition of some tendentious language about capital punishment and the cases pending in the U.S. Supreme Court which she knew would infuriate Ritter if he ever read it. She called Julie's secretary to confirm her agreement with the changes. The documents were filed in the clerk's office at 4:45 pm, fifteen minutes before the court closed for the day.

Charlotte drove back to her hotel in a daze and spent the evening checking her hate messages, which had taken on a new intensity. It had been the most exhausting three days of her life.

Tuesday, May 22, 8:00 a.m. 3 days, 10 hours to execution.

Bright sun, blue sky.

Charlotte threw back her curtains and let the morning brilliance into her room. Surely at that moment, she thought, the drama was already unfolding at the courthouse, surely serious people were considering her motions, ready to give Chris Ritter another chance. After a leisurely breakfast in the hotel restaurant — the only thing she liked about traveling was the breakfast buffet — she called Sol's office and got no answer. After she brushed her teeth she dialed again and heard a recording that said the phone was out of service. She tried his cell number but was sent directly to voice mail. A breathless uncertainty told her to hurry downtown.

She found the street blocked by police cars and fire trucks, clustered around the smoldering wreckage of Sol's office. The police wouldn't let her through. Heartsick and choking on the smoke, she made her way around the block and spotted Sol watching from behind the yellow tape, sweating in his blue seersucker suit. Tears streamed down his cheeks. Thank God he and Millie were both safe. The firebombing — that's what it was, the police said — had occurred shortly before sunrise. A gasoline can had been thrown through the window, just as the paint can had been.

Charlotte cried when she ran up to Sol and wrapped her arms around him. She cried again when he told her what had been lost.

"The earring," he mumbled. "I left it in my desk."

"Is it gone?"

"They won't let me in there, but I can't believe there's anything left of the desk. We'll never find that earring."

17.

Chris Ritter

Tuesday, May 22, 11:00 a.m. 3 days, 7 hours to execution.

Time is closing in on me. I swear the sand in my hour glass is speeding up: I have to turn it over every fifteen minutes. I'm not feeling well. Panicky, queasy, a little feverish. Not to worry, I remind myself; it won't be a long illness.

The guards take me to see the chaplain in the visitors room. "Last time we talked," he begins, barely audible, staring down at his clipboard, "you got very upset. Do you remember why?"

"I don't remember getting upset."

"It was when I suggested that Craft — whom you've portrayed as evil — was part of you. Part of your own mind."

"Naturally I got upset. Craft is real."

"He could be both. He could be real and also be part of you." The chaplain leans toward me, bashful as always, his eyes glimmering away from me like sparks over a fire. "And he could still be evil."

I watch him closely. "Did you know they call you the Devil's chaplain?"

"The guards?"

"The inmates. They despise you."

"Ironic, isn't it?" He fixes his eyes on the clipboard as if he's reading from a script. "The inmates are murderers, rapists, kidnappers. Their lives have been as evil as life can be. They've seen the world for what it is a vast penitentiary, far worse than this one, a place of suffering and mindless cruelty and death."

I can feel the anger stirring, the same anger I felt the last time I talked to him; and a deepening sense of dread. Better to end this now. "Push the buzzer, please."

"And yet every one of them — except you — believes in a God who created this monstrosity. What does that tell you?"

"I don't know. What does it tell you?"

He shrugs. "There are no atheists in Hell."

Still feverish, unsteady on my feet, I begin the trek back to my cell. Billy Bob and Bubba, as they prod me forward, also seem troubled by the geography of hell. Billy Bob, in sideburns and granny glasses, has the furrowed brow of a deep thinker. Bubba, short and squat, eyes spaced wide apart, growls under his breath whenever we pass an inmate. Neither speaks until they've locked me securely back in my cell.

"I know you've got a lot on your plate, Ritter," Billy Bob says, "but there's something I need to mention. Last night there was a story about you on the TV news. They said you're scheduled to die on Friday at the Florida State Prison in Raiford."

"I knew there was a reason I skipped that show," I said.

"You see, the problem is, that TV report was flat wrong. You're not going to die here on Friday."

I catch my breath, unable to speak. Is this how they tell you you've been spared?

"For the record," Billy Bob says, "you're incarcerated in Union Correctional Institution, in Raiford."

"Which is in Union County," Bubba adds.

"Right," Billy Bob nods. "Florida State Prison is across the road, in Starke."

"Which is in a whole different county."

"Correct. Bradford County. That's where the executions take place."

"Not here," Bubba says. "Nobody gets executed here in Raiford."

"It annoys me no end," Billy Bob says, "when I hear people say somebody's getting executed in Raiford. That's the kind of inaccurate reporting you see far too often on TV."

"Bottom line," Bubba says, "when it's time for the execution, you're going to be moved over to Starke."

"We don't want you to be under any misperceptions about where you're going to die."

Tuesday, May 22, 2:00 p.m. 3 days, 4 hours to execution.

When the fire department had thoroughly soaked what was left of Sol's office and barricaded it with plywood, Charlotte and Sol walked two blocks to a Mexican cantina where Sol knew the owner and most of the waitresses. After they sat down he had little to say and avoided eye contact. "I saw you on TV last night," he finally said, keeping his voice low. "Being interviewed in front of the prison."

"Was that on last night? I was so tired I didn't even watch it."

He glanced around to make sure no one was listening. "You told the reporter you'd be filing a motion based on new evidence. Whoever bombed my office — well, I'm wondering if that new evidence was what they were trying to destroy."

"My God, I'm sorry." Charlotte leaned closer, her face flushed with embarrassment. "How awful."

His eyes darted away. "I'm starting to believe in Craft."

The waitress brought their food and for a few minutes neither of them spoke. But Charlotte's mind raced back to the realization that had been troubling her since she saw the smoldering ruins that morning. "There's something going on here," she said, "but it's not just Craft."

"What do you mean?"

"Don't you see? Somebody's sending us new evidence and somebody else is trying to keep us from using it. There's some kind of struggle going on and we're caught in the middle."

"Good versus evil?" His tone was ironic, almost to the point of sarcasm. He'd already told her he didn't believe in evil; she wondered if he believed in good.

"More like evil versus evil," she said. "It's as if two branches of Hell are fighting over Ritter's soul."

The conversation subsided again. After they'd finished their lunch and asked for the check, Sol broke the silence on what had been troubling them most. "You're going to have to amend your motions," he said. It was as if he were making a casual observation on some point of legal procedure.

"I know," Charlotte said, her breath tightening.

"Everything about the earring has to come out."

"I know."

"Without the earring, the motions don't stand a chance."

"I know."

His face brightened. "Maybe you could add an argument about the other cases heading to the U.S. Supreme Court. After all, in a few months—"

"Forget it."

"What about all these cases stopping executions because of the screw-ups in lethal injections? The drugs don't work, they just—"

Charlotte covered her ears and bent her head down toward the table, fighting to keep the words coming. "Ritter wouldn't agree to any of that. It's actual innocence or nothing."

Wednesday, May 23, 4:00 p.m. 2 days, 2 hours to execution.

Charlotte worked all night in her hotel room revising the motions and briefs to delete all references to the earring, and emailed her work to Julie Halkins the next morning. They spoke on the phone and agreed on some last-minute changes, and Julie filed the revised motions before noon.

They were denied in a summary order, filed without opinion in the clerk's office at 4:30 p.m. The court's decision was headlined by Jenniphr Rousso on the Ten O'Clock News and widely reported on the internet.

Ritter would be executed on Friday at 6:00 p.m.

Wednesday, May 23, 11:00 p.m. 1 day, 19 hours to execution.

Charlotte had never been so depressed or had such a crushing headache. She spent half an hour on the phone with her mother, crying from anger and exhaustion. The depression, a stranglehold of futility extending to every thought, every impulse, every breath, actual or contemplated, wrapped itself around her as the anger and exhaustion ran their course. The headache would take a week to wear off — or, as seemed more likely, would last forever. Before going to bed, she left a message with her secretary saying that she would be back in the office the following week. She left a message with the Titus Foundation that she would call them in the morning. As she was making the last of these calls on her cell phone, the hotel phone rang and the operator told her she had an outside call.

It was a man's voice, a deep baritone voice she'd never heard before, with just a trace of a European accent. "You don't know me," the man said. "My name is Craft."

She dropped the phone receiver, as if she was afraid to hold it close to her ear. Even after she picked it up she could hardly bring herself to respond. "How" — her voice stuck in her throat — "how did you know to call me here?"

"That was easy, Charlotte," the man said. "I called your office in Philadelphia and asked your secretary how to reach you. Listen, I know this is coming out of the blue. But I had to call when I saw how the court disposed of your appeal. How did that happen? Weren't they impressed by your new evidence?"

He sounded so friendly and familiar that she felt her voice coming back. She took a deep breath and sat down on the bed. "We lost the earring in the fire."

"I see..." he hesitated. "I think I can still help you."

"We can't file another motion, if that's what you're thinking."

"Even if you could prove Ritter's innocence?"

She could hardly believe what was happening. "Are you going to confess?"

He barked out an unpleasant laugh. "If you're going to be rude, I could hang up right now."

"No, don't do that!" She'd made a mistake, asking him to confess. She needed to treat him with the utmost care: a flick of the fingertip and he would be gone. "I just don't know if I should even be talking to you," she said, trying to sound calm. "How do I know you're not jacking me around? How do I even know you're who you say you are?"

That brought him back to his friendly self. "I understand completely, Charlotte. Every relationship must have a foundation of trust, and that's what I want us to have, a relationship."

"OK. I'm listening."

"Asking me to confess — that's moving a little too fast. We've only just met, and it's as if you're trying to trick me into saying things I have no intention of saying."

"I'm sorry."   She hated hearing herself apologizing to a murderer.

"Don't worry about it. But believe me, I just want you to trust me as much as I trust you."

"OK." A murderer who was trying to lure her into a "trusting relationship," even though he knew, and knew she knew, that they could never have one, and that she had no choice but to pretend to go along with him. Her head felt as if it were being pinched in a vice.

"Now, let me ask you,' he went on, "what other steps are possible. Could you go back to the court?"

"Unfortunately" — she was still trying to pretend that this was a normal conversation — "the court isn't going to look at another motion. Unless—"

"Unless what?"

"Unless" — she wanted to say, unless you're going to confess — "Unless we have conclusive, incontrovertible evidence that Ritter didn't do it."

"I can't make any promises, but I might be able to give you something along those lines."

He'd baited his hook — she knew that — but she couldn't resist asking the obvious question. "What is it?"

"You're going to have to trust me, really trust me, if you want to find that out. It's a relationship, remember? You're going to have to go to New York."

Her voice faltered. "To meet with you?

"Yes. Of course, Charlotte. I'm not a monster."

"There isn't time. The execution is—"

"I know when the execution is. You can fly to New York tomorrow morning. There's a United flight from Jacksonville to LaGuardia at noon you could still get on. And give me your cell phone number, if you don't mind. I'll call shortly after you arrive and we can go from there."

"I don't know, I—"

"And by the way, don't bother trying to trace this phone. I just bought it and when I hang up I'm going to crush it and throw it away."

Thursday, May 24, 8:00 a.m. 34 hours to execution.

Before she went to bed, Charlotte booked a seat on the United flight to New York, scheduled to arrive at three o'clock the next afternoon. She felt much better in the morning: more panicky than depressed, if that was an improvement. I can't be depressed, she told herself, and I can't panic. I've got a life to save.

On the Interstate to Jacksonville she called Sol, who desperately tried to keep her in Florida. "That wasn't Craft on the phone," he told her, "because there isn't any Craft."

"Whoever he is, he's all I've got."

"If he's not Craft, you're wasting valuable time. If he is, you're walking into the arms of a psychopath."

"A psychopath who committed the crime my client is about to be executed for. I can't let that happen."

Sol was silent for a long moment, long enough for Charlotte to wonder if he was still on the line. "You're some kind of lawyer, Charlotte," he finally said. "I owe you an apology. I underestimated you."

Thursday, May 24, 4:00 p.m. 26 hours to execution.

When the plane landed at LaGuardia, Charlotte caught a taxi and directed the driver to her hotel. It was the hotel where she'd stayed before, the Marriott near Times Square, though she wasn't sure why she'd chosen it. Craft hadn't said anything about where he wanted to meet, which was fine, since she didn't plan on meeting him anyway. She'd thought about how she wanted to handle him. She needed to be in charge; she couldn't let him manipulate her. That was what had gone wrong in their first conversation. He must have wanted something from her or he wouldn't have called. Their "relationship" was going to be on her terms.

As the taxi emerged from the Queens Midtown Tunnel and made its way down 42nd Street, her cell phone rang. It was Craft. "I'm in New York," she told him. "Don't bother to ask where I'm staying."

Her tone seemed to catch him off guard. "I thought we could talk," he said.

"We are talking."

"Why did you come up here if you don't want to see me? I thought you wanted to help me."

"I do want to help you. I want to help you do the right thing."

The phone remained silent as the taxi jostled its way past Grand Central Station. She wondered if Craft was still on the phone, but she didn't say anything. She needed to show who was in charge.

"You have to trust me," he finally said. "I thought we were going to have a relationship."

"We're working on one. I could trust you more if you'd tell me what you know about Chris Ritter and Helene Varga."

The taxi stopped at a light across from the New York Public Library. A frenzy of pedestrians and traffic bolted in front of them. "It's hard to talk about," Craft said.

"I understand. But you need to try. You can talk to me. I won't judge you."

He hesitated again. "It's still hard."

The driver swung left, tipping Charlotte against the door. "A man's about to be executed for a crime he didn't commit," she said. "The least you can do is tell what you know."

"Do you think I feel good about what's happened? Don't you think I've suffered too?"

"I'm sure you have, Mr. Craft."

"Craft isn't my real name."

"What is it then?"

"You'd like me to tell you that, wouldn't you? Tricky, tricky."

The taxi glided to a halt in front of the hotel. Reluctant to relinquish control, she kept the phone to her ear as she paid the driver, climbed out with her bag and hurried past the doorman, who insisted on following her inside and carrying her overnight bag to the reception desk. She stood away from the desk, cradling the phone to her ear. "I'm not trying to trick you," she told Craft in a friendlier tone. "Honestly."

"Maybe I'll just forget I ever called you," he said, still acting sullen.

"Please don't hang up. It's just that right now I need to get off the phone. I have to check in to my hotel."

"I know," he said. "The Times Square Marriott. Go on up to your room, Charlotte. Kick off your shoes and lie down for a while. Have a drink from the minibar. I'll catch you later."

18.

Chris Ritter

Thursday, May 24, 6:00 p.m. 24 hours to execution.

It's my last night on earth and I can only imagine the moon and the stars in the sky and the swirling clouds and the seething Florida wasteland that will absorb my dust. The seconds pound into me, each with a unique timbre and sonority never to be heard again, each a spark of beauty that ignites and is gone from this earth as I will soon be. I'm burning up. My head throbs, wobbles, threatens to spin off its axis, and with each throb another piece of me is chipped off and dribbles away: this fever is my escape plan, my strategy to cheat the executioner by being gone before he arrives. How can they execute a man who has already dissolved into thin air, who has never really existed in the first place?

Six o'clock. I sit shackled to the high metal table in the visitors room, facing the Devil's chaplain for the last time. The first time I ever spoke with him, he told me that believing in the Devil would be "a good first step." I've been rolling that over in my mind ever since.

"What did you mean by that?" I ask him. "Is the state of Florida so desperate to make me believe in something that they'd send a chaplain to lure me to the Devil?"

"Just trying to save your soul," he tells me with a smile.

"The soul I never had."

"You still believe that?"

"You probably believe it too, if you'd admit the truth."

"What truth? The truth that doesn't exist?"

I feel myself puffing up, pushing against the shackles. "You sound exactly like Craft. Is that who you really are?"

"Twenty-four years you've served Craft and you don't even know who he is."

"Guards! Get me out of here!" I feel like I'm going insane, kicking and flailing against the shackles, my wrists and ankles bleeding and bruised to the bone. But the pain doesn't stop me — it seems to be happening to someone else — and the guards can't stop me. Nothing can stop me and nothing can hurt me.

Billy Bob and Bubba hold me clamped me in a headlock as they call for backup and in an instant the room fills with guards: tense, quiet, professional — not their usual brutal selves — no, not this time; they're painstakingly gentle, like a rescue team extricating a child from a car wreck. I'm a delicate flower, a priceless relic they must preserve until the ritual moment comes, when they will kill me.

Is that the chaplain still perched serenely in his chair? I can't be sure; I can't be sure any of this is really happening. But I call out to him as they carry me back to my cell: "Will you be there tomorrow? To see me off?"

"I will if you want me to be."

I try to nod but my head is immobilized by the guards' gentle stranglehold. "When it's over I want you to say: 'Ashes to ashes, dust to dust.' Isn't that what they usually say?"

"There's more to it than that.'

"But I want you to stop there. Just say that much and no more."

"Why?"

"Dust is all there is. Not dust and something more. Just dust."

Thursday, May 24, 6:00 p.m. 24 hours to execution.

By the time Charlotte reached her room on the 19th floor, her hand was trembling so hard she could barely fit the key card into its slot. Once inside, in a rage of frustration, she threw her bag across the room, swearing at the top of her lungs. She kicked off her shoes, guzzled a shot-sized bottle of vodka from the minibar and fell fully clothed onto the bed, all as Craft had predicted, or directed. She was completely under his control.

How had she let this happen? Had he hacked into her phone when she made the reservations? Or just waited for her at the airport and followed her cab? He knew what she looked like; her picture had been in the news. But all she had for him was Ritter's description — white, tall and burly, well into his fifties by now — that probably fit a hundred other psychopaths stalking around Times Square. "I'll catch you later," he'd said on the phone. Had he meant it literally?

She dialed the reception desk and told the clerk: "If anyone asks for me, I don't want to see him or have him calling me, and I don't want him to know what room I'm in."

"We would never disclose that information, ma'am."

"I'm sure. Thank you."

There was no question of leaving the hotel or even venturing down to the lobby. She ordered dinner from room service and made the waiter leave her tray outside the door. Room service was expensive but it was worth it: when she finished her New York strip, she washed off the dagger-pointed steak knife and stashed it in her purse. She called her mother but couldn't bring herself to mention what she was doing in New York. They chatted — or rather her mother chatted — about trivial things for over an hour. She downed two more vodkas mixed with ginger ale. She picked up the TV remote, wishing it was a magic wand that could transport her to some other world; instead it took her to the land of stupid cop shows. When "Criminal Minds" came on, she hit the Off button.

Kathryn, Doug and Tim met for an early dinner at a quiet East Side bistro. The hostess sat them in a dark corner booth where a small candle flickered on the table, brightening their faces with an unearthly light. They ordered red wine and bread and told the waitress they would let her know when they were ready to order. There was no joking or laughing or even the usual pleasantries. This was the vigil they had long planned for the night before Chris's execution.

"Is it really going to happen this time?" Kathryn wondered aloud.

"God, I hope so," Doug muttered.

"Doug," Kathryn began. "That's—"

"It's not that I want Chris to die," Doug interrupted, "but I want this nightmare to be over. That's what everybody wants, isn't it? Probably including Chris himself. It's time to move on."

"Move on?" Tim glanced at Doug with just a hint of a smile. "Where do you think Chris will be moving on to?"

"That was a bad choice of words," Doug said. "You know what I mean." He turned toward Kathryn. "It's the rest of us that need to move on. The main thing is that your ex-husband will finally be moving out of our lives."

"My ex-husband? Is that all he is to you?"

"At this point, yes."

The past ten years had been hard on all of them in different ways. Kathryn had suffered the most, wrestling with her anger and shame, raising the kids, trying to answer questions there was no answer to. Doug could help only so much. He wasn't one to dwell on the past, or even very much on the present. But no matter how hard he tried, he couldn't make Kathryn concentrate on what was in front of her, couldn't make her see that no matter what you've done or has been done to you, you owe it to yourself to live the only life you've got. He had no regrets — it wasn't in his nature to regret anything — but being married to Kathryn had been a surprisingly depressing experience. Sometimes he'd thought of moving on. As for Tim, he'd been depressed too — it was no secret that he'd been in and out of therapy all his life — and his outlook had darkened after Chris went to prison, for which (as Doug observed) he tried to compensate by putting on a theatrical air of naive belief, as if the world were a stage. In one way or another they'd all been living in Chris's shadow for so long that they dreaded lingering in a world without him.

The waitress paused by the booth and they waved her on.

"I'm still hopeful," Tim said.

"The lawyer said all possible appeals have been exhausted," Doug reminded him.

"Hopeful of what?" Kathryn asked. "A miracle?"

Tim leaned forward into the flickering candlelight. "Even in a mechanistic universe like the one Chris believes in, can't there be a miracle sometimes, if only by chance? In some of the ancient Greek plays—"

"Stop it, Tim," Kathryn cut him off. "This isn't some play. This is Chris's life we're talking about."

Thursday, May 24, 10:00 p.m. 20 hours to execution.

Charlotte's cell phone rang. It was Craft. She could hear traffic noise in the background. "Aren't you going out for dinner?" he asked.

"No," she said, trying to keep her composure. "I'm going to sleep. What did you want to talk about."

"I just want you to understand me."

"I'm trying."

"Sometimes people do things they can't help doing. Things that aren't really like them, who they are as people. Things that just happen. I hope you can understand that."

"I do understand that. We've all had that experience."

"Sometimes one thing leads to another," he went on. "You do one thing you shouldn't have done and then you've got to do something else. Not like it's something you've decided to do."

He seemed to be giving her an opening. "No, I understand," she said. "But right now you're in a position to do something good. You can save Chris Ritter's life. I sense that you want to do that or you wouldn't have called me."

"There's no way I'm going to spend the rest of my life in prison." The traffic noise had stopped. He must have gone inside. Was he in the hotel?

"I don't blame you," she said. "That's not my goal."

She could hear him breathing into the phone. "What do you want from me?" he asked.

"The only sure way to save Ritter's life would be by turning yourself in and confessing to the murder."

"That's not going to happen. I'm telling you, it's just not going to happen. I'm not going to prison."

"I respect that," she said. "I wouldn't want to go to prison either. There's another thing you could do. This might not work, but it's better than nothing. You could confess in front of a reliable witness other than the police. You could go to a church and confess to the priest and tell him it's all right to disclose what you said. Or you could dictate your confession to a respected lawyer or judge, behind closed doors."

"And then what?"

"And then you could disappear."

"I'd last about two days."

He was right, of course. The chances of his escaping after he confessed were almost nonexistent. But she knew she had to keep talking as if she was sure he'd come around. "There's something else," she said. "It'll take more than a confession to save Ritter's life. We'd need corroborating evidence, some objective proof that you might have committed the crime. You were at the crime scene, you knew the victim, you had a motive, an opportunity, and all that. And most important of all: You know some things about the crime that nobody but the killer would know. You can explain the gaps in the case."

"I don't know what I could say that they don't already know."

"The place mat and the photographs will be helpful, but they're not enough. You've got to make a convincing case that you committed the crime. Otherwise the court's going to stick with the jury verdict against Ritter."

There was a long silence. "I'll think about it," he said.

"You don't have time to think about it. There's only a few hours—"

He raised his voice for the first time. "I told you I need to think about it. Do you want me to hang up right now?"

"No. I'm sorry."

"I'll get back to you in the morning."

She went to bed angry at Craft and even more angry at herself, her head pounding, her stomach tied in knots, in the budding realization that the whole trip to New York had probably been one of his sadistic tricks.

19.

Chris Ritter

Friday, May 25, 4:00 a.m. 16 hours to execution.

Face flushed, mouth dry, head pounding; fever spiking ever higher by the hour. Face down on the bunk: hot, then cold, shivering under the dim lights. My escape is near completion. Must feign perfect health to Billy Bob and Bubba or they'll wheel me gently to the infirmary for heroic life-saving measures; later to be poisoned like a bug. Get it over with: there's almost nothing left of you. Turn over the hourglass one more time: go to sleep, shivering, sweating, gladly dripping away. Bad dreams, feverish dreams: lying strapped on a gurney, being sawed in half by a magician.

That jolts me awake. Fever still high, headache pounding, but still alive. It's quiet in the middle of the night: dimmed lights, rattle of keys in the distance. Buzzing lights, prisoners coughing. A night like any other. The clock in the hall is ticking, faster than usual. I open my eyes. It's 4:00 a.m. Sixteen hours to live.

There's something in the corner, something dark, filling the space across from my bunk. I squint through the dimness at an enormous dark mass until I realize: it's Teague, Teague's in my cell as Billy Bob and Bubba had promised, a last-minute visitation to send me on my way. *Some night we'll let him into your cage so he can give you a sneak preview of Hell.*

He seems half-conscious, slumped against the wall, barely able to hold himself upright. His eyes are rolled upwards, unfocused, with only the whites showing. He must have been drugged by the guards so they could drag him into my cell. "How long have you been in here?" I ask him.

To my surprise he focuses his eyes and fixes them on me with an almost feral intensity. Then he speaks: "Twenty-four years it's been" — his voice is deep and resonant, but with a surprising, archaic brogue — "and I'm here to claim what's mine."

Claim what's mine? What could he be talking about? "Did Craft send you?"

"Craft? Do you think I'd take orders from that lackey?"

"What do you want, then?"

"You really don't know, do you? Still playing innocent after all these years!"

He pulls himself up to a standing position, all six and a half feet of him, and leers down at me from the shadows near the ceiling. All I can see of his face are the whites of his eyes and his skeleton teeth. "Look at your friend Teague over there" — he talks as if Teague were a different person; I squint toward Teague's cell but of course it's wrapped in darkness — "You're practically brothers by now: the next two to die, the sharers of each other's nightly terrors. But Teague doesn't claim to be innocent. He killed his wife and kids and a prison guard. He makes no excuses. He knows what he did was evil. But you—"

"I didn't kill anybody." It's a lie, but how could he know about the Haitians?

"You" — he glares at me as if he knows I'm lying —"you are far worse than your brother. You don't even know what evil is."

At some point — I think it's when he starts talking about Craft — I become convinced that this is a dream, a feverish lucid dream I don't want to be having. I try to stand up, but I lose my balance and drop back on the bunk, my head spinning. The clock says 4:15 but I can still hear the coughing in the distance, the lights buzzing, the keys rattling. There's Teague in the corner, sneering through his skeleton teeth. I must be awake. The guards must have let him in here. "I'm innocent."

That earns a contemptuous, whispering cackle. "You keep saying you're innocent," he goes on. "As if it were that simple. As if just because you didn't kill Helene Varga — assuming you didn't — you ought to be exonerated. Even your own lawyer admits that actual innocence isn't a defense. The time is long past for that quaint argument."

"I didn't kill her."

"What about the others? What about those Haitians? You didn't even have a reason to kill them."

Again I try to stand up, this time successfully. I lurch toward him, trying to chase him out of the corner. But he doesn't budge. "You're not even real," I shout. "You're my illness. You're just a figment of my imagination."

"Dream on!"

"You're asking me if I know what evil is. The answer is yes, I know. You're evil."

He laughs out loud, his skeleton teeth flashing in the darkness. "All right, point well taken," he admits. "If I'm a figment of your imagination — which I'm not — then I'm part of your mind. What does that make you?"

"Get out of my cell!"

"If I'm who you say I am, then you should show me some respect. I've been around longer than you have."

I bury my face in my hands. "Get out of here! Leave me alone!"

"Do you really think it's fair," he sighs, ignoring my pleas, "to blame me for everything that goes wrong? What is this world, anyway? Just a bunch of matter and energy expanding at the speed of light. That's all it is or ever will be. You know that; you've said it yourself. There's no good and no evil, nothing but blind pitiless indifference. Anything, literally anything, can happen. But just because you can't find an all-knowing, benevolent Grand Pooh-Bah behind the whole thing, you try to hold me accountable for everything bad that happens. Even the disasters you've brought on yourself."

"Go away!"

He's laughing now, in his low, scornful way, enjoying every minute of the torture he's inflicting on me. "I used to think it would serve my purposes for you people to get a good dose of reality, to face the facts and give up your whole mad search for the meaning of life. Because then, I thought, you'd give me my due without looking over your shoulder for someone to contradict me. My power would be absolute, I imagined, if you didn't know I existed. But now I realize it was a poor bargain: I don't get any credit at all. I want to be known for what I am. I want you to stand in awe of my power. And I realized a long time ago that the only way to get that is to give you something to believe in, something apparently outside my power and opposed to it. There's your Prime Mover, your Grand Designer, your Father Almighty, a charlatan if there ever was one. I hung back in the shadows while everyone paid homage to Nobodaddy. And now he's gone AWOL and left you without so much as a good argument for getting out of bed in the morning. I could do the same, you know. One of these days I just might pick up my marbles and go home. And then what will you have? Do you think you can survive without me?"

By now I've fallen back on the bunk, where I lie pulling my hair, biting my lip, slapping at my cheeks — anything to wake myself up. Nothing works, nothing can stop him. "Did the guards put you in here?"

"Where did I come from?" he hisses, as if repeating my question. "I evolved, just like everything else. I began as an insignificant virus and evolved along with you, over billions of years, in a permanent arms race that neither of us could ever win. As your brain grew larger, I became more devious. I sent you gods to worship: jealous, vindictive gods who demanded obedience and killed you for sport. When you rejected them and staked your claim to eternal life, I sent in the lions; when you said 'Love your enemies,' I hired the Inquisitors and the witch burners. I turned your conscience into an instrument of torture and your freedom into a justification for slavery. When you invented socialism, I handed you over to Stalin and Mao. When you wrote the Ninth Symphony, I answered with the Holocaust. You unlocked the deepest secrets of physics; I gave you the hydrogen bomb."

I push my head against the top of the bunk, blocking my ears with my hands. "Stop it!"

"There you go again, as if you were any more innocent than I am. You drove me to my excesses just as I drove you to yours. I would never have dreamed up the concentration camps without the help of your philosophers and civil servants. I follow the same script as you do: survive and replicate, survive and replicate. We're all just following orders, aren't we?"

Now I feel the anger welling up inside me like a volcano. What makes him think he can sweep me into his evil justifications, make me complicit in his crimes? "Whose orders are you following?" I demand.

He laughs again, this time with a kind of resigned satisfaction. "There's a higher power that even I have to obey: the blind motive power of the replicators, with their insatiable will to perpetuate themselves like kudzu in a garden. I didn't plan it that way. I unleashed them for the suffering they would bring to the world, without imagining that even I would become entangled in their striving. Yes, I'm the one responsible for this clockwork nightmare you call life. I've kept a hand in it from the first amino acid right down to today, the day of your execution. I'm the intelligent designer you went to such lengths to disparage and deny. Did you really think all this came about by chance?"

"You're mocking me. You're mocking me and I won't stand for it!"

"Where does that leave us?" he jeers. "You've got to understand that I'm real. You didn't imagine or invent me. No sense pretending I don't exist And I really am in the details, as the saying goes: the atoms, the protons, the quarks, that make up the material world. I'm part of that world, just as you are. I've woven myself into your DNA and you can never, ever escape me."

With that last taunt I've reached my limit. I roll over and grab the first thing that comes to hand — the hourglass Billy Bob and Bubba gave me to count off my last hours on earth — and I hurl it at him with all my might. Lightning fast, he ducks and the hourglass bounces off the wall and lands on the cement floor.

He shakes his head in a pantomime of disappointment. "Don't take your frustrations out on me. I showed you all the kingdoms of the world but you refused to show me the respect that was due. Why? Because you didn't want to believe that I was part of you. Even though you're incapable of believing in anything outside yourself."

"Get out of here!"

To my amazement he reaches behind him and, with no apparent effort, opens the door to my cell. "We'll keep evolving, the two of us," he smiles, backing into the hall, "in our race with the Red Queen. Sometimes you'll pull ahead for a while and it'll seem like you've ground me into the dust. But I'll be close on your heels, and there'll be times when it seems that all your hopes have been dashed and I've triumphed once and for all. But of course that can never be. We're in this together, you and I. We need each other."

And suddenly he's gone. I leap out of my bunk, dripping wet, my heart pounding, but the door's locked tight. In the hall the lights are on, carts and dishes clattering. The clock says 5:00 a.m. I remember what day it is and tears fill my eyes. Yes, tears; I feel so sorry for myself I'm crying like a baby. In a few hours, I tell myself, nothing will matter. It's all an illusion, my existence is just an illusion. Is everything an illusion? No, I just saw evil and it was real.

There's my hourglass on the cement floor. And there, back in his cell across the hall, stands Teague, greeting me with his usual murderous stare, and no hint of recognition.

I retrieve the hourglass and turn it over to mark the beginning of my last day.

Friday, May 25, 6:00 a.m. 12 hours to execution.

So far it's a day like any other, the guards rattling in with the usual breakfast on a plastic tray. I'm still shaking, feverish, suddenly unable—after all these years of stoic resignation — to face what's ahead of me. Why care about it now, of all times? In a few hours I'll be nothing, and death will be nothing. From my point of view — which is the only point of view I can have — I will never have existed. I will have evened the score with God and the Devil and every other immaterial entity or idea that ever tormented me, by becoming as nonexistent as they are. And what will be left of the universe?

Billy Bob and Bubba share a laugh in front of my cell. "I'm telling you for the last time," Billy Bob says. "And I mean literally the last time — eat your damn breakfast!"

"Maybe he's saving room for his last meal," Bubba says. "You know, like you do on Thanksgiving?"

I gesture toward Teague, who glares back with psychotic intensity. "You put him in here last night, didn't you?"

Billy Bob laughs again. "Now why do you suppose we'd do a thing like that?"

"The Governor signed your death warrant, which means it's time to say good-bye," Bubba smiles. "They got a nice death watch cell waiting for you over at the prison. Your friend here'll be there soon enough."

"Though not as soon as we hoped," Billy Bob says. "His lawyers must be better than yours. They got him a stay for another few weeks."

"You're making a big mistake," I tell them. "Don't you realize you're doing this to yourselves?"

20.

Friday, May 25, 9:00 a.m. 9 hours to execution.

The phone rang again at 9:00, just as Charlotte was sipping the last drops of her room service coffee. The weather outside was as bad as the TV had predicted; she could hear rain whipping against the windows. Luckily she'd thought to bring her jacket.

"Good morning," Craft said. "I've made a decision."

"Good," Charlotte said. "I hope it's——"

"There's a taxi waiting for you outside," he interrupted. "The driver's already been paid. I gave him the address."

"I'm not getting in any taxi. Forget it."

His voice conveyed about as much emotion as a smart phone reciting directions to a restaurant. "Go where the driver takes you, which will be in Brooklyn. When you get there, he'll give you a phone number to call for further instructions."

"There's no way I'm getting in a taxi to meet you. In Brooklyn or anywhere else."

"I hope you change your mind," he said in the same flat voice. "If Ritter dies tonight, it'll be your fault."

The line went dead and Charlotte realized with furious desperation that she had no choice but to do as he said. She grabbed her briefcase and rushed downstairs and into the driving rain, jumping into the yellow cab Craft had sent for her. The driver was a cheerful West Indian who recited an address in Brooklyn but could remember nothing about the man who'd given it to him. He drove the taxi to the beat of a hip-hop track, chattering behind his plexiglass shield as she bounced along behind him trying to smear the fog off the window next to her in hopes of seeing where they were going. It was no use: the fog inside, the fog outside, the rain streaming over the windows, blocked her into an unreal, subaqueous world, disclosing only the vague outlines of bridges and exit ramps and ancient warehouses towering over narrow and increasingly deserted streets. Just the kind of day to let yourself be lured to some rundown industrial section of Brooklyn where no sane person would ever set foot.

The driver seemed to be driving in circles, as if he was trying to kill time. Then he splashed to a stop in front of a hulking brick structure that might have been a factory a hundred years ago. "This is where you get out, lady," he said, grinning at her through the plastic shield. He stuffed a slip of paper through the money slot. "You're supposed to call this number. Then I'll be on my way. The fare's been paid."

She dialed the number and immediately heard Craft's voice. "You're just in time for the grand finale," he said. "Go through the big green door on your left and take the stairs to the third floor. Then walk down the hall until you come to a door with '32' on it. Everything you want to know will be on the camera."

"The camera?"

"Forgive me," he said. "And please ask Chris to forgive me."

He hung up. She shoved a couple of twenties into the slot— "If I'm not back in fifteen minutes, call the police and send them to Room 32 on the third floor of that building, OK?" — and climbed out into the downpour. She ran to the big green door about fifty yards down the deserted sidewalk. In the shadowy foyer she grabbed the steak knife in her purse and hid it under her jacket. She ran up three flights of stairs under a leaking skylight, then down a dimly-lit corridor past a row of cavernous lofts with plank floors and bare brick walls. At last she came to the door marked "32." Did she really want to do this? She clenched the knife and took a deep breath. She had no choice.

Pushing the door open, she was pushed back by the smell of gunpowder and hot metal. On the far end of the room, she saw Craft slumped over a table in a pool of his own blood. His phone lay on the table in front of him along with an empty Starbucks cup and a jumble of books and papers. A handgun lay on the floor beside him.

She ran over and tried to sit him up but there was nothing she could do. The back of his head was splattered over the wall behind him. Blood was still pouring out of him, soaking the front of her dress when she bent over to help him. Then she noticed the camera: a digital video recorder on a tripod about twenty feet in front of the table. A red light blinked on the side to indicate that it was still recording. Instinctively she darted over and turned it off. There was something sick about recording a video of this scene. What were they going to do, put it on YouTube?

She glanced at her watch: 10:00 o'clock. Without thinking, she pulled out her phone and dialed 911.

Then she started thinking. What had Craft said? "Everything you want to know will be on the camera." She should have watched the video before calling the police. She had to know if he'd recorded a confession that would exonerate Ritter. If so, she had less than eight hours to get it to the court. Would the police let her copy it so she could send it down there in time?

She took the camera off the tripod and tried to figure out how to remove the memory disk. There was still time to get out of there before the cops arrived; maybe the taxi driver was still waiting outside. If she fled with the memory disk she'd be exposing herself to serious charges — tampering with evidence at the scene of a violent death — but what choice did she have? Yes, she'd given her name when she called 911, but they didn't know who she was. And so far they didn't even know a video had been made. If she just moved the tripod and camera out of the way....

Before she could finish her thought, two uniformed cops, one white and the other black, burst in with their guns drawn. "Freeze!" the black cop shouted. "Put your weapon on the floor and place your hands on the back of your head!"

Overcome with confusion and fear, she couldn't process what was happening. Time slowed down. "What weapon?"

"Put your weapon down now!"

She stared back at the cop for a desperate second before she realized he was talking about the camera. Still in slow motion, she set it down on the floor and raised her hands. "That's a video camera," she said. "I'm the one who called 911."

"Did you kill him?" he demanded.

"He shot himself just before I got here."

"You're covered with blood. Are you from the media?"

"No. No. Let me explain. This is really—"

"You can explain at the precinct station."

"Are you arresting me? I'm the one who called you."

The white cop was exceedingly polite, which she knew was a bad sign. "Please have a seat, ma'am," he said, opening a folding chair that leaned against the wall. "We're going to need to ask you some questions."

She walked toward the chair and the black cop called her back. "Don't forget your camera."

He handed her the camera and she asked, "Can I make a phone call?"

He laughed. "Sure, as long as it's not to a lawyer."

Friday, May 25, 10:30 a.m. 8-1/2 hours to execution.

She sat on the chair and tried to think about what to do. The white cop said they had to wait for the ambulance before they could take her to the precinct station for questioning. They acted like they had all the time in the world. She dialed Alex Lopez and prayed that he would answer. When he did, she gave him the address and asked him to drop everything and drive over there as soon as possible. "Ritter's life depends on it," she said. "How soon can you get here?"

"I can be there in twenty minutes."

The two uniformed cops were surprised and hostile when Alex Lopez showed up. Apparently they knew him and didn't much like him. As a detective he outranked them, but he was out of his jurisdiction. "The last time I checked," the white cop said, "Brooklyn isn't in the Bronx."

"When I'm the only detective in the room it is," Lopez said. "If you don't like that, call your precinct."

"She shot him," the black cop told Lopez.

"He shot himself before I got here," Charlotte said.

"If he shot himself, where's the note?"

Lopez waved him off. "Lay off. I'll handle this."

He sat down beside Charlotte and listened as she described the situation in a murmuring voice. She saw him glancing at his watch. It was almost 11:00 o'clock. "Do they know about the video?" he asked her.

She shook her head.

"When they question you, you're going to have to tell them about it. And then they're going to take it away from you."

"I've got to get whatever's on this camera down to Florida," she told Lopez. "I can email it or put it on the cloud if I can just keep it away from them. Then I've got to make a bunch of phone calls to make sure it gets to the right place."

"These jerks are going to keep you tied up for hours. Let me see your phone." He pulled a black cord out of his briefcase, attached it to the camera, and plugged it into her iPhone. "Download the video and send it wherever it needs to go."

A plainclothes detective from the Brooklyn precinct sauntered over and aimed an unfriendly scowl at Lopez. "Go back to the Bronx, Detective Lopez," he said. "I'll take it from here."

Lopez stood up, glaring at the Brooklyn detective, and before he walked out he whispered something in his ear that infuriated him. The detective followed Lopez into the corridor and shouted curses after him, joined by the two uniformed cops. While this was going on, Charlotte had time to download the video to her phone. She sent it to Julie Halkins, with a copy to the cloud; then she slipped the phone back into her purse. She knew that sending the video wasn't enough. She would need to call Julie to make sure she watched it and understood what it was. At this point their only hope was to file a motion for emergency stay in the Florida Supreme Court in Tallahassee. Julie could handle that electronically, and if that didn't work she could go to the Governor. Hadn't she said she had a law school classmate on the Governor's staff? If the police didn't let Charlotte make that call to Julie, Ritter was a dead man.

"Am I under arrest?" she asked the Brooklyn detective when he returned.

"Not yet."

"Do you mind if I try to find the bathroom?"

"That's probably a good idea. It could be a while before you get another chance."

She stood up with her purse and stooped down to pick up the camera.

"Leave that camera here."

In the corridor she turned left, ducked through a side exit and hurried down to the street, hoping Alex Lopez would be waiting outside. Instead she found three patrol cars with their lights flashing. To her amazement the taxi driver was still waiting with his engine running. "The cops showed up about ten minutes after you left," he said, "or I would've gone after you for sure. That was one weird dude who paid your fare."

"Now you tell me."

He laughed. "OK, lady, where do you want to go?"

"Take me to La Guardia," she said. "In a hurry."

On her phone she checked for the next flight to Tallahassee and bought a last-minute ticket. There was no time to make any calls in the rush to pick up her boarding pass and get through security to the plane, which departed at noon. If all went well, she would arrive in Tallahassee just before 5:00. The one-hour layover in Atlanta would give her the chance she needed to make her calls before it was too late.

Friday, May 25, 3:00 p.m. 3 hours to execution.

When the plane landed in Atlanta, Charlotte sat in the lounge and called Julie Halkins's office. There was still plenty of time for Julie to ask the Florida Supreme Court for an emergency stay, if she hadn't already done so. But when Charlotte reached Julie's secretary she realized with a sinking sensation that Julie hadn't even received the video.

"I'm sorry, ma'am," the secretary said in a country western voice. "The attorneys are all out of the office today."

Charlotte felt desperate, almost hysterical. "What do you mean? How can I reach Julie?"

"I'm afraid that's impossible, ma'am. They're on their annual retreat — you know, they do it every year about this time? — out on a boat in the Gulf of Mexico. No reception out there. I couldn't reach them if I tried."

"I can't believe this!"

Next she called the clerk's office at the Florida Supreme Court and asked to speak to one of the Justices.

"This is the Clerk's office," the receptionist said. "The Justices can only be reached in their chambers."

"Can you transfer me, then?"

"Are you an attorney?"

"Yes, I am. My name is—"

"I'm sorry. The Justices don't take calls in chambers from attorneys. You'd have to call one of the court administrators to set up a time for a conference call."

Charlotte told herself to stay calm. When you're talking to a bureaucrat, the worst thing you can do is show any sign of impatience or irritation, let alone the blind fury she was beginning to feel. "OK, I wonder if you could put me through to one of the administrators, please."

"I'll try."

The receptionist transferred the call and it rang about two minutes before bouncing back. "They not picking up," she said.

"Is anybody there?"

"I doubt it, ma'am. It's Friday afternoon."

Charlotte tried the warden's office at the Florida State Prison and was told that the warden had no discretion to delay the execution, unless they received an overriding order from the Governor or the Supreme Court.

The boarding announcement for Charlotte's plane blared over her head. She redialed Julie Halkins's office.

"This is Charlotte Ambler again," she told the secretary. "Maybe you can help me with something. Julie told me she has a friend on the Governor's staff she works with sometimes. Do you know that person's name?"

"Oh," the secretary hesitated. "I think his name is Paul Mendel. They went to law school together."

"Paul Mendel? OK, I'll call him. Thanks."

The boarding announcement was repeated, more urgently. She hurried back toward the plane and stood in line, fumbling with her boarding pass as she dialed the Governor's office and asked for Paul Mendel, who of course was unavailable.

"Is he in the office?" she demanded.

"Mr. Mendel is unavailable," the receptionist repeated.

"I realize that, but I need to know if he's still in the office. Has he left for the day?"

"Mr. Mendel is still in the office."

Charlotte limped down the boarding chute at a snail's pace, feigning disability. The flight attendant stood in the plane's doorway gesturing frantically for her to hurry up.

"OK," Charlotte said into the phone. "I need you to take this very seriously. This is about an execution that's going to take place at 6:00 o'clock unless the Governor stops it. I'm an attorney representing the man who is about to be executed—"

"Excuse me. I'm just the receptionist. I don't deal with these types of things."

The flight attendant scowled and started to close the door. "Disconnect all electronic devices before boarding the plane," she barked.

Charlotte stuck her foot in the door and pretended to stumble. "I know that," she told the receptionist. "I'm asking you to just this once go outside your job description for a minute to save an innocent man's life. Please. Find Mr. Mendel and beg him to stay in the office until I get there at about quarter past five. Tell him I'm working with Julie Halkins and it's a matter of life and death. Can you do that for me?"

"I'll try. But I leave at 4:50."

"It's a matter of life and death."

"Like I said, I leave at 4:50."

21.

Chris Ritter

Friday, May 25, 4:00 p.m. 2 hours to execution.

The death watch cell comes with a courteous staff of Billy Bobs and Bubbas who wheel in your last meal (minus the mussels and the Death by Chocolate ice cream) but who become noticeably less courteous, verging on the abusive, when you refuse to eat any of it, reminding you that an identical meal has already been served to the warden, who, you tell them, if there's justice in the world, will have a heart attack before he can preside over your execution. This enrages them, but you know their threats are idle: they can't whip you before your execution, all they can do is drag you to the next station. There's no dead man walking, no green mile, just a bullying shuffle in handcuffs and shackles down a narrow corridor to a room that looks like a doctor's office. This is the prep room, where they strap you on the gurney and stick in the IV's, four attendants wearing surgical gear in case you try to bite them or spit at them, asking you over and over again if you're comfortable, as if it would be wrong to execute an uncomfortable man. You can't see their faces, only their eyes faintly behind the goggles, so you don't know if they're smirking in there, or crying, or (most likely) not thinking too much about what they're doing. The drug they're going to pump into your veins won't be safe but you hope it will be effective. You've read the stories about the painful and interrupted lethal injections; in encouraging this hope they make you a collaborator in your own execution. The chaplain appears at your side, at a loss for words since neither of you believe in anything that will survive the next fifteen minutes, yet his presence is comforting, tears run down his cheeks and you feel like crying in sympathy with him, he's been so loyal, and you think of Charlotte, who gave you so much with so little in return, but you fight back the tears because you wouldn't want the guards or the witnesses to think you're crying for yourself. Let them think you're crying for your daughter, who hardly knew you, though you loved her so much, and your son. You close your eyes, expecting your whole life to pass in front of you, but it doesn't, so you open them again; all you see is this shiny yellow corridor they're wheeling you down, chaplain at your side, clutching your wrist in his soft hand.

You expect to see the executioner wearing a black pillow case over his head, or something like that, but no, it's just another surgical mask, only larger and more impressive than the others, as if he were chief of surgery at a leading hospital, and you wonder if, as Billy Bob and Bubba said, he might be your next door neighbor or your kid's Sunday School teacher if you had a next door neighbor or a kid who went to Sunday School, but it's reassuring to know that he's a person of high moral character who's taking time out of his busy day to perform this public service for a mere $150, which is about what it will cost him to take his wife out for a nice dinner afterwards. There are ten witnesses as required by law — also undoubtedly of high moral character — but the room is designed to hide them from you so you can't lodge a final appeal with your eyes or give them the evil eye. You can see the red phone that would ring if a last-minute call came in from the Governor — it's an old-fashioned wall phone that looks like it hasn't been used in years — and you're the only one who seems to notice it. The warden reads out some legalese (he looks a little green after finishing what might have been his last meal) and asks if you have anything to say, any last words, which the chaplain has warned you to keep short and respectful unless you want the masked surgeon to jump the gun with a quick squirt into the IV.

"I just want to say what I've said all along," you tell them, "that I'm innocent...."

That's not what they want to hear, these people of high moral character in their uniforms and hiding places and surgical masks. Your voice falters and you feel a gentle wave of drowsiness tugging you down....

Friday, May 25, 5.30 p.m.   30 minutes to execution.

The plane landed a few minutes early and Charlotte was out of her seat charging down the aisle before it stopped moving. The flight attendants threatened to have her arrested but she shoved her way past them and they let her go. She grabbed a taxi and sped to the Governor's office o n Capitol Hill, where, to her relief, a slightly-built man with twinkling blue eyes and a skeptical smile stood waiting for her at the door. It was Paul Mendel.

"I'm Charlotte Ambler," she told him.

"I figured. You're working with Julie?"

They sat down together on a bench in the lobby and watched the video together on her phone. There was Craft, staring back at the camera with the gun in his hand. He looked just the way she'd pictured him, only weaker, sadder, more like a pathetic loser than an evil genius.

And then he began to talk.

The next few days passed like a feverish dream for Charlotte, beginning that night in Tallahassee after Paul Mendel picked up his phone to call the Governor. The drama of the past two weeks — and its wrenching climax — left her a sobbing, shaking mess. Paul Mendel was very kind; he drove her to her hotel, bought her a drink in the lobby and arranged for the restaurant to send dinner up to her room. She spend most of the night on the phone with her mom, alternately falling apart and pulling herself back together until she fell asleep. The next morning, Saturday, she still felt shaky until she'd had her breakfast and coffee. She checked her email and found a message from Detective Alex Lopez of the NYPD summoning her to an inquest, scheduled for the following Wednesday, concerning the death of the man who destroyed Ritter's life and now had saved it. "Craft," of course, had been a pseudonym: his real name was Kevin McNally. She called Paul Mendel to thank him and ordered a rental car to be brought to her hotel. She had a long drive ahead of her. All the way to Raiford, to meet with her client.

Ritter had woken up in the prep room still strapped to the gurney, thinking he was dead. Two attendants stared down at him through their masks. Guards stood on either side of the gurney, in case he tried to escape. He was surprised to see the chaplain standing by the door.

"Are we both dead?" he asked the chaplain.

"Neither of us," the chaplain smiled.

"The first injection was just a narcotic," one of the attendants explained, removing the IV catheter. "You didn't get the lethal drug."

"Why not?"

"Apparently you're innocent."

Ritter felt no emotion. He could discern no difference between being dead or alive. The guards clamped him in handcuffs and leg-irons, and an hour later he was transferred back to Raiford, where Teague had kept the fire of hatred burning in his eyes. Billy Bob and Bubba, who'd handled him gingerly in the days leading up to the execution, greeted him with open scorn, as if he was more guilty by being innocent than he'd been by being guilty.

Late Saturday afternoon they escorted him to the visitors room to meet with Charlotte. Charlotte — who'd driven all the way from Tallahassee looking forward to a victory celebration with her client — was shocked to discover how little he cared about being saved. She told him the whole story, from the last time she'd visited the prison to the Governor's call at five minutes to six. The only part that caught his attention was her description of Craft blowing his brains out, which, to her dismay, he wanted to hear over and over again. "Craft's real name, by the way, was Kevin McNally," she said. "Does that name mean anything to you?"

Ritter shook his head. "Are you sure he was dead? Tell me again how he died."

"Let's try to get beyond that," she said, trying to sound cheerful. "Don't you see what this means? You're innocent."

"I already knew that."

"Maybe now somebody will believe it." The guards knocked to signal that the time was almost up. "Of course it isn't automatic," she went on. "I talked to Sol and Julie Halkins on the phone as I was driving over here. We have to file a new motion to vacate your conviction and sentence, which will require something like a trial."

"Will I get to testify at this one?"

"You'll have to testify, if you're going to stand a chance of being released. But you won't be the star witness. The star witness — thanks to the magic of digital recording — will be Craft."

Ritter allowed himself a weary smile. "Evil always has the last word."

The inquest was conducted in a windowless conference room at the Kings County Hospital Center in Brooklyn, upstairs from the morgue where Kevin McNally's corpse still occupied a drawer, by a small, bespectacled man named Samuel Hawthorne, who identified himself as a medico-legal investigator from the Office of Chief Medical Examiner. Its purpose, as Mr. Hawthorne explained, was to gather the facts concerning the cause of Kevin McNally's death; a physician would then make findings based on all available evidence, including the autopsy which had already been performed. Also present, besides Mr. Hawthorne and Charlotte, were Alex Lopez and Detective Donald Braccia, the Brooklyn detective Charlotte had escaped from in order to take the video to Florida.

Mr. Hawthorne was a precise, well-spoken man who apparently took a keen personal interest in each of the dead people he investigated. "First let me summarize what we've been able to learn about the decedent," he began. "Kevin McNally was 52 years old, born and raised in the Ridgewood section of Queens. He worked busing tables in a cafeteria on lower Broadway, where his co-workers viewed him as an oddball. He was a loner and a conspiracy theorist, more or less fitting the profile of Mark David Chapman, who shot John Lennon, and John Hinckley, who shot President Reagan. He lived by himself in a shabby walk-up on the Lower East Side, having drifted from one low-paying job to another; and yet according to his co-workers he had intellectual pretensions and delusions of grandeur, often entertaining the customers with claims to advanced degrees in various subjects, bizarre warnings and predictions of impending disaster, and boasts about his illustrious past as a writer and actor in Hollywood and his future as a celebrity who they would boast of having known. He hated minorities and immigrants and often talked excitedly about a coming apocalypse, which only he and a few others would survive. Though his past was murky, medical records reveal that he spent several months in a residential mental care facility in Florida, where he was diagnosed with paranoid schizophrenia."

The medico-legal investigator paused to let the words "paranoid schizophrenia" sink in before he went on: "He was, in short, exactly the kind of man who might take his own life. The only thing unusual about his suicide was the way he carried it off, but even that is hardly unique in my experience. You can find any number of videotaped suicide notes in our archives."

Charlotte gave a statement summarizing what she knew about McNally's death, including the history of his relationship with Ritter and the significance of his videotaped confession in preventing Ritter's execution. Detective Braccia waited for her to finish and aimed a menacing scowl in her direction. "I could arrest you right now for leaving the scene of the shooting and obstructing the investigation of a possible homicide."

Charlotte told herself to stay calm. "Am I suspected of something? Is this an interrogation?"

"Not yet."

"You would have done the same thing, Don," Alex Lopez said.

Mr. Hawthorne cleared his throat. "Is there anything else? I think we have enough information, together with the autopsy report. It's all consistent with a finding of suicide, which is what I'm going to recommend. Does anybody have anything else?"

The next day, in the visitors room, Charlotte told Ritter what had happened at the inquest and described what she'd learned about Craft. The prison had no facility for a death row inmate to watch a video, but she was permitted to bring a transcript of McNally's suicide video for Ritter to read while she waited.

"Is that all he was?" Ritter asked, lowering his eyes.

Charlotte knew what he meant without asking. After his years of suffering and despair, to which he'd attached so much meaning and importance, it was humbling, even disappointing, to realize that Craft wasn't a philosopher, an evil genius or a supernatural force.

He was just another nut case.

22.

In normal circumstances, the cycle of motions, briefs, conferences and hearings required for a post-conviction proceeding can take months to complete. But when the Governor has signed the prisoner's death warrant — which in Ritter's case had been stayed for only sixty days — the court is required to dispose of the matter as quickly as possible. For this reason Ritter would have his day in court just six weeks after the aborted execution. Judge Robert P. Castaigne, who'd handled all his post-conviction matters, would also be handling this one, which, according to Sol, was a point in Ritter's favor: Judge Castaigne was a fair-minded judge who'd be familiar with the facts of the case. Julie Halkins again served as lead counsel, with Charlotte carrying the laboring oar; Charlotte was even allowed to appear in court on Ritter's behalf. Sol and Millie had moved into makeshift quarters in a strip mall, where Charlotte paid them a visit. Sol was congratulatory toward Charlotte but still skeptical about Ritter, unable to admit that he wasn't a psychopath even if Craft had confessed to the murder. Charlotte and Julie arranged to meet with the prosecutor, Byron Paxton, ahead of time, so they could show him the video and explain the corroborating evidence, which would include Ritter's testimony to be given at the hearing. Byron Paxton adamantly refused to concede that Ritter was innocent, but after watching the video and listening to Charlotte's account of the expected testimony, he said he'd keep an open mind. Like Paul Mendel, he was a law-school classmate of Julie Halkins's.

Trials and hearings, contrary to their reputation for nail-biting drama, are ordinarily boring affairs. They are ritualized performances from which most elements of chance have been purged in advance, a series of obvious questions addressed to well-rehearsed witnesses who give the responses everyone expects. But the hearing on Ritter's petition to vacate his guilty verdict was unlike any court proceeding most of those present had ever seen. It opened with an impassioned statement by Charlotte, recounting the circumstances that led to the Governor's stay of execution, and then Ritter took the stand, testifying with a sincerity and depth of emotion that surprised everyone, including Charlotte, who'd begun to view him as a burnt-out shell. The courtroom was filled to overflowing, with an atmosphere of excited anticipation that reminded some of the reporters of a Hollywood opening. The media were there in force, along with representatives of the police, senior citizens bussed in from gated communities, and even some of the anti-Ritter demonstrators from Raiford who had relocated to a parking lot across from the courthouse. The crowd loved Charlotte's opening statement, they hung on Ritter's every word, but the real reason they were there was to see the movie. They had come to see the world premier of McNally's suicide note.

After everyone else was seated, Doug Leipzig, Tim Salis, and Kathryn's parents, Bill and Louise O'Donnell, slipped in with Sol Levy and sat down in the front row, where some seats had been blocked off as if for the family at a funeral. Charlotte made her opening statement; the prosecutor responded with some bland remarks about the sanctity of the jury verdict and the need for finality; and then Ritter testified, recounting the history of his dealings with Craft (as he still called him) and his long-standing belief that Craft had murdered Helene Varga. Judge Castaigne grew more and more agitated as he listened to Ritter's testimony, apparently struck by the realization that the original trial had been a farce. "Mr. Ritter," he growled. "Why didn't you inform the court of these facts at your first trial?"

"My attorney advised me not to testify."

"Did your attorney inform the district attorney's office of these facts?"

"I don't believe so, your honor."

The judge glared at Sol, jotted down some notes and directed Charlotte to call her next witness.

"The movant calls Mr. Sam Hawthorne," she said.

Mr. Sam Hawthorne, the medico-legal investigator from New York, proved to be as precise in his testimony as he had been at the inquest. He stated his qualifications and summarized his findings about Kevin McNally, confirming the official ruling of suicide. Then he handed Charlotte a computer disk on which, he said, he had downloaded the video files on McNally's camera. Charlotte turned to the judge. "Your honor, I would offer this computer disk in evidence, and propose that it be viewed by the court."

"Are there any objections? You may proceed."

The staff wheeled in a big-screen TV equipped with a DVD player and positioned it to be viewed by the judge and the audience. Charlotte inserted the disk, made a few adjustments with the remote control, and the show that everyone had been waiting for flashed on the screen. There was no title, no credits, just a plain brick wall behind a wide table littered with books and papers, a Starbucks cup, a cell phone; and then Kevin McNally — bearded, portly, in a tweed suit and loosely fitting tie — scooted onto a small chair behind the table. He looked exactly as Ritter had described him, with his graying, brushed-back hair and the proud, slightly crazed expression in his eyes. He cleared his throat, folded his hands in front of him and stared back at the camera like a kindly undertaker. "This is for you, Chris," he began. "I hope you don't mind if I call you Chris. I still think of you as Chris, as a friend. We were friends once, weren't we? At least I thought we were, after you overcame your initial hostility. I even became your teacher, didn't I? Maybe a little more than you imagined, or at least in a different way. You knew me as Craft, obviously a fake name. You never asked my real one.

"This video is meant for you, even though you already know most of what I'm going to say. Nobody believed you when you tried to tell this story, did they? Too fantastic, practically insane. The old lie: it's not the world that's insane, it's the gifted few — and there aren't many of us — who see it as it is, who can look the truth in the eye and not blink. I taught you how to do that—to look the truth in the eye and not blink—and they called you a psychopath. Not insane, in the legal sense, not too crazy to kill. I refuse to say 'execute.' *Killing* is what it is. That's what they're getting ready to do to you, and they say *you're* the psychopath, *you're* evil, *you* don't deserve to live! It's them that want to do this to you that are insane. You and I both know that. *They're evil*, if anything is. By the way, is there any such thing as evil? Have you figured that out yet?

"You know what happened, but you don't know exactly how it began, do you? You've had your suspicions, but you never really knew. It was in that bar on Broadway, just like you thought. I hung out there sometimes, not exactly a barfly but not exactly a graduate student either. I'd been a promising scholar once, just like you, in and out of the university for years. I was sure I'd be a famous professor someday, maybe win a Nobel Prize, but I kept getting sandbagged by my professors and the other students. I studied philosophy, law and medicine, even theology, but nobody took me seriously, because, frankly, my ideas were so far over their heads they couldn't begin to grasp them. They made fun of my research, made fun of me, treated me like some kind of wacko who wandered onto the campus by mistake, and after ten years I had nothing to show for my work. I was reduced to cleaning toilets, waiting tables, even begging on the street, until finally I found some translation work that paid pretty well. But I never gave up on my ambitions, or on my determination to show the academic world what a mistake they'd made in driving me away. And you and your friends — I'd noticed you in there before — carrying on like you had the world at your feet, a bunch of over-privileged spoiled brats. Maybe you were drunk that night, I don't know, but it wouldn't be an excuse. What an arrogant geek, boasting that you'd sell your soul for a thousand bucks because you had nothing to lose!

"I pitied you, after what I'd been through, for having such small appreciation for your undeserved success. I happened to have some extra cash burning a hole in my pocket, a thousand bucks I'd won in a poker game. What the hell, I said to myself. When the money comes that easy you've got to let it go without a struggle or it'll come back to haunt you. That's what I've always said. So I called up a girl I'd met the summer before named Helene, a receptionist where I worked. She was a drug user who was always desperately in need of cash. I paid her to hang out in the bar and give you that envelope full of cash. She wasn't to say why: that would be left to your narcissistic imagination. Helene played her part brilliantly. A little too brilliantly, as it turned out. I warned her not to get involved with you but she couldn't resist playing both ends against the middle, milking you for what you were worth and sending me the bill. I had to intervene, in the guise of Craft — a brilliant stroke, even if I say so myself. All I had to do was trim my beard, pick up an old suit in a thrift shop and practice talking like a pompous ass with a European accent. You fell for it, hook, line and sinker, giving in to all the temptations I flung in your path as if you'd been waiting all your life for me to come along."

McNally lifted the Starbucks cup to his lips and drained it, setting it back on the table. "You can't blame me, really," he went on. "I was trying to steer you in the right direction career-wise while showing you the folly of your materialistic creed. But quickly our little game turned into a struggle for your soul, though you still

didn't think you had one. You see, there were some lessons I was
determined to teach you. I studied you like the birds and turtles you
were so fascinated with, keeping you under close surveillance,
digging into every corner of your past and present life. I discovered
that you were a man of easily exploited contradictions. A scientist
supposedly committed to objectivity, yet still an egotist, a narcissist
who valued your own unique subjectivity above all else, who as
time went on came to doubt whether other people were anything
more than a cunning arrangement of molecules designed to deceive
you. The knowledge of good and evil was the one type of
knowledge you didn't crave — that tree wasn't even in the garden
as far as you were concerned — so it was up to me to teach you by
negative example. I became the spirit that negates, that incarnates
itself as evil so you could see the good in the world.

"I gave you Helene first. You already had a beautiful girlfriend
I would have given anything for. Why weren't you satisfied with
Kathryn? I sat in that bar wishing she'd just glance in my direction
occasionally. That would have been enough for me. I'll admit I
became a little obsessed with her. I followed her around more than
I probably should have. No harm done. I wasn't stalking her, just
keeping a close watch so I could make sure you treated her right.
Yes, I was jealous, especially when you started sleeping with her.
That night in the bar you'd only been friends, but before long you
were spending your nights in her apartment while I stood outside
seething with frustration. I sent Helene back into action, coaching
her to use all her wiles to seduce you away from Kathryn. The poor
girl was penniless and desperate as always from her drug habit. I
paid her well to give you what you wanted. You were far better
than some pimp or drug dealer, she knew that, and she put her
heart into the job. But you kept after Kathryn, and before long you
and Kathryn were engaged.

"I was beside myself with rage and disbelief. How could a
woman like Kathryn love a man who'd so carelessly dispose of his
own soul, a psychopath who viewed himself as a fortuitous
arrangement of chemicals? But of course there was nothing I could
do. I resigned myself to watching Kathryn become your wife. The
most I could hope for was that she would eventually see your true
colors. I encouraged you to continue the affair with Helene, which
was in fact a form of prostitution, since she was working for me.
And then even Helene started falling for you, as if it were a real
love affair! She was a whore, and I was the one paying her, but she
wouldn't let me touch her. That was the crowning insult, for which
I knew you'd have to pay. In the meantime I let you amuse yourself
with her and a dozen other women, which I knew would distance
you from Kathryn, whether she found out about them or not.
From there it was a short step to your harassment of Greta Ramos.
Oh, yes, I knew all about that. You might say I set the whole thing
up.

"Don't get the impression that I was obsessed with sex. That
was you, not me. I used sex only to expand the boundaries of your
soulless philosophy. You failed as a husband, even as a lover, but
you also earned failing grades in sympathy, loyalty, ethics and so
many other subjects. By the time you gave the so-called
Raskolnikov interview — another brilliant stroke on my part,
sending in that right-wing nymphomaniac Amy Pierce to record
your nihilistic pillow talk — you'd gone so far down the road of
egotism that there was no turning back.

"You understand, I wasn't out to destroy you. I wanted to help
you, to show you how mistaken you were about the nature of
things. But you were incapable of grasping the enormity of the
mistake you had made; I realize that now. It was a kind of original
sin you couldn't overcome without some kind of miracle. So when
Helene tried to turn the tables, my first thought was for you.

Whether, if she did what she was threatening to do, you would ever have a chance to work out your salvation.

"She came to me one day — we always met in a little bar on the West Side — and said she wanted out of the game. Her conscience was bothering her and she'd decided to tell you the whole truth about what had been going on. In effect she was blackmailing me. You had become a celebrity: your picture was on the cover of *Time* magazine. If Helene exposed my plot, including her role in it, you would have gone after me and made my life a living hell for years to come. That was as far as her thinking on the subject had gone. Wait a minute, I said. You're blackmailing the wrong guy. If you want to tell Chris that you've been getting paid to have sex with him, go right ahead. Even if you want to tell him who's been paying you, I wouldn't mind. Maybe I'll send him a bill. Don't you see? It's him you should be blackmailing, to keep you from selling your story to the National Enquirer. The poster boy for Neo-Darwinism, the man who unlocked the genetic key to altruism, has been carrying on a decade-long affair with a prostitute, using the University's money to entertain her while he cheated on his wife, sexually harassed graduate students, falsified study data and sabotaged his colleagues' careers. He could get his picture in *Time* magazine all over again."

McNally reached over to touch his phone, which lay face up on the table, as if he wanted to check the time. "So here's the bottom line," he said. "I told Helene: You blackmail me, you get peanuts. You go after Chris, you could be set for life. And I'll help you do it. Blackmailing can be a dangerous game, especially against a victim with no moral scruples. I'll be your life insurance policy. I'll set it up so you have all the documentation and proof you need, deposited in a safe place he won't be able to reach, and you won't even have to tell him my name. I'll pay you to keep me out of it. I like you, Helene. You've done a good job and you deserve to be compensated for it. I'll make sure you get what you deserve.

"As I talked to Helene I could practically see the wheels spinning in her bleary addict's eyes. She could always be depended on to calculate her own maximum advantage. I didn't trust her, even when she agreed to go along with my proposal.

"We decided — or rather I decided — that the best time for Helene to confront you would be on one of your junkets to Florida. There was one coming up in a month. That gave us enough time to gather the evidence — we had dozens of photographs, hotel receipts, email messages, handwritten notes — and stash it in a safe deposit box where it would be quickly discovered if anything went wrong. Before leaving the city I bought a cheap digital camera and an extra memory card from a street vendor near Times Square just in case any more pictures might be needed.

"Helene flew to Ft. Lauderdale on your corporate card and rented a Toyota Camry at the airport. I took the precaution of flying to Miami and driving a hundred extra miles to meet her at the Denny's near my hotel in West Palm Beach. I noticed that she was wearing a pair of unusual earrings you had given her. We made our final plans and I met her at a mall near your in-laws' townhouse, where you and she had stayed many times. I left my rental car at the mall and rode the rest of the way in her Camry. We knew you weren't at the townhouse. You were spending a couple of days out looking at sea turtles and had told Helene to expect to see you in the morning. She had her own key to the townhouse and the code for the garage door opener.

"We parked in the garage on the first floor and let the garage door shut behind us. Upstairs we poured ourselves a drink and I reminded Helene of our deal. I wouldn't be there when you arrived and she wouldn't reveal my name no matter how hard you pressed her. For the first time she started to waffle on that crucial point. She was afraid of how you'd react, unsure of her ability to withstand your anger and the pressure you'd exert on her. I was sympathetic at first and tried to reassure her. Then she made a big mistake. She suggested that if I paid her more — a lot more — she'd be better able to withstand your pressure. I told her she was lucky to be getting rid of you, and she wasn't losing anything because she'd still have me. She laughed in my face.

With an angry gesture, McNally swept a pile of papers onto the floor, clearing a spot on the table. "I was absolutely beside myself with fury. All the anger I'd accumulated over the years — toward you, toward her, toward all the idiots I'd had to contend with all my life — came pouring out in a torrent. Without thinking, I picked up a marble statuette that was on the coffee table and threw it at her. It hit her in the head but didn't kill her, though it left her groggy and bleeding on the floor. I was still in a rage. I pulled off her clothes, lashed her wrists to her ankles with my belt and took pictures on my new camera while I finished beating her to death. I cleaned the statuette thoroughly and put it back where it belonged on the coffee table. One side of her face was relatively untouched by the beating. I arranged her arms and legs in a sexy pose — even her face looked sexy, on the good side, with the earring dangling over her neck — and shot a few more pictures with my camera. I removed the memory card from the camera and wiped it clean and hid it in the back of a bureau drawer in the master bedroom. Then I put my spare memory card in the camera and took some more pictures, as identical to the first set as I could make them. I wanted something to remember her by.

"I took another souvenir: one of the earrings you'd given her. Then I asked myself — I remember laughing when it came to me — 'What good is one earring?' So I ripped the other one out of her ear and hid it in the suitcase you'd left behind in your bedroom.

Then I poured myself another drink and cleaned up the floor and the rug with bleach so there wouldn't be any fingerprints or DNA. Just after midnight I wrapped up Helene's body and clothes in a sheet and dragged it downstairs and locked it in the trunk of the Camry. I went through her purse and her pockets and suitcase to make sure nothing in them would point to me. I kept the key to her apartment in New York, so I could check it out when I got back. The key to the safe deposit box I stashed in her suitcase where the police would find it. Then I drove to a swampy area near the mall where I'd parked my car, and dumped the body and the purse and suitcase in the swamp. It was after midnight and nobody was around. I left her car at the mall and drove mine back to my hotel. I never went back to the town house.

"I want you to know that I didn't intend to kill Helene. She shouldn't have said what she said. She shouldn't have tried to go back on our deal, which was to blackmail you, and try to squeeze more money out of me. She could've got plenty from you without bringing me into it. When she said what she said, I realized I could never trust her to keep her mouth shut. She shouldn't have laughed at me."

Frowning, McNally reached in his pocket and pulled out a gun, setting it down carelessly on the table in front of him. "I didn't want to hurt you either, Chris," he said, shaking his head. "I was hoping the alligators would eat Helene's body and they'd never know she was killed, or at least they wouldn't connect her with you. But if they did find her — if there was going to be an investigation — then unfortunately it would lead to you. They'd find the memory card in the townhouse and the earring in your suitcase, but only if they knew enough to search for them. And then they'd go to the safe deposit box in New York and that would tell them everything they needed to know. They'd never come looking for me.

"I've been living with the consequences for over ten years and it's been torture. I hope you appreciate that, Chris. Helene didn't really suffer. She didn't know what hit her. But I've been suffering every day, because, remember, I was the one who became a murderer for your sake. It's ironic, isn't it? It's really ironic. You've suffered too, of course, but I doubt if you've suffered any more than the rest of us. Where we are is Hell, and where Hell is, there must we be. I never thought they'd try to kill you. I assumed you'd be out after a few years like most murderers. And now I won't let myself do it again, even in self-defense. I won't let you go to the electric chair or the gas chamber or whatever they have down there on account of what I did. You've been there for me all these years and now I'm going to set you free. I'd stop the earth from turning but I don't know how. The stars move still, time runs, the clock will strike, the Devil will come."

He sat waiting for a moment until his cell phone rang. He raised it to his ear and said, "You're just in time for the grand finale. Go through the big green door on your left and take the stairs to the third floor. Then walk down the hall until you come to a door with '32' on it. Everything you want to know will be on the camera. Forgive me. And please ask Chris to forgive me."

Without hesitation, he set the phone down on the table. Then he picked up the gun, stuck the barrel in his mouth, and squeezed the trigger.

23

The courtroom hovered in shocked silence as the video exploded to its climax. Charlotte clicked it off and returned to her seat beside Ritter, who stared at the blank screen, his face pale and expressionless. Judge Castaigne also seemed to have been momentarily incapacitated by the video, gazing around as if waiting for something to happen. The prosecutor, who had fumbled noisily with his papers right up to the moment when the shot was fired, took Judge Castaigne's silence as his cue to stand up and start talking, but the judge waved him back into his seat. Another long moment passed before the judge began to talk. "There's always some doubt in these cases," he said as if he were musing to himself. "I know what the prosecutor would say — will say, when it's his turn to speak. I've been there myself, when I was a prosecutor. Finality, respect for the jury system, unreliability of witnesses who materialize years later: it's all true as far as it goes. There are some real issues here. What's the standard for evaluating the evidence after so many years? Who has the burden of proof? How much deference is owed to the jury verdict? Actual innocence is the hardest argument to win at this stage. Better to claim some procedural flaw that at least doesn't put the whole system in jeopardy. But that's all backwards, isn't it? The state has no interest in putting an innocent man in jail, let alone executing him. There's no constituency for that, so far as I know, even on the Supreme Court."

Judge Castaigne peered at the prosecutor as if daring him to stand up again. "Mr. Paxton, I'll share my thoughts so you can frame your arguments accordingly. I'm inclined to rule, based on the evidence presented, that there's a high probability, nearly a certainty, that if this evidence had been presented at the trial, the jury would not have reached a verdict of guilty beyond a reasonable doubt. In fact, there's a good chance Mr. Ritter would have been acquitted on a directed verdict. Therefore — subject of course to anything you might wish to add to my analysis — I'm going to vacate the judgment and sentence and direct the Warden of the Florida State Prison to release Mr. Ritter from custody as soon as reasonably practicable. Do you disagree with that analysis, Mr. Paxton?"

The prosecutor stopped fumbling with his papers and lurched to his feet. "No, your honor," he said. "The state takes no position on the merits and accordingly will accede to the court's recommendation."

"It's a ruling, Mr. Paxton. Not a recommendation."

"Yes, your honor."

The judge banged his gavel, the bailiff shouted "All rise!" and suddenly it was all over. Ritter was a free man — except, of course, that he had to go back to jail. He would remain in the state prison until it was "reasonably practicable" for him to begin a new chapter of his life. The marshals clamped their grip around his arms, in case he tried to escape.

Before they could turn around, Doug Leipzig darted forward with Kathryn's parents a step behind him. "You'd better stay away from my kids," he warned Ritter. "You'll be in court again if you go near them."

"They're my kids."

"You stay away from them!" Kathryn's mother hissed.

"Liam isn't your son," Doug said. "If you want to get a DNA test, go right ahead."

"You haven't seen the end of me," Ritter said as the marshals pulled him away.

Tim Salis stayed in his seat, shaking his head at the way Doug Leipzig and the O'Donnells were behaving. He moved away from them and stood up to greet Charlotte as she made her way out of the courtroom. "I'm really sorry about that," he told her, frowning toward Doug. "It's way out of line."

"I know," Charlotte agreed, a little coldly.

Tim stayed with her, walking beside her to the lobby and out into the summer heat. "I came down here to support Chris," he said, "not to make things worse for him. I didn't know Kathryn's parents were going to be here. Please tell Chris I said that." He smiled warmly and held out his hand to say goodbye. "And thanks for all you've done for Chris. You've done a terrific job."

She appreciated the compliment and the friendly attitude. "I'm sure Chris appreciates your coming down."

"Listen," he said, squeezing her hand, "I don't know what Chris is planning to do next, but if he comes to New York he's welcome to stay in my apartment. I'm going to be up in the Berkshires most of the rest of the summer. I'm doing a play up there."

"Thanks. I'll tell Chris."

"And Charlotte, I hope to see you again too. Let me know when you come to New York."

"OK," she smiled. "I'll do that."

Charlotte felt an inner glow as she walked away from Tim and crossed the street to where she'd parked her car. For the first time in months she could allow herself to relax, to feel good about herself. She'd survived her ordeal, she'd accomplished something as a lawyer that she could be proud of. The law has its flaws, enormous flaws, in fact: there are times when it's inhuman, almost diabolical in its cruelty, but there are also times when it soars above the injustice of the world with a majesty all its own. She could hardly wait to tell her mom and her colleagues at the law firm in Philadelphia.

A pair of protestors — the law protected them too, in their meanness and ignorance — came toward her, still waving their placards. She recognized the puffy-haired blonde from Raiford and her beer-bellied boyfriend, and wondered if they were coming to apologize. She welcomed them: at that moment she could have forgiven everyone and everything.

They stopped about ten feet away. The man stood chopping with his placard like a tomahawk. The woman screwed her face into a hideous mask of hate. She lurched toward Charlotte and spit on the front of her dress. "You ought to be ashamed of yourself," she said.

Ten days later Charlotte flew to Jacksonville and drove out to Raiford to pick Ritter up. She parked her car and met him at the security station. The weather was stifling, humid enough to make time stand still. Ritter didn't seem overjoyed or even particularly happy. He blinked and squinted at the first daylight he'd seen in years. They didn't give him a suit, just a pair of jeans and a T-shirt. He carried everything he owned in a small plastic bag.

Charlotte tried to be more cheerful than she felt. Her initial excitement had worn off, as everything does. She still had to decide what to do with her life. Ritter couldn't help her with that.

Before long they were cruising toward Jacksonville on the blacktop road she had driven before. She glanced in the rear view mirror, half-expecting to see the red pickup speeding up to run her off the road.

"So is it done, then?" Ritter asked.

"What do you mean?"

"Did the judge sign the order?"

"Yes, he did," she assured him with a bright smile. "You're home free."

"They can't undo it, or have me tried again?"

"No, of course not," she laughed, a little less brightly. "Why do you ask?"

He stared out the window, looking away from her into the tall trees, studying the trees and the sultry rays of sunlight that probed the spaces between them, as if his mind, like the red pickup, might escape down one of the dirt roads that branched off into the woods. "The man on the video," he said without turning around. "That wasn't Craft."

Part III: Victory

"We skeptics have our enemies, our Satans who undermine our doubting and plant seeds of faith in the most cunning places."

— Irvin D. Yalom, *When Nietzsche Wept.*

24.

No, of course it wasn't Craft. The man who blew his brains out in that video was an alcoholic loser named Kevin McNally, and you're the only one who knows he wasn't Craft. You and I, rather; it's our little secret, a common bond that will keep us from drifting apart. I've done everything in my power to keep you alive. I hope you appreciate that. If it makes you feel any better, McNally was himself a murderer, as he once confessed to me. He had to be sacrificed, a life for a life, to keep you on the planet a while longer. You still have some lessons to learn before you can be released.

Now that you're out of prison, maybe you could go easy on the innocence theme. We're all innocent, aren't we, when you come down to it? There's nothing either good or bad but thinking makes it so. No good, no evil — I agree with you about that. So don't blame me for your crimes and misfortunes. Nobody can make you do anything you don't want to do. You create the devil you don't believe in and then succumb to his temptations. As for the other fellow — I don't believe in him either, so don't think that's what this is all about. Out here in the world you'll be on your own. Things aren't black and white, the way they are on death row; they're ambiguous, indeterminate, hard to grasp. You're going to wish you believed in something. Eventually you'll be searching high and low for me, but you won't find me.

I don't exist, remember?

25

Charlotte gave Ritter a hundred dollars and put him on a plane to New York. The money would buy him a couple of meals and bus fare to the halfway house where he was to live in Queens; after that he'd be on his own. Like any ex-prisoner, especially one released from death row, he was detached, distrustful, anxious about venturing back outside. And he faced the additional burden of knowing that his exoneration had been a hoax, facilitated by the murder of a stranger. At the hearing, when the video began playing on the screen, he immediately saw the horrible truth: Craft was not Craft — and worse, Craft was not dead. He was still alive and he'd shown that he would go to any length, even making an innocent man kill himself, to get Ritter out of prison. What new deceptions and tortures waited for him on the outside?

There was very little out there for him, as it happened. He had no family; even his miserable uncle had passed away. Kathryn refused to see him, and Doug had threatened him with prosecution if he went near his kids (one of whom, according to Doug, wasn't even his). The academic world wanted nothing more to do with him; they probably would have liked him better if he'd been guilty. The only friend he had left was Tim Salis, who'd generously offered the use of his apartment while he was away for a summer theater festival. Ritter had politely declined. "I need to do this on my own," he told Tim. But then he asked himself: To do what? What was he supposed to do? After ten years on death row there wasn't enough left of him to do anything. No goals, no ego, no personality, no self to speak of. The life had been drained out of him, drop by drop, with only the last bitter taste remaining when the reprieve came. Charlotte didn't seem to like him; she tolerated him out of a sense of responsibility, like a dog she'd rescued from the pound. What he needed to do, whether he liked it or not, was to bring himself back to life. He had to rebuild himself one molecule at a time.

His room at the halfway house was practically identical to his cell on death row. What was the halfway house half way to? he wondered. In his case it was probably half way — meaning the rest of the way — to hell. He began every morning with an hour of calisthenics, which he'd never bothered with in prison. Why was it any less pointless now? What was he training for? Sometimes he thought lying on the bunk in his room was no different from lying on his bunk on death row. He studied the sky, which was all he could see through his window; there were no stars, thanks to the ambient light, and when he closed his eyes he could imagine, as he often did in prison, that he was alone in the universe. But at other times the experience was utterly different. To be alone in the universe and think yourself free is utterly different from being alone and knowing that you live in a cage. He thought about that often, meditated on it, for lack of anything better to do. Concrete and barbed wire — was that all that stood between him and freedom all those years? Or was there something more? Knowing that the door to his room was unlocked made his life almost seem worth living. But why?

He prowled the steamy August streets, rode the buses and subways, supposedly looking for work. Drank coffee in train stations, cheap bourbon in seedy bars. Talked to stray dogs and cats when they didn't run away. Avoided the eyes of women and the stares of children. As time went on he sensed a growing Zen-like strength in his detachment, as if the secret of non-being was almost in his grasp. As if, someday when he needed to, he could break rocks with his bare hands.

He knew better than to share that fantasy with the Ex-Offender Support Group he was required to join in order to live in the halfway house. The group met in a church basement and was led by a sixty-year-old priest called Father Al, who often reassured its members that he had seen everything. You could have boasted that you'd served time for the rape and massacre of a hundred disabled children and Father Al wouldn't have batted an eyelash; but Ritter, who never "shared" with the others, clearly rubbed him the wrong way. The other men confessed their crimes, their addictions, their abuse of their families; they paraded their remorse and their determination to turn their lives around, often crediting Jesus or God or Allah for leading them back on the right path. But they remained wary of Ritter, who never spoke about himself. They respected him because he'd been on death row, and he played his part well; but he felt like a fake. A fake criminal because he'd been released on the basis of innocence, a fake penitent because he'd never owned up to his crimes, a fake ex-offender because he'd never stopped being an offender. Unlike the others, he'd never really served his time. Only his guilt was real.

One evening after the meeting, Father Al asked Ritter to stay, leading him back to his cluttered office. "You never say anything in the group," he said, offering an uncomfortable chair. "Why not? I'm sure you have a story to tell that the others could benefit from."

"I'm afraid we don't have much in common."

The priest sat down at his desk and folded his hands in front of him. "This program won't help you if you hold yourself aloof from the others. A support group means all the members lean on each other. Everyone is stronger because he has the others to lean on. It's based on empathy and compassion."

"I spent ten years on death row."

"That must have been very traumatic and dehumanizing. And now you face a new challenge. The attitudes and behavior that ensure survival in prison — toughness, aloofness, distrust — don't do you much good on the outside. It's a kind of culture shock and it can be almost as traumatic as being incarcerated."

"I was in prison for a crime I didn't commit."

"You should talk about that in the group. The injustice of our justice system is a perennial theme for ex-offenders."

"But that's just it," Ritter shrugged. "I'm not an ex-offender because I was never an offender. I was innocent."

Father Al smiled the kind of wry, skeptical smile that priests do best. "I wish I had a nickel for every ex-offender who said that."

"No, I mean it. I was framed."

"What about your drug problem? Most ex-offenders—"

"I never had a drug problem."

"Alcohol?"

"Not really."

"So you're unique," Father Al said, his skepticism verging into sarcasm. "You're better than everybody else, you've never been guilty of anything, never had a drug problem, never abused your family. Just an average white guy who's been victimized by the legal system. Does that about sum it up?"

"I never said any of that."

"You did, in so many words." The priest stood up but kept his eyes down, fiddling with the clutter on his desk as if impatient for the meeting to end. "And on second thought I agree with you. It wouldn't do the others any good to hear you talk about yourself, and you're obviously not interested in them." He lifted his eyes and smiled at Ritter for the last time. "I'm going to ask you not to attend any more meetings."

From the moment Ritter's execution was halted, Kathryn and Doug began a new vigil: the anxious, determined struggle to keep him away from the kids. He had left messages on Kathryn's cell phone, tried to reach Doug at his office, loitered in front of their building until the doorman threatened to call the police. Kathryn knew it was only a matter of time before he would get a legal aid lawyer to sue them. She couldn't sleep and spent hours every day on the phone with her mother, which only made her more anxious. Doug was supportive but surprisingly detached. Conflict didn't bother him; he was used to dealing with lawyers and litigation in his business deals. He favored going to court to obtain a protective order, but their attorney cautioned against aggressive tactics that might alienate a judge.

They joined Tim for dinner in the same quiet restaurant where they'd met the night before the scheduled execution. Same booth, same flickering candlelight, even the same waitress. But this time the atmosphere was more tense. Tim was the only one who showed the least bit of sympathy for Ritter.

"I don't care what the lawyer says," Doug said. "No judge is going to let that ex-con spend time with our kids."

Tim couldn't help smiling. "Chris isn't your typical ex-con, Doug. He's innocent, remember?"

"There's nothing innocent about him," Kathryn said. "Even if he didn't kill that prostitute, he'd be just as depraved as he was before he was arrested."

"Unless you think ten years on death row has improved his character," Doug said.

"Some people find Jesus in prison," Tim suggested with an impish smile.

"Then I hope Jesus tells him to stay the hell away from our kids."

"If not Jesus," Tim added, "let's hope he can find *something* to believe in. For Chris that would be a first."

"I'll take the kids to China before I let him get near them," Kathryn said.

"I'm renting a house in the Berkshires for the summer," Tim said. "Maybe I can convince him to stay up there until everybody calms down."

Kathryn's eyes flashed. "We're not calm enough for you?"

"No, no, it's not that," Tim stammered. "It's just — Chris has to get his feet back on the ground, figure out how to live in this world. Don't you think we should help him with that?"

In planning her return to Philadelphia, Charlotte had expected to resume her law practice, spend time with her mom, and clean up the mess in her apartment. What was supposed to be a two-week pro bono assignment had consumed two months and changed her life forever. Finding Kevin McNally's body and watching him die again and again on the video had been traumatic enough, but the revelation that he wasn't Craft had unnerved her and demolished every lesson she thought she'd learned from the experience. Before that she liked to say the case had restored her faith in the law, if not in the human race; now she felt equally sickened by both, and tinged with the same evil that Ritter had wrestled with for so many years. Double jeopardy might protect him, but it wouldn't protect her. She had perpetrated a fraud on the court — inadvertently, though no one would believe that. If the truth came out, she would lose her license and probably her freedom. And she had no doubt that the truth would be revealed, in a manner that would inflict as much suffering on Ritter and herself as possible. After all, Craft was still out there.

She'd come to like Ritter more after the reprieve. He was gentler, less cynical, as if maybe someday he would become human again. She couldn't blame him for not telling her the truth about the video until his exoneration was final. She wished he hadn't told her at all, but she trusted him more because he did. They talked regularly on the phone. She tried to help him readjust, without sounding like a social worker or someone in his ex-offender group. But sooner or later, all their conversations came back to one terrifying theme: Craft was still out there.

"Are you going to look for him?" she asked Ritter.

"I don't need to. He'll find me."

"Aren't you afraid of him?"

"If he wanted me dead, he would have let me get my lethal injection."

"Unless...." She remembered what Andy Wagner had said when she questioned him in the high school parking lot.

"Unless what?"

Unless he's saving you for something a little more cruel and unusual. "Never mind."

For her the punishment began a few days later, when the threatening phone calls started again. The caller — it was the same indistinct male voice she'd come to dread — identified himself sometimes as Craft, sometimes as McNally, and his message was always the same. She had helped a murderer to escape, and even if she'd been able to block Ritter's punishment, she wouldn't escape her own. Did she remember the explosion at Sol Levy's office? The next time that happened, it would be her pieces they'd be picking out of the rubble.

She called to warn Sol. "I thought you ought to know," she told him. "The guy said, 'the next time that happens' — after asking if I remembered the explosion at your office."

"Charlotte," Sol said after a pause, "I think it's you he's threatening. Not me."

"You're probably right."

"I can't imagine why he's doing this. Isn't the Ritter case over? Didn't Ritter's nemesis Craft blow his brains out on prime time TV?"

Charlotte hesitated. She couldn't tell Sol the truth about McNally and Craft.

"If you believe that," Sol added in an undertone.

"What do you mean?"

"Charlotte," he said, "you did a great job representing Ritter. I want to congratulate you on that, if I haven't already. But I still count myself as a skeptic. I still think Ritter's a psychopath, and I still think he's guilty."

"Then you think McNally was some kind of impostor?"

"Maybe he wasn't the real Craft. Maybe there's never been a real Craft."

26.

Who am I?

I am the Other you loathe and fear but can't live without. We're bound together in creation like prisoners on a chain gang. You eluded the executioner at Raiford, but you can't escape from me, or from yourself. You will always be what you are.

Am I insane? Call me insane if you will, but don't call me evil. In your universe, evil doesn't exist; even malignity is motiveless. Animals share your materialistic worldview, and the devil has no power over them. You must have some intuition of the good before evil can tempt and defeat you. To be truly evil, you must have a refined moral sensibility; you must be a person of the highest ideals.

27

Ritter walked the streets, mostly in the seedier parts of Queens, away from the money-fueled frenzy of Manhattan and the yuppie dominions of Brooklyn. He sat on park benches as long as the police would let him, drinking pint bottles of bourbon out of brown paper bags. He stared at women — young mothers with strollers, buxom nannies, thirtysomethings in running suits — and lowered his eyes if they glanced in his direction. (In those moments, with a twinge of embarrassment, he often thought of Charlotte.) His thoughts ran in circles like greyhounds at a dog track, breathless and noisy but not sure just what they were chasing. One thing was certain: he had to find some way to make a living. In a desperate, self-destructive moment he applied for a job bussing tables at the cafeteria where McNally had worked, but the next morning he was too ashamed of himself, or too afraid, to show up for work. Instead he took a job at a cafeteria three blocks away, wondering when Craft would catch up with him. He called a few of his old colleagues at the university, who all promised to help, though he never heard from them again. It occurred to him that he might be able to find a research job if he could revive his computer skills, so he went to a local branch of the public library every day and sat with the rest of the homeless guys, surfing hungrily for the knowledge he used to have at his fingertips. He tried to avoid reading about himself, but sometimes the temptation got the better of him. The whole saga was a Google search away (he even rated a Wikipedia article): his arrest, his trial, his years as the most hated man in America, and with lesser prominence, his exoneration, presented as a quirky factoid like a one-armed violinist or a woman giving birth to sextuplets. The only thing out of his

past that interested him was the fate of Teague, whose last round
of appeals was spinning toward the inevitable crash landing. A firm
execution date had been set for October 15.

His mood of detachment protected him on the mean streets
where he spent his time, fending off winos and hookers and drug
dealers and even cops, who saw a broken man that was better left
alone. One night on his way back to the halfway house he was
cornered under the elevated train by a gang of teenagers who
demanded his money but would have settled for his life. The
money he couldn't afford to lose; the life he had scant use for,
since at the deepest levels of memory and imagination he had
already lost it. He'd been strapped to a gurney and wheeled in to
face the executioner, who gave him a taste of the lethal draft that
would lead him down to death. Consciousness ceased: in effect he
was dead. And after waking up, he knew he would never spend
another moment in fear of death. He had nothing to fear in this
world. A cold wind must have blown off him on that hot summer
night when the teenagers cornered him under the elevated train
platform. He laughed at them and stared them down. He pushed
his way through them and they stood aside in fear and amazement.
But when he was safe in his room he broke into a sweat. What had
given him the power to do that? Was it courage, or insanity? Had
the last ten years turned him into the psychopath his accusers
claimed he was?

The calls could come at any hour. Charlotte didn't answer them,
but the man always left a message she had to listen to in case his
threats became more specific. Anxiety and migraine attacks kept
her from concentrating on her work. She stayed with her mom,
who was recuperating well, and spent hours on the phone with
Ritter and Sol. All of them encouraged her to take some time off.

She was still struggling with her career, traumatized by what she'd experienced and disturbed by the hostility and distrust that lingered between Ritter and Sol. Her boss approved an unpaid leave of absence and she decided to spend it in New York, where she could lose herself in shopping and museums and a little legal sleuthing. The mystery of Craft, she sensed, could be solved if she knew more about Kevin McNally and Helene Varga. She'd spoken to Tim a few times and liked him more and more. He worried about Ritter as much as she did, and about her, especially when she told him about the phone calls. She could have his apartment all to herself while he was up in the Berkshires.

Once in New York she found herself enjoying Ritter's company more than she thought she would. He still wasn't quite human, but he seemed to be heading in the right direction. Together they walked up Fifth Avenue and visited Central Park Zoo. Charlotte had almost forgotten that Ritter was a zoologist; she was amazed at his wealth of knowledge and excited when he offered to take her to the Museum of Natural History, even if she'd have to pay for it herself. She sympathized with his struggle to see his kids, whom Kathryn shielded from him as if he were a leper; it was a struggle 'he had no hope of winning without a lawyer he couldn't afford. He never cursed Kathryn, but reserved his harshest words for Doug Leipzig, whom he hated as much as Craft (even suggesting, one afternoon over a beer at the Blarney Stone, that they might be one and the same). Sometimes she felt Ritter was flirting with her, or at least treating her a little more gallantly than she would have liked to be treated by a man who'd spent the last ten years in prison. She was both flattered and annoyed that he seemed jealous of her budding relationship with Tim. "He's old enough to be your father," Ritter cautioned her when she told him Tim was returning to the city for a couple of days. "True," she said. "But then again, so are you."

The phone calls interrupted every quiet moment they managed to share. One of the nights when Tim was in town, the three of them had dinner at an Indian restaurant in Brooklyn Heights. Charlotte described her trip to the Cloisters museum in upper Manhattan; Tim touted the success of his production of *Measure for Measure* in the Berkshires. Even Ritter seemed engaged and relaxed, as if he might actually be enjoying himself. They had finished their curry and were digging into scoops of cardamom ice cream when a metallic melody jangled over the table.

Charlotte stared at her phone. "It's him."

"Aren't you going to answer it?" Tim asked.

"He'll leave a message."

She waited until the phone signaled that a new message had arrived. Her face tightened with fear as she listened. "My hourly two minutes of hate."

Tim reached for the phone. "Could I listen to that?" She handed him the phone and he held it to his ear. "This is horrible," he said. "Who is it?"

"I wish I knew," she said. "I've been getting these calls off and on since I went down to Florida in May. Usually he threatens to kill me."

Tim pushed the phone toward Ritter. "Listen to this."

Ritter answered without picking it up. "I've listened to some of these messages before," he said. "Some evil sicko, obviously." He had to be careful not to say it could be Craft. Craft was dead.

"But who? Do you have any idea?"

"It's not like there's any shortage of evil sickos walking around," Charlotte said. "Either here or in Florida."

"But why is this particular one threatening you?" Tim asked. "And how did he get your cell number?"

"I don't know. He also knew where I was staying in St. Augustine."

Ritter glanced around as if he thought the call had come from within the restaurant. "Sounds like Sol Levy," he said, glancing back at Tim. "Or your pal Doug Leipzig."

"Don't be ridiculous."

"Or maybe Kathryn's father. Charlotte gave them her number."

"Come on, Chris!" Tim laughed. "You've been in jail too long. You think everybody's evil."

"Whatever," Ritter smiled. He might have said: "Yes, I *have* been in jail too long. And I know everybody's evil." But what he said was: "There's not much we can do about it, is there?"

Tim bristled at his resignation. "So you're just waiting for him to carry out his threats? Charlotte's a sitting duck."

"Tim," Charlotte said, "I'm OK. You don't need—"

"Chris, don't you think you should try to protect her? I mean, look what she's done for you."

Ritter smiled again, this time a little sadly. "Charlotte," he said, "you don't have to stay in New York. At least not for my sake, if that's why you're here. It doesn't matter."

She lowered her eyes and pretended to be concerned with her ice cream. After what she and Ritter had been through, it hurt to be so lightly dismissed.

Tim, who must have perceived this reaction, reached out and touched her hand. "I can see you two are a couple of wrecks," he said. "Why don't you both come up to the Berkshires for a few days? You can stay at my house on the lake. I'll be at the theater most of the time and you'll have the place all to yourselves."

The incident in the restaurant changed everything for Ritter. He'd been playing a waiting game, expecting Craft to make an appearance when it suited his purposes. Now, as he thought about the threatening calls, he realized that Craft was using Charlotte as his cat's paw, tormenting her to lure him out of his passivity. And he was ashamed — and a little jealous, though he wouldn't have admitted it — when he considered that it was Tim who'd grasped that when he suggested she leave New York. He didn't want her to feel unwelcome or unappreciated, but he did care about her safety. The next day she made things worse when she told him she'd launched her own investigation. The McNally inquest had raised more questions than it answered, she told him, especially in light of the suicide video. She wanted to find the truth about McNally's claim that he'd been a graduate student and met Helene Varga at an office where she worked as a receptionist.

"What difference does it make?" Ritter asked. "Everything McNally said in the video was probably a lie. We know he was a fake."

"I want to find out how he knew Craft," Charlotte said. "And I want to find out more about Helene."

"Why?"

"The one thing we know about Craft is that he knew McNally and Helene."

Charlotte had a law school classmate who worked in the Manhattan DA's office. She told her friend she was working on a death penalty case and asked if she could have access to the records database. They set her up in a cubicle with a terminal and she spent most of an afternoon researching the dozens of Kevin McNallys who'd found their way into the city's police and court records. The one she was looking for — the one who'd been featured in the recent inquest — had only one blot on his record, a dispute with a neighbor about a dog. But "Helene Varga" was a much more unusual name, and when Charlotte searched her records she hit pay dirt. Twelve years earlier, about a year before the woman's death, she'd been arrested on drug and prostitution charges, which were dropped before she came to trial.

The arresting officer was Alex Lopez.

28.

"You've got to understand," Ritter told Charlotte. "Alex Lopez should be considered armed and dangerous. He comes from a very tough background and he was in the Marines. You don't want to mess with him."

"Something's been bothering me about him," Charlotte said. "When I walked into that loft and found McNally's body, I called Alex because I needed help getting the video to Florida in time to stop the execution. He was there in fifteen minutes, even though he's based in the Bronx. How did he get there so fast? And why did he slip away so quickly?"

"Maybe McNally didn't shoot himself. Would Alex have had time to shoot him and duck out before you got there?"

"I'm sure he would have."

"Listen, Charlotte. I can protect myself but I can't protect both of us."

"I don't need your protection."

"You've got to get out of the city. We were planning to go up to the Berkshires anyway. Why don't you go on up and I'll be up in a couple of days?"

"Why don't you come with me? What are you going to be doing here?"

"I'm meeting Alex tomorrow and anything can happen."

Ritter had arranged to meet Lopez in a bar near Penn Station called The Tatler. It was the sort of place lawyers take their secretaries after work: faux elegant, predatory, with shadowy booths along the wall. A few losers who didn't even rate secretaries sat hunched over the bar, washing down drafts of Sam Adams as they fixed their eyes on a Mets game. Alex Lopez sat alone at the end of the bar, shunning the Mets as he nursed a glass of amber beer. He looked like a loser himself, with his receding hairline and the panda-like paunch bulging under his cheap suit. When Ritter swiveled onto the barstool beside him, he acted as if he'd never seen him before.

"Come in here often?" Ritter asked.

"Often enough," Lopez said. "Not usually to meet another guy." Without being asked, the bartender set up two shots and two beers in front of them. Lopez raised his shot glass in a quick salute and emptied it in one gulp. "You're looking relaxed, Chris. Considering where you spent the last dozen years."

"You got something against Florida?"

Lopez shrugged. "At least you were in a gated community."

Ritter drank his whisky — it was cheap bar bourbon that burned his throat — and chased it down with a sip of beer.

"What's on your mind, Chris?" Lopez asked.

"Helene Varga."

"I can understand that." Lopez turned to face him for the first time. "How'd you ever get that guy McNally to confess and shoot himself? Did your hot lawyer set that up for you? She sure was Johnny on the spot."

"So were you, I heard."

"Just doing my job."

"You got there sort of fast, I heard, even though it was out of your jurisdiction. Left in a hurry, too."

Lopez turned back around and signaled to the bartender for more drinks. "What's on your mind, Chris?"

"You knew Helene. You arrested her on drug and prostitution charges about a year before you arrested me for killing her. But you let on like you didn't know her."

"We don't go out of our way to educate murderers about the life stories of their victims."

"But I wonder, why were those charges dropped before she came to trial? She didn't even have to cop a plea. I wonder why."

"She was a cooperative witness."

"Very cooperative, I suspect."

They sat quietly while the bartender brought the next round of drinks and glided away.

"What are you getting at, Ritter?"

"I'll tell you." Ritter picked up his beer and took a sip. "Any prostitute who gets arrested can offer sex in exchange for dropping the charges, but Helene faced serious drug charges, so she had to offer more. I think she offered up her number one customer. Me."

"She felt trapped. Off the record."

"What does that mean, 'Off the record?'"

"It means if you tell anybody we talked about this, I'll deny it and probably kill you."

Ritter knew he meant it. "Why did she feel trapped?"

"Because she was trapped between you and this guy Craft who was paying her to have sex with you. You didn't know that. You thought she was your girlfriend or whatever. But Craft was paying, so she felt caught in the middle."

"So she asked you to help her."

"Right."

"And you agreed because you hated me."

"Wrong. I didn't hate you yet."

"Anyway you liked the idea of her betraying me the way I betrayed you and your family."

"Couldn't have put it better myself."

Lopez was through his next shot and half his beer, and his tone was getting belligerent. He waved to the bartender for more.

"You knew a lot about me," Ritter went on. "A lot more than Helene did, including the fact that I was sort of famous. So you suggest a way she can get free of her trap: Come to me and say she wants out, ask for enough money to go a long way away. If I don't pay up, go public with everything she's got on me. Was it your idea to put it all in the safe deposit box? Maybe you helped her with that so you could make sure there was nothing in there about you."

Lopez kept his eyes down as the bartender set up the next round. "You're not drinking?"

"I'm drinking." Ritter downed his shot and waited for the bartender to disappear. "What did Helene tell you about Craft?" he asked in a quiet voice. "When did he hire her?"

"She told me she was originally hired by a guy named Doug."

Ritter felt his breath tightening. "My ex-wife's current husband."

"I wasn't going to mention that."

"Thanks."

Lopez kept his voice low as he filled in the details. "She met Doug in an office where she worked as the receptionist. She was always sort of a whore, I guess. She started sleeping with Doug, probably for money, or not, until his girlfriend caught them together. The girlfriend broke up with him over it, and he was so pissed he wouldn't go out with Helene again. Sounds a lot like the McNally video, doesn't it?"

"Except McNally didn't mention Doug."

Lopez nodded and went on: "No, but Helene did when she was telling me about it. Doug felt guilty about breaking up with her so he sent some business her way. He paid her to give you an envelope full of money and lure you with sex. "

"Did she say anything about Craft?"

"After the night she gave you the money, Doug never contacted her directly again. But she started hearing from this guy named Craft who said he was working for him."

Craft working for Doug — Ritter felt a little chill when Lopez said that. "How did she describe Craft?"

"Tall, heavy guy with a goatee. He knew a lot about you and your work — must've got it from Doug — and he coached her on what to say to you. He had her meet you at the Four Seasons and from then on she just did whatever he paid her to do."

"And by the time you met her, she desperately wanted out. Were you in love with her?"

"She had a major drug habit," Lopez hesitated, "and she needed money. Apart from that, all she wanted was to escape. She wanted to go down to the islands and get lost."

Lopez picked up his shot glass but didn't raise it to his lips. His belligerence had dissolved into uncertainty and sadness. He turned to face Ritter and in his brown eyes Ritter saw the boy he'd known so many years before. "Yeah, I was in love with her," he said. "I wanted to help her."

Ritter gave him a chance to explain. "So you encouraged her to blackmail me?"

"No, that was her idea. She was all set to blackmail you before I met her. What I came up with was a better scheme, I thought. I told her, why not get money out of both of them? Ritter and Craft. Play both ends against the middle."

"It's what got her killed."

Lopez looked away. "I'll never forgive myself for that. But then I was the one who was trapped. I couldn't let it come out that I had anything to do with Helene. I couldn't let my wife find out I was sleeping with a whore."

"So you let me go to prison without bringing any of this up."

"I was sure you killed her. I still am."

"You killed her yourself."

He spun toward Ritter with hate in his eyes, knocking over an empty shot glass with his trembling hand. "Why would I do that? I was crazy about her."

"To get back at me. To send me to the death house."

"I didn't kill her." Lopez stood up uncertainly and groped in his pocket. Ritter hoped it wasn't for his gun.

"Were you in touch with Craft after she was killed?" he asked.

Lopez pulled out his wallet and fumbled inside it. "I was never in touch with Craft."

"Did you send the new evidence down to Florida? The place mat, the earring—"

"No. Your lawyer asked me that. No."

"I think you followed her down to Florida and killed her."

Lopez yanked a fistful of bills from his wallet and tossed them on the bar. "If you really didn't kill her," he said before he headed for the door, "then you know what I think? I think you should talk to Doug."

29

Ritter met Charlotte at a White Castle on 8th Avenue, where paper-thin hamburgers had evolved into sliders while he was in prison. They ordered a dozen and sat on plastic chairs that reminded Ritter of the furniture in the death house. "Doug set the whole thing up," he told her. "He'd met Helene in the office where he worked the summer before. I remember him talking about that."

"She was the receptionist," Charlotte said. "That was in the McNally video."

"Everything she did — probably including sleeping with him — he paid her for. When his girlfriend broke up with him, he hired Craft to continue what he'd started with me."

"This is a new twist," Charlotte said. "The idea that Craft wasn't acting on his own."

"I know. I'm not sure I believe it."

Ritter tried calling Doug's office a dozen times but could never get through to him. Finally his secretary politely threatened to notify the police if he didn't stop calling. The next morning he waited under an awning across from the Leipzigs' apartment building on the East Side. After half an hour Doug stepped out in his Italian suit and the doorman waved to a cab, which stopped instantly in the middle of the street, and when Doug climbed inside, Ritter darted forward, opened the opposite door and slipped in beside him.

Doug held his ground. "Get out of here before I call the cops."

"I'm not going to kill you," Ritter said. "I'm not a murderer, you know."

"How do I know what you are?"

"I'm the father of your children, for one thing."

"We're not going to discuss that. You have to go through my lawyer."

"That's not what I'm here to talk to you about."

"What's this about, then?"

"I spoke with your old girlfriend Alana."

"Really?" Doug missed a few beats as he adjusted his face not to show his consternation. "How's Alana doing?"

"She's doing fine. She told me about you and Helene."

"Helene?"

"You're a piece of work, Doug. Always have been."

They rode in silence down 79th Street and turned southbound on FDR Drive, which was clogged with traffic. It would be a fifteen minute drive to Doug's office near Wall Street, giving him plenty of time to play dumb, avoid eye contact, feign anger and spin lies—and maybe, in spite of all that, come a little closer to the truth. "You never mentioned that you knew Helene," Ritter said. "I was on trial for my life and you never mentioned that you knew her. Not only knew her. Slept with her."

Doug gazed across the East River at the red and white Con Ed smokestacks in Long Island City as if they were one of the Seven Wonders of the World. "It was ten or twelve years before you got arrested. Why would I bring it up?"

"Well, you introduced us, didn't you?"

More silence, layered over honking horns, police sirens, and the driver's radio with its cryptic bursts of static to which he seemed to attach deep meaning.

"I know all about it, Doug," Ritter said. "You got Helene to give me the thousand dollars."

Doug turned to face him for the first time. "I was doing you a favor."

"Was Kathryn in on it? How about Tim?"

"Tim tried to talk me out of it. Kathryn didn't know anything about it. I hope we can keep it that way."

Ritter laughed. "Now you're asking me for favors?"

"You were desperate for the money, remember?"

"Getting me involved with a prostitute? That's your idea of doing a friend a favor?"

"It was just a joke. You started it with your stupid ad."

"You knew what you were doing, Mr. Art of the Deal."

"What did I get out of it?"

"You got Kathryn, which was what you wanted. I'd say it was one of your more successful transactions."

Doug's face reddened and he turned away. "I was in love with Kathryn. I still am."

"So you paid Helene to lure me with money and sex, and Craft to lure me with power, until Kathryn turned against me—"

"That was your own doing."

"And when Helene wanted out, you killed her and framed me for the murder."

Doug made a show of struggling with his fury. "You're nuts!" he shouted. "I didn't kill anybody. I broke it off with Helene right after she met you at Dominick's. Alana caught us together and wouldn't have any more to do with me. By then I was in love with Kathryn anyway. I never wanted to see Helene again."

"No, after that you let Craft do your dirty work."

"I never knew anybody named Craft."

"Then, when I was arrested, you paid Sol Levy to lose the case."

"I paid your attorney fees, for Christ's sake! Over fifty thousand dollars out of my own pocket! I can't help it if he lost."

The taxi swung off the expressway just before the Brooklyn Bridge. "Take a left on Pearl," Doug barked at the driver. The driver turned sharply left, throwing the two passengers on top of each other. They pushed each other out of the clench and huddled in their corners.

"You and Kathryn stole everything I had and spent part of it to keep me in jail," Ritter said. "But execution was a little more than you'd bargained for, wasn't it? So at the last minute you started sending the missing evidence down to Sol. The place mat, the second earring—"

"And then what? I blew my brains out in a loft in Brooklyn?"

"No, you got somebody else to do that."

"Right here, driver. Just pull over anywhere." The cab stopped at the corner of Pearl and Wall and both men climbed out. "I'm known around here as a guy who can get things done," Doug said with a forced smile. "But that one's a little beyond my powers, Chris. There are limits to what money can buy."

Are there really? Ritter wondered as Doug stalked away. The encounter with Doug had left his head buzzing with violent scenarios. He wished he was still under sentence of death so he could do anything he wanted. Doug deserved to be gunned down on the street. He found a bench on the Wall Street pier and watched the commuters marching in from the ferries and water taxis. He tried to reach Charlotte. When she didn't answer her phone, he dialed Alex Lopez.

"You saw the McNally video," he said to Lopez after they'd exchanged their mutually distrustful greetings. "Was there anything on it that contradicted what Helene told you about Craft? Anything important that was left out?"

"I can't think of anything," Lopez said.

"Doug admits what you told me: that he hired Helene to give me the thousand dollars. But he says that was the end of it."

"That's not what Helene said. She said she kept taking orders from Craft and Doug paid for it. "

"Did she say Doug?"

Lopez hesitated. "Somebody was paying for it. Craft didn't try to hide that. She assumed it was Doug, but I don't think she really knew. All she knew was that the guy Craft was working for hated you."

"Hated me?

"Yeah, I remember her saying that. He hated you for ruining his life."

Ruining his life. The phrase echoed in Ritter's mind. He'd ruined plenty of people's lives, but there was only one who had confronted him with those words: Andy Wagner.

"The high school biology teacher," Charlotte said.

They'd met for coffee at a Starbucks in Chelsea, near Tim's apartment where she was staying. "He's a high school teacher now," Ritter said, "but he was a professor until I ruined his life." He burned his tongue on a scalding sip of coffee. "Which I really did, by the way."

"Could Wagner be Craft? "

Ritter shook his head. "They do look alike — Craft could be Wagner's evil twin, or vice versa — but they're not the same person. I knew both of them."

"Maybe they're brothers. Maybe Craft told Wagner about what he was doing for Doug, and when Doug wanted out, he kept it up and Wagner took over the payments."

"That would explain how Craft knew so much about me and my work. I never understood that."

Outside Starbucks, pedestrians surged around them and spilled into the street. Ritter wanted to walk Charlotte back to Tim's apartment, but she wouldn't let him. "I think I can get there on my own," she laughed. She was beautiful when she laughed, but her laughter scared him. He'd learned to live with his own fear, but this was something new: he was afraid for Charlotte. She could so easily be lost in the pitiless chaos that was New York. "You've got to listen to me, Charlotte," he said. "There's something bad going on here. Alex is lying, Doug is lying. I don't trust them or anybody else. Tomorrow I'm going to look for Wagner and he could be dangerous. You need to get out of New York."

30.

"The Devil's Chaplain" — *it must have been unnerving to hear your fellow inmates use that phrase. Was Dawkins's book in the prison library? Or were they aware of what Darwin had said — "What a book a devil's chaplain might write on the clumsy, wasteful, blundering low and horridly cruel works of nature!"—? Darwin had observed a billion years of predation and mass extinction in the fossil record; he hadn't seen the human horror show of the twentieth century or the twenty-first. If he had, his devil's chaplain would have been busier still, chronicling the low and horridly cruel works of man. To call them clumsy, wasteful and blundering would have been shamefully dishonest, even for a devil's chaplain — because man, unlike nature, intends what he does, and most of what he does is evil. Do you agree with that? Or do you still think there's no such thing as good and evil? Are you still one of the few who can look the truth in the eye and not blink?*

31

Ritter had finally persuaded Charlotte to get out of New York. She took the Greyhound bus to Stockbridge, where Tim would pick her up, leaving her car for Ritter to drive up in a couple of days. He parked it in a garage near the halfway house and spent a restless night staring at the starless sky. At 6:00 a.m. he retrieved the car and retraced Charlotte's trip to Nutley High School in New Jersey, where he hoped to find Wagner. As he arrived in the parking lot, some teachers were weaving their way through the parked cars toward the entrance security gate. Wagner was not among them, and fifteen minutes later he still hadn't appeared. Last to arrive was a white-haired man in a tweed jacket who looked like a sixty-year-old Harry Potter. "Excuse me," Ritter said, stepping toward him as he climbed out of his car. "I'm looking for a friend of mine."

"And you are?"

"Sorry," Ritter smiled, extending his hand. "Chris Ritter."

The man nodded but didn't shake his hand. "Dr. Ash Brown. Chairman of the English Department. How can I help you?"

"Do you know Andy Wagner?"

"Biology, isn't it? Looks like Mephistopheles?"

Ritter hesitated as he tried to place the allusion.

"You know. The Devil in Goethe's *Faust?*"

"Oh, yeah," Ritter stammered, suddenly queasy. "That's Andy."

Dr. Brown glanced around the deserted parking lot and stepped toward the security gate. "He must have arrived early. I'd suggest you check at the office."

Ritter checked at the office. The secretary informed him that Mr. Wagner would not be coming in that day. He had called in sick.

In Manhattan that afternoon, Ritter headed for the public library to do some internet research. He'd never read *Faust,* but he had the impression that it was about a man who'd sold his soul to the Devil. In fact, as he learned, in Goethe's play the bargain between Faust and Mephistopheles was more a bet than a sale. In Christopher Marlowe's version, the learned Dr. Faustus actually sells his soul to the Devil and seals the deal with his own blood. Reading this on the screen brought back the sinking feeling Ritter had experienced that morning when the English teacher compared Wagner to Mephistopheles. He might as well have been talking about Craft. Could that have been a coincidence? Was there something in those plays that could lead him to Craft?

The McNally transcript was the only written record he had of Craft's words. Ritter began typing it into Google, in hopes that the search would reveal what he and everyone else had failed to recognize. And with mounting excitement and dread he starting finding phrases in the transcript that led to Marlowe's *Doctor Faustus:*

"I gave you Helen first."

"Where we are is Hell, and where Hell is, there must we be."

"The stars move still, time runs, the clock will strike, the Devil will come."

When Craft put those phrases in McNally's mouth, he borrowed them from Marlowe. Ritter kept typing in searches until he'd found every production of *Doctor Faustus* in the past twenty years and every actor who'd ever played Mephistopheles. Sometimes there was a picture of the actor, and after an hour he found what he was searching for: a picture of Craft in the role of Mephistopheles, some twenty years earlier, at the Shakespeare festival in Stratford, Ontario. The actor's name was Hal

Morgenstern and what Ritter found was his obituary, which said he'd committed suicide around the time Ritter was arrested. The role of Mephistopheles had been something of a specialty for him. He'd played it in Stratford, San Francisco, Atlanta, Houston, Chicago. And he'd played it in New York.

At GlobeSpace, the theater founded and directed by Tim Salis.

32

You'll be coming to look for me soon, Chris. I can feel it in my bones. You've searched everywhere, except possibly in the soul you don't think you have. Questioned the usual suspects — Alex Lopez, Doug, Kathryn (by the way, have you considered Kathryn's parents? They hate your guts) — and you'll be coming after me next. I'm surprised you haven't already done that. Is it because of Charlotte? You like her, and I don't blame you. She's a very nice lady. It's just a shame she got mixed up with you.

She's with me now. Tonight she thinks I'm taking her to see Measure for Measure. *It's a play about morality — as I've explained to Charlotte — and its lesson is: Sometimes you have to do evil to spare others from a greater evil. The magistrate Angelo asks a pious young woman, Isabella, to do something evil — have illicit sex with him — in order to avoid a greater evil, her brother's execution. She refuses. Is she virtuous for that reason? Or merely vain and heartless? You could argue that Angelo is more virtuous than she is. At the end he not only accepts his punishment, he begs for it. He embraces, even loves, his fate.*

Who am I?

I am the fantastical duke of dark corners, who manipulates the characters' fates from behind the scenes. I am Angelo, the man who sacrifices himself by becoming evil to permit the salvation of others. I am the spirit that negates, that incarnates itself as evil so others can see the good in the world. A Christ of Evil, as it were.

And I've been doing it all for you.

33.

Ritter could feel a catastrophe unfolding inside him as he stared at the computer screen. A catastrophe of past, present and future, a slow motion upheaval of what had been, what was now and what would be. It was a déjà vu moment like no other, a vision of evil he'd foreseen in death row premonitions and alcoholic nightmares in New York, a shadow that fled the light. Now it rose before him, horrifying and unavoidable: The man behind Craft was Tim Salis — had he suspected it? had he known it all along? — and Charlotte had fallen into his power.

He grabbed his phone and dialed her number. There was no answer, no connection: the automated voice said her mailbox was full. It was after 8:00 p.m. She was supposed to have reached Stockbridge at 5:15, to be met by Tim for an early dinner before seeing *Measure for Measure*. Maybe her cell phone was in a dead zone in those mountains, or maybe she'd turned it off during the performance. Ritter called again with the same result; then he dialed the theater and heard a recorded message that tonight's performance had been cancelled. He jumped in Charlotte's car and sped out of the city, following the expressways north to the Taconic Parkway. Two hours later the GPS led him to Tim's house, an elegant cottage surrounded by towering evergreens. There were lights on inside, but no one was home. Taped to the door he found a note: "Sorry to have missed you, Chris. You'll find us at the theater."

The theater was ten miles away over dark, twisting roads. Ritter glided into the parking lot with his lights dimmed and ran to the entrance, where a door had been left ajar. The theater was dark but he could hear voices inside. Stepping through the lobby, he saw a stage dappled with spotlights as if a play was in progress. He padded down the aisle past rows of empty seats and saw Tim on the stage under a spotlight, sitting behind a long table with his hands folded in front of him. He wore a loose-fitting hooded cowl; the set suggested a medieval monastery. A dozen feet to the right, in front of the table, Ritter saw something he didn't recognize at first. With a start he realized it was Charlotte, tied to a chair with her hands behind her back and draped in a blanket. A gag was drawn tightly across her mouth; blood dripped down her chin. She looked half-conscious, as if she'd been tortured or beaten. Ritter rushed up the steps at the side of the stage.

Tim had picked up a gun, which he held pointed at Charlotte. "You'd better stay where you are, Chris," he said.

Ritter obeyed. "What are you doing? Put that gun down!"

"It's loaded, by the way" Tim's voice sounded friendly and unemotional, as if they were in New York discussing a menu. "And the safety is off."

Two other items stood out on the shadowy stage: a digital video camera on a tripod, with its recording light blinking, and a small table or pedestal on which lay a knife with a long, sharp blade. The pedestal stood under a spotlight about a dozen feet to his left, on the opposite side of the stage from Charlotte. Tim could have shot them both if Ritter made a move toward the knife.

Charlotte squirmed in her chair, grunting and shrieking through her gag and jerking her head from side to side, as if trying to warn Ritter to escape. It was all he could do to keep from rushing toward her. "What did you do to her?"

"Nothing so far," Tim said, leveling the gun at Charlotte's head. "But I'll shoot her if you don't stay right where you are."

"What is this? Some kind of crazy play you're putting on?"

"Yes, it's a play," Tim said, nodding proudly. "Not crazy, though. Possibly the greatest play of our time, of any time: the masterpiece I've been working on for almost twenty-five years. And it's all been for you, Chris. You're the only one who'll ever see a complete performance. Do you realize what a privilege that is? I gave important parts to Hal Morgenstern and Helene Varga and Kevin McNally, but they had to make early exits. And now Charlotte—"

She shrieked again, raging unintelligibly under her gag.

"What did you do to her?"

"Easy now!" Tim crooned, turning the gun in Ritter's direction. "We wouldn't want to see the stage littered with corpses before the last scene."

Ritter struggled to recapture the state of mind he'd achieved when the gang surrounded him under the subway platform in Queens: an intimation of detachment he'd honed in ten years on death row, a presence of mind that was the absence of mind. Tim Salis was insane, and he knew he had to humor him, had to keep him talking at all costs. He pointed toward the camera on the tripod. "Are you recording this, Tim?"

"Of course," Tim chuckled. "This isn't just a rehearsal. That's what McNally thought, you know, when he stuck that gun in his mouth and pulled the trigger. Just another rehearsal, only he didn't notice the gun was loaded. He thought he was going to star in an independent film."

"What is it, then?"

"It's the denouement. Last act, last scene. The grand finale."

Ritter forced a smile. "I can't wait to see how it ends."

"That's up to you," Tim smiled back. "Let me stop the action for a moment and explain your choices in how to play the last scene."

He stood up and gestured with the gun in his hand, swinging it around to aim at Ritter or Charlotte to illustrate the particular point he wanted to make. "You could turn around and drive back to

New York," he said, "in which case I will shoot Charlotte as soon as you leave. If you don't call the police, no one will ever know you were here. If you do, the world will learn that the McNally confession was fake. Maybe you'll go back to prison."

Ritter felt an overpowering anger and disgust welling up inside him as he listened to Tim discussing Charlotte's murder as if it were a bit of minor stage business. It brought back his last hours on death row, when men of high moral character made their preparations to kill him — they were professionals, all honorable men, who went about their business with the same quiet competence that Tim had cultivated as a director, rehearsing and explaining and justifying every step of the production — but now he was in danger of being overwhelmed by a righteous rage he'd never felt in prison, even when they were wheeling him in for his execution.

"On the other hand," Tim went on, "you could stay and end the play as a tragic hero. You see that knife on the pedestal? You could grab it and try to free her, or come after me with it. In either case I would shoot both of you. You first, then Charlotte."

The knife gleamed under the spotlight, its blade pointed away from Ritter, its black handle beckoning him to the desperate leap that Tim was tempting him with. Should he try it? The pedestal stood at least twelve feet to one side and another ten feet in front of Tim. Charlotte huddled on her chair at the opposite end of the stage. It would take a few seconds to run to the pedestal, grab hold of the knife, and leap across the table at Tim — and before he could get there he'd be dead.

"Now, before you decide," Tim said, "let's get Charlotte's point of view. She's a virtuous young woman who would do anything to save you, or almost anything. Just like Isabella in *Measure for Measure*. How would you like Chris to play the last scene, Charlotte?"

Instead of what Ritter expected — another outburst, warning him away — she lowered her eyes and remained silent.

"Ah!" Tim exclaimed. "She's telling you: Why not give it a try? Of course she has nothing to lose. You do, though. If you walk away, you'll still be alive."

Ritter felt his skin burning, his body twitching and twisting, as if he were being pulled apart with hot pincers. "You're evil."

Tim smiled, pointing the gun at his face. "There's no such thing as evil, remember?"

"You're insane, then."

The smile faded to a sneer. "Don't tell me what I am," Tim said. "I am not what I am."

Ritter heard the coldness in Tim's voice and his attempt at detachment failed him. Suddenly he wasn't a dead man, he was alive, with just enough presence of mind to know what he had to do.

He leaped to the pedestal, grabbed the knife and ran toward Charlotte, flinging himself over her as he cut the cord that bound her to the chair, then pushed her down to the floor out of Tim's shooting range.

It was a suicide mission. He knew it was the last thing he would ever do. But when it was done he was still standing, knife in hand, Charlotte sobbing on the floor beside him. Tim had not fired the gun.

Tim faced him with a wry smile, the gun still in his hand but pointed away from them now. Ritter gripped the knife, breathless, sweating, confused. For the second time his life had been spared at the last minute and he didn't know what it meant. Had this whole thing been a sadistic trick? Or was Tim just prolonging the torture? Was Charlotte in on it? Had she been in on it since the beginning?

"Put down the gun, Tim," he said.

Tim stared back with his inscrutable smile.

"I know you're not going to shoot me," Ritter said, "so put the gun down."

Tim turned around and set the gun on a shelf behind him. Ritter couldn't reach it there, but neither could Tim.

"You could kill me with that knife," Tim said, turning to face him again with his mocking smile. "I wouldn't be able to reach the gun in time to stop you from cutting my throat."

Ritter stood still, wondering if he would kill Tim.

"Can't bring yourself to do it?" Tim jeered. "Why not? I ruined your life. I killed Helene and framed you for it. I killed McNally and Hal Morgenstern. And now look what I've done to Charlotte."

He certainly deserved it. A monster, the kind of criminal no litany of mitigating factors could excuse, but clever enough to avoid falling into the clutches of the law. If I don't kill him, Ritter thought, no one will.

"What kind of man are you? Don't you have any self-respect? Any emotions? I think you really are a psychopath. You're pathetic, that's for sure."

And it wouldn't be hard to do. A sudden leap, the plunge into his throat, a short struggle, and it would be over.

"Do you think I'll ever stop torturing you? Not to mention your loved ones, if you have any. How else can you stop me? Are you going to call the cops and tell them I faked the McNally video?"

Could he really kill someone? Ritter asked himself. Why not?

"Think about it, Chris," Tim said. "No one will know you were here, except Charlotte, and I doubt if she'll blame you for killing me after what I did to her before you got here. Next I'll find your kids, if they're really your kids—"

"Shut up!"

Ritter dropped the knife and bent down to help Charlotte to her feet. "Let's get out of here."

Tim held the gun in his hand again. "Bravo!" he shouted. "Does this mean you believe in something?"

Ritter ignored him, staring into the gun as he backed Charlotte away, sobbing and stumbling as she went.

"I'll take that as a yes." Tim's smile was a real smile now, not mocking or ironic or even embarrassed. "I knew you could do it, Chris. You're a free man." He set the gun down on the table in front of him. "As for the next step, you'll have to figure that out for yourself."

Ritter glared at Tim and turned his back on him for the last time.

"A word or two before you go," Tim called after him. "It's a shame so many people had to be sacrificed for you to get to this point. Honor their memory, and don't forget me, Chris. I did it for you. The question is, can you live without me?"

He picked up the gun, stuck the barrel in his mouth, and squeezed the trigger.

34.

The next few weeks were a nightmare of ambulances, police cars, jail cells, reporters and lawyers. Charlotte, roughed up but not seriously injured, was hospitalized with post-traumatic shock. Ritter — disoriented, angry, depressed, aggressive — was held in the Berkshire County Jail until the video camera and Charlotte's insistence persuaded the DA to release him. Both refused to talk to reporters until the coroner had ruled Tim Salis's death a suicide. Before the details were made public, the theater community in New York held a memorial service attended by over five hundred people, including Kathryn and Doug Leipzig and the psychiatrist who'd treated Tim for twenty-five years. Everyone agreed that his death was a tragedy.

Charlotte's mother stayed with her until she was discharged and then drove her home to Philadelphia. Ritter returned to the halfway house, still unsure whether he was half way to hell or half way back. He could see no purpose in continuing to live. The joy and relief he'd expected to feel on being liberated from Craft was obliterated by the images of violent death that visited him day and night. Tim's last words echoed in his dreams: *Can you live without me?* Every dream ended with the gunshot, jolting him awake. He would stare into the darkness, wondering if he could live without the malign spirit who'd been directing his life for as long as he could remember. The starless sky had nothing to say on the subject. He was going to have to figure it out for himself.

The weather was unusually hot for mid-September. Ritter spent his afternoons at the public library among his new friends from skid row. He'd given up the illusion of honing his computer skills to find a job. It was just something to do. The only news story he followed was the build up to Teague's execution, which was scheduled to occur in three weeks. All appeals had been denied.

One morning Alex Lopez intercepted him outside the halfway house. Alex had spoken with Charlotte — she was doing well — and she'd told him where to find him. The two men were uncomfortable greeting each other. The hostility of their last encounter had dissipated but not disappeared. "I'm surprised that you'd want to talk to me," Ritter said.

Alex ventured a smile. "Everything that's ever happened between us is ancient history."

"Yeah, and you're looking at one of the ruins."

They walked a block to the Korean diner where Ritter usually breakfasted on fried eggs, a grilled corn muffin and coffee that tasted like turpentine. It reminded him of the place Alex's parents used to run, but he didn't mention that to Alex. They sat beside each other at the counter so they could avoid eye contact. "They sent us the video Salis made at the theater up in Stockbridge," Alex said.

"You didn't watch it, I hope," Ritter said.

"You come off as quite a hero."

"Don't believe what you see on TV."

Alex took a sip of his turpentine coffee and set the cup down. "I wouldn't believe it except for what Charlotte says," he said. "We reopened the files on Morgenstern and McNally. They've both been ruled homicides. Salis's second and third victims, after Helene."

"I'm to blame for all of them. Especially Helene."

Alex hesitated. "We're both to blame for what happened to Helene." He tried another sip of coffee and pushed his cup away. "Did you know Hal Morgenstern?"

"I knew him as Craft. Apparently he enjoyed the role so much he made a whole career of playing Mephistopheles."

"I talked to Doug Leipzig," Alex said. "It's pretty much what you thought. He started the whole thing with Helene. Salis found out about it and paid her to keep it going, then later he put Morgenstern on the payroll. Between the two of them, he paid out a pretty significant chunk of change over the years."

"Family money. Tim never had to work."

"At the end they both must've been blackmailing him. That's why he killed them."

"To keep them from talking to me."

"I still don't get it," Alex said. "Why Salis did all this."

"I don't either. He tried to explain — you saw the video — but it didn't make any sense."

"He was crazy."

"Is that an explanation for anything? If it is, then we're all crazy."

The counterman set their eggs in front of them and they bowed over them as if moved to silent prayer. "What do they put in this coffee?" Alex asked Ritter.

"Turpentine."

"By the way," Alex said when he had finished his eggs, "it was Salis who sent the place mat and other stuff down to the attorneys in Florida. We located the messenger service he used down there for the hand deliveries. He got the name of Charlotte's hotel from her secretary in Philadelphia."

Ritter pushed his plate away and turned to face Alex, who stared straight ahead. "You know, Alex," Ritter said, "I suspected you at one point. I'm sorry about that."

"I not only suspected you," Alex nodded, "I helped send you to death row. So don't bother to apologize."

"Did you talk to Kathryn?"

"I don't think she was in on the joke, if that's what you're wondering. Have you talked to her?"

"Not since I got back."

"How about the kids?"

"Luckily for them, they don't know me."

Alex picked up the check and tossed a few bills on the counter. "This is on me." He stood up to leave, making it clear that he didn't want Ritter to follow him outside. "Your life has been a train wreck, Chris. For you and everybody you've ever known. I'm hoping you can do a little better from now on."

"Is that a vote of confidence?"

Alex grinned as he stepped toward the door. "I'll send in an absentee ballot."

Ritter called Charlotte that afternoon on a throwaway phone he bought near Times Square. She was doing well, as Alex had said, still staying with her mom and still on leave from the law firm. The question was whether she would ever go back. The rest of her life was up for grabs, she told Ritter. Having seen what she'd seen, could she really go on with a corporate law practice? Ritter had no words of wisdom that could help her, though he hoped he would see her again. She was able to clear up one loose end that Alex had failed to explain: the threatening phone messages, which had continued to arrive on her phone for several days after Tim's suicide. Sol Levy had called with the news that the local police had made an arrest in the bombing of his office. The suspects were a middle-aged couple, Lisa Kane and Walter Housevogel, who spent their time protesting at abortion clinics and prisons, against death in the one case and for it in the other. When Charlotte saw a picture she identified them as the puffy-haired blonde and her beer-bellied boyfriend, the protestors who'd spit on her after the hearing that resulted in Ritter's release. They admitted (it was not so much an admission as a boast) that they'd followed Charlotte from the prison in the pickup truck and firebombed Sol's office, and Walter Housevogel admitted making the threatening calls. Apparently a couple of garden-variety wack jobs, except for one thing: Lisa Kane claimed that she'd been given Charlotte's cell number by Kathryn's parents.

After talking to Charlotte, Ritter called Kathryn, who unexpectedly answered the phone. Not unexpectedly, she wasn't overjoyed to hear his voice. "My parents don't even know this Lisa person," she said. "Is that what you're calling about?"

"No."

"What do you want, then?"

"I know it's a little late for this, but I want to apologize for everything I've put you through. You didn't deserve it."

"Chris," she said, "I'm not going to let you see the kids unless you have a court order."

"I'll fight you on that if I have to."

"You have to go through our lawyer."

"I'm not a criminal anymore, you know."

"Don't call again, Chris."

"I never was."

A week later Charlotte called to tell Ritter that she'd resigned from her law firm and joined an advocacy organization dedicated to representing prisoners on death row. "It's not like the Titus Foundation," she explained. "We represent all prisoners facing the death penalty. Not just the innocent ones."

"You've changed your philosophy, then?"

"I have you to thank for that."

Her first assignment was to return to Florida to represent Teague in his final appeal, and she asked Ritter to come with her.

Two days later they stopped at Sol Levy's new office in the St. Augustine strip mall. Sol came out to greet them in his seersucker suit and escorted them into the conference room, where Millie served cookies and iced coffee. "I owe you an apology," he told Ritter. "I did my best to defend you, but I never doubted that you were guilty. I thought Craft was a figment of your imagination."

"In a way, he was," Ritter said.

As to Teague, Sol offered his support for Charlotte's appeal but rated its chance of success at somewhere between zero and hopeless. "Teague has one possible argument," he told her. "That at the time he committed his crimes he suffered from extreme mental or emotional disturbance, and this factor wasn't adequately addressed at the trial. How are you going to prove that?"

"He's completely insane," Charlotte said. "Chris can attest to that."

"I still wouldn't make that argument unless he agrees," Ritter said. "It's better to die with dignity."

"What dignity?" Charlotte asked. "He's a murderer."

"He's a guilty man, not a broken one."

They discussed the case against the office bombers, which Sol hoped would result in long prison terms. Lisa Kane had revealed the motive for her actions. Eleven years earlier, she claimed, she'd had a one-night stand with Ritter. He left without saying goodbye and she soon discovered that she was pregnant. At first she kept this discovery to herself, agonizing over what course to take, but a few weeks later, when Ritter was arrested, she saw his picture on TV and realized that the father of her unborn child was a vicious murderer. She decided to have an abortion and had been tormented by remorse ever since. Over time the remorse hardened into hatred, first hatred of herself, then of abortion, and then of Ritter and anyone who tried to stop his execution.

"I think I know who she is," Ritter said. "She's not making it up. I never knew about the pregnancy, though."

"Did she really get my phone number from Kathryn's parents?" Charlotte asked.

"She met them at an anti-abortion rally," Sol said. "They've admitted that they gave her your phone number, but they deny knowing she had any connection to Ritter."

"Just a coincidence," Charlotte said, shaking her head.

Sol chuckled as he took a sip of his iced coffee. "I'm sure they feel terrible for what they did. '

After leaving Sol's office — it was late afternoon, the sky was gray but not threatening rain — Charlotte drove with Ritter to their hotel, where they had booked separate rooms. Having checked in, they put on their bathing suits and drove a short distance to a public beach. They dropped their towels on the sand and walked barefoot across the beach to the ocean, wading in until they felt the undertow hollow out the sand under their feet. They stood in the surf until the footprints they'd left behind them had been washed away. Staring into the empty sky, Ritter made a confession he'd been holding inside him for a long time. He told Charlotte about his last trip to Baxter Island and the Haitians who'd cried out for help before he watched them sink to the bottom. "It was the day I didn't kill Helene," he said. 'The morning of my one-night stand with Lisa Kane. The last day of my life." His voice trailed off into the roar of the breakers.

There was nothing Charlotte could say. She couldn't judge him: the path she'd chosen didn't lead in that direction. Neither could she forgive him, even if she'd wanted to. She wasn't the victim of his crimes.

They watched the restless waves, the gulls swooping carelessly in the wind. "I can imagine myself out there, being swallowed by the water," Ritter said. "The same way those people were."

"And then your sins would be washed away?"

"No, but I could forget that I ever existed."

"Forgive and forget. Don't they have to come in that order?"

"There's an ocean of forgetting out there," he said. "But no forgiveness."

She resisted the temptation to touch his hand. "No blame either."

35.

The next morning they drove to Raiford in a steady rain. A crowd of protestors — smaller than the one that had gathered for Ritter's execution — occupied the designated area at the end of the parking lot, huddling under umbrellas or sitting in their cars. "Teague is much less hated than you were," Charlotte told Ritter. She saw in that a ray of hope.

To one side stood Paul Young, the Devil's chaplain. Unlike the others, who aimed their signs and slogans at each other, he faced the building where the execution would take place. The crowd stirred when Charlotte climbed out of the car, moving to block her path. She faced an impossible, possibly dangerous task; Ritter doubted that Teague would even talk to her. "I may be a fool, but I'm going in there to do what I can do," she said. "Even if they spit on me."

The protestors recognized Charlotte — she'd been in and out of the prison many times — but they didn't know Ritter, whom they'd never viewed as a real person. He walked over to join Paul Young and stood beside him in the rain. Neither had a hat or an umbrella, and the rain was falling harder. The chaplain welcomed Ritter with a hug, as if he'd been expecting him. He had read about the shooting in Massachusetts and the revelations that followed, and he listened eagerly as Ritter told him the whole story. To Ritter, responding to the chaplain's gentle questioning, the story started making sense for the first time.

"Do you remember the first time you talked to me?" Paul Young asked, his face brightening with the memory. "I came to save your soul and you insisted that you didn't have one."

"You said believing in the Devil would be a good first step. That seems to have been Tim's strategy too."

"He was truly a Devil's chaplain. Much more so than I. I give him credit for that."

Ritter stared at the prison and recalled his vision of Teague in his cell, the night before he was to die, expounding evil. "He wanted me to believe in something, even if it was evil."

"Did he want you to believe in God too?" the chaplain asked.

"If that was his goal, he didn't succeed. I still think we're alone in the universe."

"Then why didn't you kill him when you had the chance?"

"I felt sorry for him."

Paul Young nodded as if weighing the pros and cons of this motivation. "Compassion," he said, giving it a name. "Then you risked your life to save Charlotte. Why did you do that?"

"I didn't think I was risking anything."

He smiled at Ritter's clumsy attempt to avoid the imputation of selflessness. "You attached no value to your own life," he said, "and yet again you chose compassion." His smile broadened as he turned to face Ritter. "I think you've learned more than you realize."

"What do you mean?"

"I'm a skeptic like you. More than a skeptic. Why do you think I'm chaplain to the non-believers?" The chaplain pulled out a handkerchief and wiped the rain from his forehead, then handed it to Ritter, who did the same thing. "But one thing I know is this: you have to believe in your own mind, your consciousness. It will last only as long as you live, but it's all you have. And you can't have consciousness without contraries — good and evil, guilty and innocent, love and hate, true and false — even though every one of them is false. You have to live as if you believed in them, but at the same time you have to get beyond them. You have to love your neighbor as yourself, even when you hate yourself."

He wrung out his handkerchief — it was useless against this weather — and stuck it back in his pocket. "What kind of faith is there for people like you and me? Only forgiveness and sympathy, even for those we most despise."

Their vigil would continue until Charlotte came out, and it will continue, rain or shine, until the day Teague is either killed or spared. Ritter can envision everything that will happen inside the prison. Teague stands in his cell, the roar of evil or madness in his eyes. He is subdued by the guards — it takes four of them — and clamped in manacles and leg irons, dragged to the visitors room. Would he talk to Charlotte? Would he agree to another appeal? Ritter can see it all: he is Teague. The van to the death house, the prep room, the gurney, the IV tubes, the narrow corridor to the execution chamber, the witnesses behind the curtain. The man of high moral character, wearing a mask. The warden. The red telephone.

Charlotte emerges from the guard station and strides past the weary protestors into the rain. She approaches the two men, wondering if what she sees is rain or tears streaming down their cheeks. With a sweet smile she reaches out to squeeze Ritter's hand.

"Does he have a chance?" he asks her.

"Only a miracle can save him."

THE END

ACKNOWLEDGEMENTS

Many thanks to James A. Drummond, Esq., for his patient and invaluable guidance on the intricacies of death penalty law and practice. I have not always followed that guidance, having taken certain liberties in the interest of dramatic interest and narrative flow — the most salient liberty, of course, being the premise that someone like Christopher Ritter would ever face the death penalty in the first place. Subject to that, I hope that my portrayal is reasonably accurate; any mistakes are all my own. As to the workings of capital punishment in Florida during the relevant time period, I am indebted to *Heinous, Atrocious and Cruel,* by Terence M. Lenamon, and *Now I Walk on Death Row,* by Dale S. Recinella.

In writing this novel I have profited from books too numerous to mention, some of which may be obvious to the reader. The book referred to by Sol Levy in Chapter 9 arguing that Hitler was a failed artist who consciously imitated Ibsen's plays is *Ibsen and Hitler,* by Steven F. Sage; in a similar vein is *Hitler and the Power of Aesthetics,* by Frederic Spotts. Of the many books I've read about evolution, I would especially like to acknowledge *Darwin's Spectre: Evolutionary Biology in the Modern World,* by Michael R. Rose, specifically the author's discussion of immanent Darwinism and his image of our subjective experiences as dogs on a leash held by a Darwinian master. Many thanks to Irvin D. Yalom and *Free Inquiry* (a publication of the Council for Secular Humanism) for their kind permission to quote from published works. (The "Declaration in Defense of Cloning and the Integrity of Scientific Research" was promulgated in 1997 by the International Academy of Humanism and authored by Pieter Admiraal, Ruben Ardila, and Sir Isaiah Berlin.) I would also like to acknowledge and thank Professor Richard Dawkins for his writings on evolution and religion (including his collection of essays entitled *A Devil's Chaplain*).

ABOUT THE AUTHOR

Bruce Hartman is the author of seven previous novels, including *The Rules of Dreaming*, *The Philosophical Detective*, and, most recently, *Potlatch*. A graduate of Wesleyan University and Harvard Law School, he lives with his wife in Philadelphia.

www.ingramcontent.com/pod-product-compliance
Lightning Source LLC
Chambersburg PA
CBHW020236180626
46810CB00006B/2217